THE TRUE STORY OF MANSE JOLLY
PART I

D1713683

Guidon of Company F, 1st South Carolina Cavalry, based on a drawing by Private Bright Burrell and sent home in a wartime letter to his wife.

Company L guidon cited in Chapter Twelve, stitched in April 1865 by Private Farrell from two old shirts.

THE TRUE STORY OF MANSE JOLLY PART I

As told by The Hon. A.W. Fries

The War Years, 1860-1865

Steve Biondo

Writer's Showcase
San Jose New York Lincoln Shanghai

The True Story Of Manse Jolly Part I
As told by The Hon. A.W. Fries

Writer's Showcase
an imprint of iUniverse, Inc.

For information address:
iUniverse, Inc.
5220 S. 16th St., Suite 200
Lincoln, NE 68512
www.iuniverse.com

Any resemblance to actual people and events is purely coincidental.
This is a work of fiction.

ISBN: 0-595-23800-9

Printed in the United States of America

This Book

is for my father, Michael,
and especially my mother,
Jeanette Marie Dahly Biondo 1927-1996

Contents

Preface

The writing of "The True Story of Manse Jolly," Parts I and II, began in 1981 when I was a daily columnist and reporter for the morning Anderson, S.C., Independent-Mail.

Through more than two decades of research, writing and writer's block, I leapt undocumented gaps to unlock the key to the enigmatic personality of Upcountry South Carolina folk hero Manson Sherrill Jolly, a man who really lived and died much as Ansel W. Fries relates in the following volumes.

Other writers have been intrigued by the historical persona of Manse Jolly, about whom so much, and so little, is known. There were long feckless periods when the manuscript did nothing but gather dust, but the book progressed to its inevitable end.

The research required to document Manse Jolly's life was extensive. His only extant papers—eleven letters, all post-war, and one 1861 Civil War furlough—are in the Olin D. Johnston Library at Anderson College, including the final 1869 letter sent home from Texas by his cousin.

I first read the collection in 1982. To the best of my knowledge, it still contains a thin lock of red hair wrapped in a swatch of blue gingham, the last remaining physical vestige of Manson Sherrill Jolly.

The late historian E. Don Herd Jr. wrote a perceptive 50-page essay about the man and his myth in his second volume of "The

South Carolina Upcountry, 1540-1980." It remains the best factual published account of Manse Jolly's life.

My study is fictional and takes fictional license, but it is based on contemporary newspaper accounts, letters, memoirs, local lore and published documents, such as the 128-volume "War of the Rebellion: A Compilation of the Official Records of the Confederate and Union Armies."

The OR details the 1st South Carolina Cavalry's baptism of fire on Johns Island, S.C., its debut with the Army of Northern Virginia against Sigel's troops, unit organizations, battles and campaigns. The OR also showed where the 1st South Carolina Cavalry served in the chaotic closing days of the war.

Purists may criticize my description of the regiment's fight at Brandy Station, specifically its dismounted charge up Fleetwood Hill, which is based directly on Colonel Black's after-action report in the OR. This action foreshadowed the growing importance of dismounted cavalry as the war progressed.

It is ironic that, although Jolly saw plenty of horse fighting, this self-styled knight of the Confederacy participated as an infantryman in the greatest engagement of mounted troops ever seen on the North American continent.

I have attempted to give life to the true historical characters, but created others based on real lives. For instance, the roster of Company F includes both fictional characters and men who actually served in Jolly's outfit.

The narrative is salted with stories and anecdotes drawn from Upstate South Carolina history and tradition, unpublished memoirs, diaries, letters to the author and items taken from the newspaper column I wrote for ten years, from 1981 until 1991.

My thanks for access to these richly varied sources of Upcountry history goes to author Hurley Badders of the Pendleton Historic Commission; researcher Donna Roper; a true daughter, the late Miss Nettie Ducworth; a dedicated and United Daughter, Peggy Carr of

Pendleton; the Olin D. Johnston Library; journalist Terry Dickson, who instructed me in the Southern way; and Earle Josey's indomitable uncles, the erudite S.H. "Jack" Earle and the late E.J. "Shorty" Earle.

Thanks also to Anderson County photo historian Fred Whitten; that much esteemed lover of accurate history, Beth Klosky, now of Columbia; the living historians I came to know as comrades in Sherman's Bummers; my Confederate friends in the Palmetto Light Artillery, McBeth's Battery and the reactivated 1st and 2nd South Carolina Cavalry; our beloved editor emeritus at the old Anderson Independent, the late L.S. "Slim" Hembree; the regretfully late but eternally delightful Louise Ervin of Honea Path, S.C.; Nancy Stein, former owner of the restored Manse Jolly home, and many others. I must also thank my son, Zach, for his able assistance with the graphic illustrations, and my sister, Karen B. Hayes of Alexandria, Virginia, for her careful and thoughtful reading of the manuscript.

I hope I have given them a book that captures the spirit of the times and helps breathe life into the images of the 1860s generation. Their faces haunt us still.

Steve Biondo
Anderson, South Carolina
Summer 2002

A Word

A clipping from the June 1, 1923, Cameron City Times of Cameron, Texas, enclosed within a 1930 letter to the editor from Dr. B.F.L. Jenkins of Killeen, Texas, General of the Texas Commandery, United Confederate Veterans:

> "Particulars On The Life
> & Death of Manse Jolly,
> Rebel & Outlaw
>
> Great Feats During The
> War Between The States
>
> How A Rascal Yankee
> Captain Was Laid Low
>
> Bloody Remembrance Of
> The Last Comanche Raid
> In Milam County
>
> And, A Plea For Temperance
> By The Former Circuit
> Judge For Milam County,
> The Hon. A.W. Fries"

"That brittle piece of newspaper hung by a tack on the wall of the judge's water closet all the last years of his life. He read it morning, noon and night, seated on the French porcelain stool that gave him as much comfort as a well-made saddle when he was younger.

"He was not the sort to compare clippings, like some fag actor, but he liked this story, because it was printed very much as it was told by him and, as he often said, that is a rarity for a newspaper.

"Judge Fries was my good friend. My purpose in writing is to praise your editorial judgment in commemorating the life and death of this gallant soldier, pioneer, Indian fighter and jurist. That generation is now nearly gone, and those of us still left wonder if all the hardships endured and sacrifices made will soon be as dust in the prairie wind, scattered and forgotten.

"As the City Times so eloquently reported, the judge passed in a year that began with the St. Valentine's Day massacre in Chicago and ended with the great stock market crash on Wall Street. His ending came not long after the latter event, at the age of 89, and, though generally unreported outside Texas, was, with proper dignity, noted at length in the newspaper of his adopted hometown. Judge Fries was a man esteemed as a relic of the times he had survived, and was valued by his friends and colleagues as a compassionate witness of both the good and evil that men do.

"But in the familial sense Judge Fries was not, in his own estimation, a complete man. He never married nor fathered children, in spite of the scurrilous legal action that plagued him shortly after his retirement, and, in his own words, suffered late in his life for his extreme probity.

"In this, as in most things, however, he refrained from complaint and remained philosophical and cheerful to his last breath."

Headlines from Judge Fries' front page obituary in the November 25, 1929, Cameron City Times:

"Death Of Judge Fries, At 89

Last Rebel Veteran In Milam
County Is Laid To Rest

Old Trooper Served Under
J.E.B. Stuart,
Wounded At Brandy Station"

Oh, true enough, those printed words, fragments of a life every bit as inconsequential as the columns that reported it.

All except that folderol about being wounded at Brandy Station. Trust the newspapers to screw up the facts, not that it matters a damn. No, I came through that scrape more or less intact; it was at Kellys Ford that I left part of an elbow, and several ribs later along Moccasin Creek.

But, all in all, true enough. I was another old man for whom no one was left alive to mourn. When such a man—any man—shuffles off this mortal coil, who notices? It's the young ones who get mourned, and rightfully. Might as well take the old ones, stuff them and prop them up in a glass case at the museum, like Stonewall Jackson's horse.

I can say that because I am the honorable A.W. Fries, in his boniest incarnation, now dead these many years. Would I have the temerity to even presume to say it if it were not true? I am not solicitous of your sympathy—what a ludicrous concept to those who have passed! Might just as well curse an amoeba, or tear out hairs over a breath of unwanted breeze—but seek only to underscore the veracity of my tale, for a dead man can have no purpose but truth.

And if your mind is such that it cannot suspend disbelief and leap the picky and mundane questions, such as, "How can ectoplasmic thoughts from the ethereal plane be translated to tangible pages in a book?", or, more to the point, "How can a dead man write a book?", then read no further. My story is wasted on you. By way of defense I shall say only that, if brain-dead politicians, fattened by public graft and the noxious swill of foreign influence, who lie, swindle, cheat, and destroy countless lives, and then merrily retire to public approbation, hiring professional hacks to sing their putrid life praises, may write books, then by God a dead man may also. Let us leave it at that.

I should mention here my contact, intermediary and secretary, Mr. Julian K. Dent, Esq., of Fort Worth, Texas, a noted expert on the afterlife and the processes of automatic writing, who located my consciousness through his ceaseless cosmic probings and first excited my interest in producing the memoirs I should have written while alive.

Of course, the condition of being dead has its natural drawbacks, but also its advantages. I have no need for records, books, memoirs or notes because my memory is complete and virgin-pure, cleansed of lies and bias by the redeeming blood of the Lamb and full in the sensual richness of remembered sounds, smells, tastes and touches. Memory among the dead is akin to a brilliant kaleidoscope of life moments, blending and shifting one into the other as if in a constant and eternally moving picture show. A gate occasionally opens in this breath-taking vista and diademic wisps of other things intrude. I cannot say whether these are pieces of lives once lived, or other men's memories loosed from their souls and floating free in the unknowable cosmos.

Already I have given lie to my purpose, rambling on like a demented old soldier, which I am. For three long years, the most terrible and wonderful of my life, I was a private soldier in General R.E. Lee's Army of Northern Virginia, serving under men such as J.E.B. Stuart, Wade Hampton, M.C. Butler and John Logan Black, colonel of my old regiment, the First South Carolina Volunteer Cavalry.

Oh, we were bully lads, virgins and rapists, killers and choir boys, but mostly children, smooth-faced children who were expected to become men. And we had the demeanor of children in the beginning, at least most of us did. Those who lived, maimed and unmaimed, did become men, and I think good men for the most part. They are with me still.

Being in mortem decedo, I may relive those days. Now, I may not embrace old comrades nor sit on a cloud watching events below. Heaven is not like that, if heaven this be. But, immersed in these gently flowing cosmic streams, I can live again the good times and the bad, relive any moment simply by thinking, and not as I remembered it but as it was. That can mean sweet bliss or sights unholy. 'Tis the price one pays, for this is a kind of immortality, is it not?

In these dreams I breathe again, speak in fondly remembered conversations, see again and touch, lovers, my father and brothers, my poor doomed comrades of the Lost Cause. We laugh, joke, rage, comfort one another, weep. There are faces loved and valued, and one or two despised. Still, the journey is an unexpected delight—a physiognomic exercise extraordinaire—unique to the afterlife.

Again I digress. Verbosity was my Achilles heel as a young trial lawyer.

It is my pledge to female readers that my work does not appeal by intent or plan to prurient interests. But at the same time I cannot censor what I know occurred, from some misguided sense of propriety. For, as Mr. Sherman said, war is unbridled cruelty and cannot be refined. He might as well have said the same of "life" as war, and been just as accurate. I said that.

This, then, is my story, and also by definition the story of many others, but of one other in particular. He was Manson, who was called Manse, and I, who was a living man called Ansel W. Fries, his friend and comrade.

Sworn, Witnessed & Faithfully Transcribed
by J.K. Dent, Esq.
29 March 1940
in the County of Milam, Texas

CHAPTER 1

Remembrance Of Days Past

Strange fits of passion have I known;
And I will dare to tell,
But in the lover's ear alone,
What once to me befell.

—Wordsworth

Seventy-five years ago, I helped to kill a man.

It is my guilt to confess it now and I don't have even the excuse of war. This happened after.

He was not the first man I killed, I am pretty sure, though I possess no proof that any enemy soldier ever died directly at my hand. There were several others afterward as well, in Texas; all were Comanche but one.

I remember this man because he was a soldier who died unnecessarily, and badly, a long way from home. I would recognize him now if I could just see a likeness, because a duplicate portrait exists deep in my brain and has since the moment before he died. It was imprinted there by the same process the chemist uses to produce an image on japanned tin or glass. I remember him because the way in which he died was no incident of war; the war had been over for months. This had been murder. Some nights I can still see the scene being very clearly played out before me, only dimmer now, as if on a stage with dying footlights.

He was a Union soldier with a face like many, his features absurdly exaggerated in the heat of the fight, his skin sunburned by campaigning, his eyes wide in excitement and mouth half-open. His animal sounds of fear.

Weeks afterward I read about the murders in the newspaper, three Federal soldiers shot to death at a ferry on the Savannah River while guarding a shipment of confiscated cotton that had been branded as contraband.

One of the dead men, Reames, was too old to be this man; he was forty-six. The second, P.X. O'Malley, was Irish, too short, too slight, too red headed. So the third, an H. Brown, had been my man. He left a bare epitaph.

A private in the 1st Maine Battalion, Brown—first name Henry? Harry? Harvey?—was a seaman by trade, an orphan and a Presbyterian with no surviving family. He was twenty.

The triple internment was held with full military honors at the First Presbyterian Church, West Whitner Street, Anderson Court House, So. Car., on Wednesday at two o'clock in the afternoon, October the 18th, 1865.

A dead man could do worse. It was said that schoolteacher Nora Hubbard tended those graves with great devotion for many years. Decades later, the moldering soldier's bones were dug up and reinterred at the national cemetery in Marietta, Georgia.

But I have reason to remember Private Brown, and many others: My older brother, Tom, for one, and Manse Jolly's five brothers, and our friends and comrades, the half a million who died and whose deaths still burden this country's conscience. It happened early in October; the night air still smelled of summer green. Cowardly

Walter Largent, stunned by the violence of recent minutes, sat rigid in his saddle, making odd barking sounds with every ragged breath that erupted in the pine-scented darkness.

We had not been expecting an army guard at the river ferry. Largent had panicked, opened fire, and the Yankees shot back. Manse dropped one of them; the other we found slumped behind a bale of cotton. The third soldier fired his musket, threw it away and broke for the cover of the woods.

Pursuing on horseback, we quickly surrounded him while all around us the Savannah River murmured its ceaseless song.

We turned to the tall figure whose face was hidden by the forest's night shadows. Manse exhaled with finality, and with his right thumb cocked his single-action Colt revolver. I couldn't see it, but I heard it, and I knew from long experience what the sound meant.

"Draw, all of you, and throw down," Manse commanded. "It is all of us together, or none."

A voice said, "Manse, the war is over." A shrill, piping voice. My voice.

Herb Williams: "We already killed two. Ain't it enough?"

But time was pressing, and the night air already smelled coppery with blood.

"I didn't see nothing, I swear," begged the Yankee. "I only 'listed in the army to get out of jail."

There was an uneasy stirring, the creak of leather.

"Boys." The party raised its weapons, sitting mounted in a ragged circle, with the Yankee slumped forward at the circle's opening.

"Steady."

Private Brown sank to all fours, frantically patting the pine needle mat covering the forest floor with his hands. Then he reared up, shook his fist at his murderers and wailed, "I'm supposed to be at sea, not here at all!"

The sudden concussion of pistol shots made the killers wince. The horses jumped and snorted. Before the pall of smoke had cleared,

Henry Knauff and Largent dismounted and, each grabbing an arm of the body, limp and leaking like a sack of hog innards, dragged it through the underbrush and down the riverbank and rolled it with some difficulty into the gurgling river.

The corpse did a pirouette in the blood-dark water, drowned in a wave of foam, resurfaced and was carried quickly downstream.

Manse always said there is killing and there is killing.

Some killing you never think twice about, and one may nag you to your dying day. Which proves to me that Manson Sherrill Jolly had a conscience.

For years, people told the most ridiculous stories about him, that he killed a hundred Yankees, or twenty or ten or five, for each of the five brothers he lost in the war. Nonsense. Manse did kill, during the war and afterwards, too. I knew him for a killer by any law, civil or moral, you may cite; I will offer no excuse for the man some called South Carolina's Jesse James.

But it was because, for Manse and for many of us, the war did not end at Appomattox Courthouse or Bennett's Farm. It kept on for years, a blood feud sparking and flaring up like a stubborn brush fire.

Why did I stick with him when I was old enough to know better, when most of the honest fight had been beaten out of me by the war? I don't know. It may be because I came by many hard ways to learn that, among men, compassion sometimes binds itself to cruelty and thereby tempers it. When you fight alongside a man, sleep with him, share his coffee, cartridges, miseries, exultations and hates, when his leadership makes you a reluctant brother, it is like signing a marker. Manse held my marker.

My name is Ansel Wilhelm Fries. The surname is meant to be pronounced in its original German to rhyme with "freeze," but the American Fries as "pies" was how I heard it for most of my life. I was born on the western edge of the old Pendleton District of South Carolina in 1840, the same year as Manson Sherrill Jolly.

My father settled in the foothills of the Blue Ridge mountains, after leaving Westphalia in Germany to avoid royal conscription in some European war. His people were mostly Lutherans seasoned with a few Bavarian Catholics who founded a town called Walhalla.

Shortly before I was born, my family moved farther south to Townville, South Carolina, on the Seneca River, where Mr. Fries opened a profitable dry goods business, shipping cotton and lumber down the Seneca to the Savannah River and thence to Augusta, distributing and selling the goods sent upriver from New York and even Europe across the Upcountry.

My mother, Anna, died of consumption when I was three. My only memory of her is from an old ambrotype: a gentle, pallid face and dark almond eyes. She was buried behind the Baptist church, in a plot separated from the Baptist dead because she had been Catholic. I only just remember the red clay of the grave and the pallid faces of my older brothers, Tom and Newton. Big men huddling like cattle in their somber coats. Cottony streams of breath in the raw spring air.

My father, who read Darwin, was a progressive man when it came to his boy's education. He was determined I should finish my schooling at Mrs. Hart's Grammar Academy and go on to college. He wanted me to study law and become a man of some worth, ambitions I eventually fulfilled but which he never lived to see. He was a good man with a shopkeeper's soul and I tried my best to please him.

At eighteen, I entered the College of William and Mary in Williamsburg, Virginia, and after three lonely years of study took my degree in humanities and the law. That was in the sweet and turbulent spring of 1860, when the country was astir with talk of secession and civil war.

Mstr. Ansel Fries
Mdm. Stantons' Boarding House
Williamsburg, Virg
May the 2nd, 1860

My Dear Son, Ansel,

Many thanks for Yours of the 28th ult.——it was received and read with great interest. Your Brothers, Tom and Newton, are crazy for Bruderkrieg and spend too much time with their worthless friends, riding round the Circuit speaking on behalf of the Democrats, telling their praises, and no doubt Drinking some. That is a man's pleasure, to be weak in his Youth. But I tell you I tire of their antics. Both are older than you, Ansel, and yet still are boys in many ways.

Oh I wish you were here, Ansel, with your gutte Sense and steady strength. You are small in body, Son, but you have the Geist of a Giant. That is why I determined to send you to the finest schule, of American law, in Virginia. I hope the Bluebloods have not given you too hard a time. One day you will sit among them. Of this I feel sure.

Yr Loving Father,

Augustus Fries

As Always, Direct letters to:
  Fries Mercantile Co.
  C./of Postmaster
  Anderson Court House, So. Car.

John Brown had been hanged in December—the Southern students gaily toasted his execution at my dining club while I quietly sat in a corner and read Boswell—and a bushwacking border war was raging in Missouri. Military companies were forming in every district in anticipation of war, and when Lincoln was nominated that summer the warhawk's numbers swelled.

Some of the most strident voices were from my home state, a circumstance that caused ill feeling between me and my closest friend at college, Parker W. Pope.

Parker was a handsome, well-heeled young fellow from Fayette County, Virginia. He pretended not to understand the differences between the fire-eaters, who were mostly Lowcountry slaveowners, and Upcountry yeoman, who were not and tended to be Unionist in sympathy, although a similar situation existed in his own state of Virginia and eventually would split it in two. Parker and I came to an understanding.

Parker despised slavery, and while I was no proponent of the "peculiar institution," I saw nothing wrong in letting it die a natural death, as many said it would. We argued bitterly over the subject, but at the time I was not aware he was estranged from his own father because of his views. Parker, of course, enlisted in the Union army at the first opportunity.

I returned home after graduation to help my father with the family business, which help he hardly required. My older brothers Tom and Newton were there, fellows rougher and hardier than I was as a youth. I occupied myself reading for the bar and clerking for visiting attorneys when circuit court was in general sessions at Anderson Court House.

I was not a total liability to my father. That autumn I sued a ferry operator who cheated my father by inflating his ferry charges for bulk freight, agreeing to one rate then billing at a higher rate. I won the case with damages, and I will never forget how my father's mustache bristled with pride when the judge ruled in my favor. Unfortunately, the rascal ferryman left the state and we never collected a penny of what was due us.

Yet I worked little. I read, hunted, and fished in the muddy Rocky River on hot summer days, and often trekked over the countryside looking for flint arrowheads and spearheads around the old Indian mounds that peppered the region.

Manson Sherrill Jolly, the fifth of seven brothers, was a complete stranger to me until 1860, the summer of our twentieth year. The first time I saw Manse he was riding along the old Cherokee trace west of Anderson Courthouse one evening that July.

My brother Newton and I drank some whiskey after supper and had gone out into the cool of the evening to shoot some rabbits, when we saw a tall rider coming toward us down the sunken path on a fat gray mare. We hunkered down in the brush, free young white men, who were armed, but common sense dictated prudence.

Manse rode by us like a medieval baron surveying his fiefdom, his wool sack coat buttoned at the throat and showing his flannel shirt underneath when the coat flew back. His long legs were swathed in corduroy, the cuffs stuffed into the tops of his boots. The setting sun made his jouncing shoulders and fiery head burn with a golden glow.

Newton said, "I know him."

But when I started to rise, he pushed me back down.

Manse looked hard, as if carved from wood. His eyes were a clear, calm blue; his sinewy hands threatened, like oaken clubs, in spite of one noticeable peculiarity: He lacked the first joint of his right index finger, the result, I later learned, of a cotton gin accident many years before.

We were both twenty years old, but if you had stood us side by side we would have looked like mismatched shotgun barrels. Manse grew to a strapping six-foot-four, while my growth stopped forever at five-foot-five.

A glass image of Manse exists that is as true as life. Others surfaced long after his death, showing a slope-shouldered fellow with a weak chin, but they bore no resemblance to the Manse Jolly I knew. The likeness I know shows Manse in his high-collared uniform frock coat, glowering at the photographer, gripping a homemade D-guard Bowie knife in one hand and his Colt pocket revolver in the other. You can clearly see the missing tip of his right index finger, and the collar of the corduroy shirt his sister Mary made for him to take to war.

Manse Jolly rode by us that day, unaware of our presence. It occurred to me long after that I could have killed him then and saved many people considerable trouble.

Manse Jolly and I grew up within fifteen miles of each other and for twenty years one never knew the other existed.

I attended Mrs. Hart's Grammar Academy in Townville with five other children whom I can still name. Manse went to the one-room Lebanon community school when his father could spare him from the farm.

Me and my two older brothers lived comfortably in rooms at the rear of father's store. Manse had six brothers and four sisters, all but one of whom survived to adulthood. Two of his four older brothers married before the war, fathered children and helped their father work his two hundred forty acres of land north of Anderson Court-house. The Jolly clan lived in a clapboard-sided cabin with two rooms downstairs—subdivided after dark by horse blankets hung from tenpenny nails for marital privacy—and a crowded attic above in which the younger children slept.

Manse's great-grandfather came to this country from Ireland in the 1760s, trekking first to Pennsylvania and then going south to what is now Union County, South Carolina. He moved to the Pendleton District in 1798, staked out a land claim for his ninety day's militia service at Cowpens and followed the Bible's command-ment to be fruitful and multiply.

South Carolina's Upcountry was a virgin land in those days: green, forested with pine, rolling to the dark ridges of the southern Blue Ridge. In spring, the air smelled of pine resin and honeysuckle vine.

Joseph Moorhead Jolly built his home on land bequeathed him by his father on the road between Anderson Courthouse and Pickens. A natural spring bubbled out of the ground near the house; the red earth produced an abundance of corn, cotton and even peaches. Joseph and his wife, Anna, never owned slaves and were prosperous by the standards of the time. They had to be.

Manse, a literate young man who wrote with a refined hand, kept his father's ledgers and figured that every week the family consumed forty gallons of milk (from three cows), ten pounds of butter and eighty to one hundred pounds of flour and corn meal, not to mention sidemeat, wild game and sixty gallons of sorghum a year.

Manse was the fifth born of the Jolly boys, of whom one only survived to middle age, Freeman Liberty, the seventh son. His lifelong slowness was attributed to an accident at birth in which the baby's cord was compressed, depriving him of oxygen. Yet Freeman served in Hampton's Legion during the war, married and fathered five girls. He ended his life at his own hand in Hart County, Georgia, in 1885.

Manse's other five brothers died in the war: Joseph Jr., John, James and William Enos perished on battlefields from Virginia to Tennessee; Jesse Alfred died in an army hospital of brain fever. After the war, the Jolly girls—Ruah, Martha Anne and, Manse's favorite, Mary Jane—married men of good reputation, Ruah and Mary to the Syms brothers, George and William. Margaret, the first Jolly girl, had died in infancy.

Everybody in the district knew of the Jollys. As the saying went, you could not throw a rock north of Anderson Courthouse for fear of hitting one. My father had some dealings with Joseph Jr. and James Jolly, who around 1857 bought on credit a specially-ordered length of tanned leather to make a belt with which to power a sawmill they hoped to build. Nothing ever came of the scheme, and the boys had to pay off their debt with hard-earned bushels of peaches and corn seed.

Some of that happened before and some happened later, long after the war which consumed our youth and was the center of our times, a great magnet that held our fortunes and mixed our atoms in some mysterious way so that things were not the same ever again. None of us were aware of that subtle chemistry then. We were only conscious of a great stirring in the land, but it all seemed to be happening so far away.

My father growled through his mustache at the newspapers which arrived upriver from Savannah and Charleston. He did not like talk of war and defiance of federal authority; it upset something basic in his orderly German mind. Not that he was a Unionist, and there were many in the Upcountry at that time, but Augustus Fries knew in his shopkeeper's heart that war would be very bad for any business that depended upon the river trade, as his did.

The news of Fort Sumter struck my family and our small community like a thunderbolt. That happened on the evening of April 14, 1861; I was two months short of my twenty-first birthday.

I was returning home from a visit to the McCormicks, where I had intended to spend a pleasant hour or two with young Lettie. Her father was an attorney at Anderson Courthouse and a rabid fire eater who had signed the secession ordinance. Instead of hours mooning with almond-eyed Lettie, my ears were filled with all the Yankee-hating invective her old man McCormick could muster. I had to endure his tobacco-fouled breath with nothing stronger than sugared lemonade.

Cantering past the handful of whitewashed plank buildings that was Townville in 1861, I saw lanterns swinging from the front of my father's store, throwing a weird yellow light on the hand-painted sign of Augustus Fries & Sons. Groups of men crowded the narrow lane, talking loudly and wildly gesticulating.

Brother Tom grabbed my reins as I rode in and gripped my knee with his other big hand.

"It's war, Ansel!" he cried. "The Yankees have fired on our forts in Charleston harbor and were soundly whipped. Governor Pickens is calling for troops and we are all going. It will be a fight to the finish!"

Brother Newton was at the center of a group of excited young men, each jostling for the broadsheet newspaper Newton was trying to read by lantern light. Shadows outlined the smallpox scars on his angular face. Newton threw the newspaper to his friends and I could read the vision in his eyes. He saw banners and marching columns surging through the wreckage of war, a terrible, heroic tableau with himself at the center.

Father was sitting in darkness at his desk in back of the store; the scent of paint, pitch, tobacco and raw leather mixed with the animal musk of our stabled mules and horses. He had unbuttoned his linen vest and crossed his legs, so that the glow of the match with which he lit his best clay pipe flared for a moment on the scuffed toe of his boot.

"I suppose, Ansel, you will be galumphing off, too, with the rest of them," he said softly, sucking the pipe stem. The bowl glowed brightly. "I don't blame you. You boys want to feel the elephant."

"See the elephant, pa."

"It is a natural thing and I should feel proud my boys want to fight." He paused and seemed to struggle with a thought he could not adequately express. He aimed the pipe stem at me. "Some say this war will be good for business, some say bad. I say it will be bad, Ansel. In the end it will be a bad thing for us out here. I been reading all the papers and listening to the speeches, and Gott help me if I can figure out what the blamed hell this is all about. All the boys are going off to fight and not one of them knows what for. Do you, Ansel?"

He looked at me so fiercely I dropped my eyes.

"It's for our home, pa. For South Carolina."

Father sat and sucked his pipe, which had gone out, then tucked it into a pigeonhole on his desk, and slowly stood and stretched.

"As long as you have it straight in your head, Ansel," he said. "As long as you think you know, this old man will keep his mouth shut.

I'm going upstairs to bed. Close up the store when those people have gone home."

That was the last time I remember my father saying anything about the war. What was there to say? Our very atoms were being mixed and interchanged by powers beyond our control; there was no way to tell which capricious way Nature or God would hurl us. Great change was coming, bearing down on our lives like a runaway train. One might just as well try to stop the sun and moon.

Two weeks later, Colonel John Baylis Earle Sloan began recruiting three companies of a regiment that would become the 4th South Carolina Volunteer Infantry at Anderson Court House.

Father, Tom, Newton and I rode the freight wagon to town on Saturday morning. Tom and Newton strode to the captain's muster desk, set up on the courthouse square and decked with red, white and blue bunting. My brothers swore they were over seventeen and healthy in mind and body, then signed their names as privates in the rolls of Company C, the Palmetto Riflemen.

They swaggered back to us under the admiring eyes of old men and barefoot boys, and smiling young ladies carrying tiny Stars and Bars flags, or wearing handwoven palmetto cockades made from palmetto fronds. They swung their haversacks over their shoulders, lovingly equipped by father with woolen socks, tobacco, soldier's housewives (complete with English pins and good strong thread) and an extra muslin shirt.

"Well, Ansel?" father inquired. But I shook my head.

Newt asked me if I was just naturally yellow, so I punched him hard in his lanky upper arm. Tom protested the war would be over before I had a chance to get into any of it, and asked me to reconsider.

"Captain said I was right popular with the boys, so that makes me good officer material," Tom boasted. "Come on, Ansel, join up. Why, I'll make you a corporal and won't little Lettie's eyes get big."

I had no doubt Tom was right. He was the kind of man other men liked to be around; tough in a fight and possessed of considerable brains. He could have gone to college and been a judge or a state senator.

Maybe Newt was right. Maybe I was yellow, deep inside. Something was holding me back.

I did not know it at the time, but Manse had been in the service of South Carolina for more than three months. He joined the 1st South Carolina Regulars in February and was stationed at Fort Moultrie on Sullivan's Island the day the war began. He retrieved one of the first cannon balls fired at Fort Moultrie from the heavy Federal guns at Fort Sumter, an 18-pound iron shot that he picked up from the sand parapet and took home as a souvenir. For years afterward, the cannonball was displayed every Fourth of July in the window of Fant's pharmacy at Anderson Court House.

In July, the first great battle of the war was fought on Manassas plain. Father and I rode to Anderson Court House to get the latest papers with the casualty lists. To our relief, their names were not to be found, though we recognized those of neighbors and near kin.

Tom's letter home arrived three weeks later, full of triumph and grim news. Tom and Newton were in that fight with their regiment, the 4th South Carolina; Tom was already a first sergeant and, true to his promise, Newt had made corporal. They saw their brigade commander, General Barnard Bee, of nearby Pendleton, shot down, and dozens of mutual acquaintances whom Tom listed by name. He was not so sure anymore that he liked fighting and soldiering, but wrote, "I will stick to it to the end." The end of his life, he meant. Newton asked pa to send him a new shirt; his had been saturated with the blood of a friend.

August that first year of the war was uncommonly hot. Drought burned out crops around the district, which we knew would drive up the price of grain at harvest and make fodder scarce in winter. That month I delivered a load of dry goods to Ulmer's store in Anderson Court House, then took a stroll around the square, munching boiled peanuts.

I wandered over to the Benson House Hotel and stepped down into the darkened saloon. I was immediately hailed by Henry Knauff, who was two years younger than me, pimply-faced and frail-looking as a girl. Henry bought me a lager, cool and frothy in its earthenware bottle, and we sat, smoking and drinking, and spitting on the hard-packed dirt floor.

"I'm going to join up," Henry announced. "I don't like some of the looks I've been getting. Even Hepsibah gave me some lip today about hanging around and I durn near cuffed him. Glad I didn't; probably would've killed him. But I get the feeling my Petey feels the same way, Ansel."

Pietra Zenker was Henry's little Dutch sweetheart. Strange, but neither of us thought it odd that Southern women were so anxious to chase their men off to war, to be mangled or killed.

"I don't know, Ansel. After Charlie Bibeau come back with most of his face gone, I started thinking a little deeper about this enlisting thing," Henry said. "I don't know whether I would be better off in the army, living in a tent, or staying here and taking my chances with the citizenry. They are hostile, Ansel."

Henry leaned back, pipe dangling from his mouth, clutching his dirty linen suspenders and burying his soft chin in the open placket of his shirt. I tried to imagine Henry as a soldier and could not.

Just then a tall, rangy man in a dark blue frock coat with brass buttons stalked in and made for the inelegant bar of polished pinewood set atop three stout barrels. He took off his wide-brimmed slouch hat and the curly red hair on his head caught a shaft of afternoon sunlight slanting through the open doors.

"That's Manse Jolly," I said, half to myself.

Henry turned. "By God, so it is. Do you know him? He is a cousin of mine on my father's side. Hello, Manse!"

"No, don't call to him."

"Sorry. I will go to him then." Henry stepped to the bar, rapped the big soldier on his shoulder and was warmly greeted. Henry indicated our table and after Manse gave me a quick glance they sauntered over.

"Ansel, this is my cousin, Manson Sherrill Jolly. He is home on a 15-day furlough. Manse, Ansel is an old school chum of mine."

Manse nodded curtly and took my hand. I was immediately aware how soft and effeminate my right hand seemed compared to his. His hand was huge, rough as emery and fairly crushed my poor paw. He seated himself with some grace in one of the narrow caneback chairs at our table.

"Your daddy runs the dry goods store over to Townville," Manse stated. "The German who sells the red fireman's shirts?"

Father was famous for those shirts. He had ordered them all the way from Boston months before Sumter, and sold not a one. Then a local militia company took a shine to them—martial-looking in their double-breasted, button-down fanciness—and purchased the whole lot. They were blood-red wool flannel and cost seventy-five cents apiece. But father could get no more on account of the Yankee blockade.

"Yes, sir, Augustus Fries is my father," I replied, feeling the effects of the lager, "and if you require a good shirt I just brought to Ulmer's today a shipment of gray governors, reasonably priced at sixty cents."

"Oh, no, Mr. Fries, you will not sell me so easily," Manse laughed. "I have been home a week now and have successfully eluded the drummers in the Upcountry; all have something to sell a poor soldier. I needed stockings and a good pair of boots, and both needs are nicely met, thank you."

Manse ordered beer all around. We talked mostly of the war; Manse did most of the talking. He told us of the fight in Charleston harbor and how glorious was the cannonade. He admitted he was more a spectator than a combatant, however. Manse spoke proudly of his cannonball; he had seen one just like it take the foot off a foolish trooper who stuck it out to stop the ball's bouncing progress across the parapet, thinking it harmless.

"That poor fellow screamed for quite a while before he fainted from loss of blood," Manse said. "It sure made a deep impression on us all."

Henry quickly put the mouth of his beer bottle to his thin lips; for a moment I thought he was going to be sick. He was merely steeling himself for the question.

"Manse, I want to join up. When you go back, can you take me with you?"

Manse did not even hear the question. He was watching a stocky, broad-shouldered man who had just ducked into the saloon, went directly to the bar and ordered whiskey. Manse left our table and walked up to him, his right arm akimbo as if seeking something inside his long coat. When his hand swung free again at his side, it was extended by the length of a .41-caliber Colt pocket revolver.

Manse heavily tapped the man's shoulder with the pistol barrel. The man spun about and gazed at Jolly with the face of one looking at death, nosehair to nosehair.

"Ezra Johnston, where is my money?" demanded Manse.

Johnston's grizzled face seemed to age a decade. He choked and his face turned beet red, Manse all the while poking him with the pistol barrel.

"You have money to drink with but not money enough to pay me," Manse growled and cuffed Johnston across the face.

The man dug into the waistpocket of his vest and produced two gold double eagles, which he pressed into Manse's outstretched hand. Manse pocketed the money, put away his pistol and made some crack about the prompt repayment of loans made in good faith.

"He tried to cheat me," Manse said, only partly in apology, as he again eased into his seat. "He is vile, low-life scum, and if he had thrown down on me I would have ended his miserable life."

I had no doubt Manse meant exactly what he said. Henry shifted uncomfortably in his chair. I tightly gripped my beer bottle so no one would notice my hand trembling. I had nearly witnessed a murder.

Nonchalant, Manse drew out one of the double eagles and proposed a party, on him, to include liquor, supper and perhaps even a visit across the river to Mrs. Creel's famed boarding house. Henry and I managed weak, willing smiles.

That was my personal introduction to Manse Jolly.

CHAPTER 2

The Great Joiner Of Things

In our youths, our hearts were touched with fire.

—Oliver Wendell Holmes

Before I relate the reasons that compelled me to join up, let me explain a few things.

A great war was simmering far away; a great adventure was beginning. The lightning flickering in the clouds on summer nights, and the following rumble of thunder, I imagined as the vestiges of some desperate and terrible battle.

I held no solid notion of the great issues of the time. I was ambivalent toward slavery. My father refused to own them. "A big expense," he said, but his own ancestors were not far removed from serfdom. At the same time I certainly did not like the idea of armed strangers invading our state on any pretense. It seemed an honorable fight, one that came to possess our minds, our every thought. All planning and effort was directed toward it, all gossip and conversation centered about it. It was the biggest thing that had ever happened. It simply could not be ignored.

Father posted the broadsheet pages of the latest Anderson Intelligencer and the week-old Charleston newspapers on a board outside the door of the store every Saturday. Most all our customers had sons, brothers, husbands or fathers serving in Virginia, like our neighbor, Amos Sterling, who sent three sons into the army. Fortunately, there were few great battles that autumn and the war news often consisted of soldier's letters to their hometown papers, describing the joys of camp life. However, I read with consternation one newspaper account which described the Union army's occupation of Williamsburg, Virginia, and the subsequent ransacking of the college's ancient buildings.

There were families we knew well who cared not a flip for the war, who thought they could carry on as before and not feel even the ripples from the big stone that had been thrown into the pond. Some were Mennonites, peaceful people and good farmers who settled in the Upcountry to escape the ever-present face of slavery. Others were Unionists, rooted in the Upcountry, who had no choice but to lay low for fear of reprisal from the hotbloods, young toughs who roamed the district, professing patriotism but noticeably absent from the recruiting office. Their courage was fueled by whiskey and manifested itself in the burning of Union barns. Late in the war, these bands of bushwackers turned to robbery and murder, hid out in the hills and were only rooted out by regular Confederate infantry and cavalry diverted from the front.

That first autumn of the war, the train depot at Anderson Courthouse was constantly crowded with soldiers coming home on furlough or returning to the various fronts—Virginia, Tennessee or the Lowcountry—to rejoin their outfits. A new breed of civilian was springing up, one with which Southerners were not well acquainted: the bureaucrat, a class the Confederate government found it necessary to create and which plagued the daily lives of soldier and civilian alike throughout the war. They crop up in every war and once in place are there to stay; the man who tries to fight them is battling a hopeless tide. That was one lesson Grant taught the South: Bureaucracies can win wars. His was just more efficient than ours.

And yet there was a feeling this war was a great joiner of things, of human beings great and small who were being swept along by a surging, irresistible wave of portentous events. Anything seemed possible, and soon every day in my father's employ became a chafing reminder of the great chapter of history that was passing me by. I gradually came to feel there was something shameful in tending store while beyond those blue hills the hugest struggle in American history raged.

Manse returned to his regiment at Sullivan's Island in August and I saw no more of him for awhile. I thought of him now and again, tall and cocky in his uniform, guarding the forts by day and escorting the pretty belles of Charleston along the Battery by evening. How he would hoot if I had told him that! But, that is how I pictured army life then.

I talked to my father frequently that autumn about joining up. As always, he remained silent, tamping his pipe, relighting it with a wooden match, tamping again. I did not then have the courage to say, tomorrow or the next day, I was going.

October was a golden month, breathtaking in the red and yellow mosaic that spread over the forested hills. Winter, when it came, was dry and mild, leaving no room for excuses.

One day in early April I read in the Anderson Intelligencer of a company of cavalry forming in Pickens, a half day's ride north of Anderson Courthouse; Captain Elam Sharpe of Pendleton was recruiting men and horses. The next day, I told my father over breakfast that I intended to offer myself to Captain Sharpe and his command.

Father said nothing. He chewed his sausage, sipped his coffee, then pushed away his plate and stood. He began to walk by me, then, on impulse, gripped my shoulder and pressed his lips to my temple. Then he straightened and went in the store.

I started off for the war on a warm, sun-dappled day in April of 1862. There was twenty-five miles of objectionable road between Townville and Pickens, so I saddled up my roan stallion, Siegfried, with the aim of enlisting the both of us in Captain Sharpe's company.

I had decided, on the excellent advice of my brothers in the infantry, that the odious chore of experiencing battle from the same sawed-off vantage point from which I had viewed the previous twenty-two years of my life was not for me. I was built to be a cavalryman; everyone said it. I stood five-foot-five in my stocking feet and weighed in at one hundred thirty pounds. I was somewhat bandy-legged but had relatively sinuous arms, owned one bad tooth (an upper right molar), and had no known social diseases. I also possessed a first-class brain, which I intended to use to my best advantage.

Besides a linen haversack crammed with fresh clothing and toiletry articles, and topped with liver sandwiches and squares of gingerbread wrapped in waxed brown paper (a farewell gift from father's occasional cook, Eastie), father produced from the back room a heavy Prussian saber he insisted his father had carried in the days of the alliances against Napoleon. He pressed the thing upon me and I had to accept it. Here was the old German sending his youngest son to war, doing it with as much style as he could muster. Later, I recognized he was giving me a shield, so to speak, made of the hide of the dragon, a weapon that he imagined had been forged in fire and tested in battle and perhaps retained a portion of its old power.

I secured the sword to my saddle and waved as I cantered off, promising to write. I did not look back. It was a long ride to Pickens.

I had one stop to make, however, at the home of Miss Lettie McCormick, who, I understand, had been showing considerable interest in several young fellows of the Anderson District who were strutting around in finely-tailored uniforms that complemented their swollen chests and waspish waists.

Lettie was as pretty a girl as the Upcountry produced in those days, pale complected with luxurious, raven-black hair and emerald eyes, and the most charming habit of dropping her voice when she made serious conversation. She was well-schooled as well and quick with apt quotations from Tennyson and Shelley. Her little sister, Tessie, was a pretty little thing, too, but had the tartest tongue I have ever heard on an eleven-year-old.

I hoped to impress the whole family with my farewell. Except for Lettie, they considered me a malingerer and a tiresome bore for hanging around so long after Sumter. I thought I might add a blood oath for good measure.

But our best laid plans "gang oft' aglay," Mr. Burns wrote, and he must have known Elmira, Lettie's sullen black housemaid. She met me at the door, a storm cloud on her brow.

"Go away now, young mister. You looks like trouble and Miss Lettie don't need no more of that."

"What's wrong?" I demanded. "You act as if I were a stranger. Give me a reason or let me in."

Seems that Lettie was mourning the death of Captain Jack Sherrill, Tom and Newton's company commander, who died in winter quarters in Virginia of brain fever and whose body had just been sent home. He was a dashing and arrogant fellow, who no doubt caught his fatal fever prowling barefoot to some camp follower's cabin for "horizontal refreshment." I wondered callously if his death meant Tom now had a chance at promotion.

I did not press my case; that would have been bad form. But I left with Elmira an important message she was to convey to Lettie alone. This included my admiration for her, my grief at her sadness and, of course, my blood oath. I was determined not to waste it.

"Where the marks from that blood oath, boy?" Elmira inquired insolently.

I showed her a painful blood bruise I had raised on my left arm while unloading sacks of feed at the store the day before and she seemed satisfied. I even pressed two bits into her palm to seal our confidence. I found out later she never delivered my message; she forget about it the moment she slammed the door in my face.

A mile or two north of Anderson Courthouse, the old Pickens road, furrowed and sunken with use, narrowed into a lane shaded by beech and oak. It made for a pleasant ride, the sun just hot enough to wring a trickle of sweat from my neck, the sky cloudless, the shade cooled by a light breeze. Siegfried picked his way along the road, taking his time, while I composed letters in my head to Lettie and father.

"Better walk that horse, boy."

The voice, a deep, baritone growl, had come from the trees crowding the parapet of sunken lane just ahead. I had no weapon but that old Prussian saber, tucked beneath my suddenly taut right leg. Then a dark rider on a huge gray mare nosed his way out of the cover of trees and clambered down the embankment. The sunlight showed him to be a tall man with red hair, pistols stuck butt-up into his wide army belt.

"Manse!" I cried.

Manse Jolly appeared to have seen hard service since our last meeting. His frock coat was patched with various materials, mended with odd-colored threads. His brown leather belt and cartridge box were worn and cracked, his brass buttons and palmetto belt buckle dirty and dim. But his fiery blue eyes were alert, if mildly amused.

"Hello, Mr. Fries," Manse called. "Pardon my manners, but it pays to be careful on these lonely country roads. Where are you going, so far from home? Business trip?" His eyes settled on the sword my thigh vainly protected.

"I'm going to Pickens, Manse, to enlist in Captain Sharpe's company," I announced, summoning my finest oratory. "I have determined to smite the Yankees and win my spurs on the field of battle."

Manse's face split wide in a deep belly laugh.

"Then save the horseshit for the correspondents, Ansel, and ride with me because it seems we are fated to be comrades in arms."

As we rode along, Manse explained that he had tired of the infantry life in garrison, drilling and walking endless hours on sentry. Manse finally gave up his rank of sergeant and, in spite of the pleadings of his captain and colonel, left the regular infantry in February when his one-year enlistment expired. He came home to reacquaint himself with the smell of raw earth and the feel of hard farm work. But after two months he had grown restive. Three of his brothers were with General Joe Johnston in Virginia, fighting the real war, he said. But he also missed the army routine, the camaraderie and the smell of powder—"smoking action," he called it.

When Manse's youngest sister, Mary, told him of the horse company forming in Pickens, he caught the fever.

"Cavalry's the thing, Ansel. It's going to win this war, not the poor boys slogging through the mud," Manse maintained. "This horse outfit is heading straight for Lee's army. We're going to be under Wade Hampton, the biggest, meanest, cussedest old Sandlapper you ever saw. And Hampton is under J.E.B. Stuart, my friend, which means lots of hot, smoking action. You'll be tangling with all the Yankees in creation, Ansel, you wait and see. Oh, you'll wish you stayed home and minded your daddy's business."

Manse and I trotted into Pickens Courthouse a few hours after sunrise. It was a fresh, clear, blue-skyed morning, the sort of day the history books say greeted Napoleon at Austerlitz. Pickens was the seat of its own district, a pretty town of dirt streets, clapboard houses and picket fences, budding dogwoods and a red brick courthouse in the federal style that commanded a steep hill at the center of town. The square was roiling with men and horses, carriages, gentlemen and ladies, darkies in field clothes and servant's livery. A band was playing a martial air. Manse grinned at me and quickened his mare, Dixie's, pace. My heart began to beat at a canter.

I gawked at the handsome officers in their superbly fitted uniforms, no two quite alike in color or cut. That was the way of it through the war; Confederate gray never existed, for officers or men. Even the wealthiest colonel's frocks ranged in hue from charcoal gray to cadet gray to bluish-gray to, later in the war, the home dyes that ranged from deep walnut brown to yellow-brown butternut and everything in between.

The officers chatted with their ladies, grand in their finest hooped skirts and outlandish bonnets, carrying gaily-colored parasols. They stared arrogantly at the less opulently clothed enlisted men.

At any rate, I guessed the other men milling about the courthouse square were enlistees. They did not look much like soldiers. Most brought with them their own horses, for which they were paid a bounty by the state, along with some forage money. Some had paid for regulation cavalry trousers, reinforced with leather in the seat, or nine-button shell jackets rakishly cut to conform to a lean young man's waist.

A few sported soft leather English boots that rolled to mid-thigh; others wore simple working man's clothes, woolen trousers, brogans, sack coats and a variety of hats: straw boaters, slouches, bowlers and bee hives, peaked or cut.

Their mounts, too, represented a wide range of horse flesh: sleek, finely-muscled Arabian thoroughbreds, western quarterhorses, frisky little ponies, tired plow animals, huge but gentle draft Belgians, even a mule or two.

The weapons they carried were just as diverse: smoothbore muskets, double-barrelled shotguns, revolvers and hideaways, some flintlock, some percussion. A few cradled long hunting rifles their ancestors had carried in the Revolution; most carried powder horns, shot bags and a plethora of knives that could be variously described as dirks, on the low end, to crude iron Bowies that weighed three or four pounds.

Even stranger, there was an effusion of musical instruments among the mob: brass bugles, penny whistles, hunting horns, mouth harps and ancient Masonic drums. The band was trilling and thumping away beneath a small clump of trees in front of the courthouse, but it was hard going for them to make an impression through the wall of noise.

> It is my great delight
> To march and fight
> Like a Dixie volunteer…

Captain Elam Sharpe of Pendleton sat uncomfortably on a camp chair behind a table confiscated from the courthouse, set up on a section of wooden sidewalk at the base of the building's front steps. South Carolina's deep blue banner of crescent moon and lone star snapped overhead, catching the morning breeze next to a home-stitched Stars and Bars, a rather nondescript cloth for a national flag, I thought.

Manse made right for the desk, shouldering Dixie through the crowd of men and horses. I felt awful conspicuous. We dismounted in the street's urine-stinking gutter and patiently waited our turn while Sharpe and a consumptive lieutenant signed up two brothers, Pendleton boys fresh off the farm whom Manse evidently knew well: Robert and Ezra Sitton, the sons of Gus Sitton.

"By God, Manse, now I know I'm doing the right thing if you're coming along," cried Ezra. "I'll put your name up for sergeant."

When Manse stepped up to give his vitals, he drew a long steady gaze from Captain Sharpe. The captain was also a big man, who wore his beard long and untrimmed; his unbuttoned, heavy wool tunic flopped over at the collar. He offered Manse a pencil and told him to render his full name, age, occupation and previous military experience.

"You are one of Joe Jolly's boys," Sharpe stated.

"Yes, sir," Manse replied, scribbling, "and I believe the Reverend Silas Sharpe was your daddy." Sharpe smiled.

Manse was possessed of a rather elegant handwriting style, which I admired in a man whose life work had been with plough and ax. He gripped the wooden pencil so powerfully it snapped in two. Manse brushed away the residue and asked for another.

"Son, I hope you are not as hard on horses as you are on government writing materials," said Sharpe.

The Sitton boys laughed and Manse grinned. "I'm even harder on Yankees, cap."

Sharpe grunted with approval when he saw that Manse had already served a year in the regular infantry. He appointed him provisional corporal on the spot.

"Captain," said Manse, putting his hand on my shoulder, "this here is my friend and comrade, Ansel Fries. He was with me at Sullivan's Island during the Sumter fight."

I nearly choked at the bald-faced lie, but I was grateful. Several recruits turned their heads to regard Manse and I with mingled curiosity and respect.

"Mr. Fries, sign your name," the captain sighed. "You must be one damn sight ornrier than you look. At least you won't wear out a horse like this big old boy. Right there."

I solemnly signed my full name, Ansel Wilhelm Fries, and the lieutenant filled out my voucher for "one horse and assorted equipage, present for duty." My chest swelled with emotion as we led our horses to a water trough in front of Draisen's newly-painted undertaking parlor, where a gang of recruits were lounging and cavorting like children on a Sunday picnic.

I spotted a familiar form sitting lonely and forlorn on an unfinished coffin. I called his name and he looked around, bewildered. Then his pimply face lit up. It was Henry Knauff.

Henry hugged me like a long-lost brother.

"Great God Almighty but I never hoped for luck as good as this!" whooped Henry. "I been up here three days waiting for the company to fill up."

"Henry, I am profoundly disappointed. I thought you had given up any idea of living the life of a common soldier."

Jan Zenker had delivered Henry an ultimatum, threatened, in fact, to haul him by his britches to the nearest place of muster if he did not join up within the week.

Henry had no family left to speak of. His father was only a mouldering limestone marker in the Presbyterian churchyard, and his mother had passed the previous year of a melancholy thought peculiar to the Knauff family. When old Zenker gave him hell, Henry jumped like a frog in a frying pan, emancipated his only slave, Hepsibah, and packed his worldly goods. He even wrote out his will, leaving his mother's house on Rose Hill to the Zenkers in the event of his untimely death. Until then, Hepsibah could live there and work to maintain the place; Henry promised to send home money every month.

Henry greeted his cousin, Manse, who was preoccupied showing the Sitton brothers his homemade Bowie knife. So Henry and I bought a jug of apple cider from a huge black woman, leaving our horses with two of the town boys, who fought for the privilege. We sauntered over to a crowded general store where a white-bearded grandfather was handing out greasy bags of boiled peanuts and pungent squares of sweet potato pie. Thus, had we our breakfast.

"Look here, Ansel. What's that?"

A small but boisterous group of men had gathered in front of a small shop. As we watched, the store front window suddenly shattered. The men threw their hats in the air and cheered. Jagged shards of glass slowly fell from the unbroken frame, then came the crash of more breaking glass, and following every crash the men cheered.

"They're rousting out old John Johnson!" someone cried.

I button-holed a waistcoated gentleman and asked what was going on. He glared at me unkindly and snapped that John Johnson was editor of the Pickens Register, the worst abolitionist rag to be found south of Boston.

"Our boys will deal with the rascal," he snarled, "and whatever fate he receives, I can promise you it is one he richly deserves."

Pieces of a hand-powered printing press came vaulting through the remnants of the newspaper's store front, followed by reams of paper that fluttered in the breeze like a flight of birds before scattering over the mob. Two sturdy young men poured out a barrel of black ink from the door. It splashed in an obsidian river over the plank sidewalk and swirled in wide, opaque eddies into the dirt street.

An elderly man was shoved out of the office, a wizened, red-faced septuagenarian who squinted in the sunlight but bore himself with great dignity in spite of the fists being shaken in his face. His broken wire-rim glasses swung from one swollen ear. His face bore fresh bruises. He had been beaten.

Arms clawed at Johnson's torn vest and there were calls for a rope. Johnson went stiff and for the first time appeared to be afraid.

Just then a square-shouldered officer hunched onto the sidewalk; men backed away from the steady gaze of his coal-black eyes. His beard ruffled like a flag halfway down his broad chest. Two men cradling shotguns flanked him. The Sitton boys, by God.

Elam Sharpe addressed the mob. "As the senior military authority in the Pickens District, it is my duty to read you my standing orders. 'Mob violence of any sort is not to be tolerated.' You will therefore disperse immediately, or face the consequences."

Sharpe glared at individual faces in the crowd, staring one down, then the next, until these composite parts drifted away invisibly like meadow mist at dawn. Sharpe signaled for the Sitton boys to follow and encourage those who dragged their feet.

The captain turned to Johnson and his demeanor softened.

"My apologies, sir, on behalf of the state of South Carolina. If you will, please indicate those who assaulted you. You understand, of course, that you must see a constable to register a criminal complaint. I have no civil jurisdiction."

Johnson pointed his finger accusingly at several men still slouching about, and Henry stepped up to name two of our recruits he had recognized. Sharpe ordered the suspects to help clean up the Register office, under guard. Then he and Johnson shook hands.

That behavior, I learned, was typical of Elam Sharpe. He was the bravest man I knew while in the service, bar none, even Manse. Their brands of courage were of different types. Manse came to respect Sharpe but he never understood the captain's value system. Manse despised gentlemen, and yet aspired to be one. That would make for trouble down the line, though I could not see it then.

One day much later I chanced to comment on the seeming incorruptibility of Captain Sharpe's character, and Manse turned on me. He asked me if I had been with Sharpe every moment, read his deepest thoughts, walked around in his boots.

"Everything is corrupted," he snapped. "Nothing escapes the world's evil, no man nor woman. We all hide demons in our secret innards."

By the end of that memorable day in April of 1862, Company F of the 1st South Carolina Cavalry Battalion mustered a full complement of ninety-three officers and men, and an equal number of horses and mules. Recruits without mounts were ordered to join us in camp in Columbia, where mounts might be found for them. Those who were never horsed became teamsters or cooks.

It was common practice for volunteer companies to elect their officers. But Captain Sharpe brought with him two Anderson boys, J.B. Whitner—the consumptive officer who was at the muster desk—and Baz Hilliard, who already had their first lieutenant's commissions and lacked only a fighting regiment to join. Nobody argued with his choices.

Baz and I became good friends, but Whitner—well, he and I developed what people today call a basic personality conflict. We hated each other's guts. I will say more about that tiresome relationship later.

At Sharpe's recommendation the boys elected Buddy Dunn of Pendleton a second lieutenant, along with a popular, athletic youth from the Pickens District, Willie Grew. Both were fated to die at Brandy Station. The election of sergeants and corporals would wait for camp, where the chaff would be separated from the wheat.

In the afternoon, Captain Sharpe assembled the company and told us we were marching to Greenville in the morning, there to leave our mounts and baggage and entrain on the Greenville and Columbia Railroad for Camp Hampton in the capital city. After our mounts arrived, we would begin training in cavalry drill, tactics and deportment and draw weapons, uniforms and accouterments.

"It is my opinion our company will eventually train for the Low-country, to act as pickets against Yankee incursion into the many inlets and rivers around the Holy City of Charleston," Sharpe said. "Our troops there skirmish daily with the enemy. If you truly wish to fight, that is the place to be. "Not a few of the boys grumbled in protest, which Sharpe ignored.

"Hell-fire and damnation," complained a yellow-complected recruit who wore a black sombrero and new silver spurs. "I joined to follow the feather of Stuart. Just what does that man Sharpe mean to do?"

Manse spat with contempt.

"You boys are green as baby shit and about as pretty," he sneered. "Don't you know the army means training? You think you piss-ant peckerwoods would stand a chance against organized cavalry in the field, even if they was Yankees? The captain has my vote. He is going to drill you bastards until you can wheel by fours into column and back into line of battle in your sleep. He is going to march and coun-termarch you until your arse puts roots in the saddle."

Manse concluded his speech by pushing the sombrero-wearing recruit backwards into a horse trough, where he choked and spluttered and kicked his musical spurs to the wicked delight of the troop.

That evening we marched out to a peach orchard on the edge of town to make camp, passing as we did the sobering scenario of three recruits whom Sharpe had ordered bucked and gagged for the ransacking of the Register office and beating Mr. Johnson. It was not a light punishment. The guilty party's hands were tied and secured over his knees, and a stout stick was slid through the space over his straining arms but under the knees. Three hours in that position and you were painfully sore for days, butt, back, thighs and shoulders.

We had no tents, so we built small cooking fires and threw our blankets under the trees. We fed and watered our mounts, using hay and feed donated by local farmers. Before retiring, Manse rubbed down Dixie, then used his saddle as a pillow, Texas-style. He bedded down with the Sitton boys and other friends from Pendleton, while Henry and I rolled out our blankets nearby. Henry lit up and shared with me puffs on half a cigar that he produced.

We savored the thick, rich taste of the tobacco, and dreamed. It was a night for dreaming. Peach blossoms scented the air; the sky was a crystal-studded expanse of black velvet.

"You know, Henry, I believe I am a failure. My father went to considerable expense to send me to a fine center of learning to study law, and how do I show my gratitude? By running away to join the army. Leaving my father alone to manage his business. All alone."

Henry lay on his back, watching the sky with half-lidded eyes. The orchard smelled pleasantly of woodsmoke.

"There's a falling star, Ansel," he murmured.

I am not homesick, I told myself. It was exciting, but also disturbing, to feel so rootless. Supper had consisted of half a day-old liver sandwich and tepid water from a canteen. Breakfast would be spare indeed. I thought of the panned cakes and fried sausages father ordered from Eastie every Sunday.

Somebody in the camp, as if reading my thoughts, began singing acapella in a strong yet sweet voice. The song was "Lorena"; the soloist soon was joined by a guitar and mouth harp.

A hundred months 'twas flowery May
When up the hilly slope we climbed
To watch the dying of the day,
And hear the distant church bells chime.

We lay there a long while, listening to the music, until the camp hushed, and Henry started snoring. I lay awake for a long while, thinking about Tom and Newt in Virginia, listening to the muted thunder that rolled like gentle drums in the night.

That night, I had a dream. We were at the swimming hole on Bear Creek that we had frequented as boys; it ran brown and deep and shade-cool in the hottest days of the Carolina summer. Tom, Newton, Henry and myself were swimming and shouting, all naked, our buttocks and loins white as a fish's belly, our heads, necks and forearms seared brown by the sun.

Then Tom and Newt were at the center of the muddy pool. They were sinking, their arms raised above them as if in supplication. Slowly they sank, their sculpted martyr's faces streaming water, and when they were gone the reddish marl of the creek surface bubbled once and was still.

I woke up, trembling.

CHAPTER 3

Johnny's Gone For A Soldier

We're tenting tonight on the old campground
Give us a song to cheer our weary hearts,
A song of home and friends we loved so dear.

—Walter Kittridge

I woke up in a gray misty dawn to see Henry huddling with other blanketed figures by the fire, boiling water in tin cans to make coffee. My woolen shirt and heavy coat made a fine, warm sleeping cocoon, though the top of my brown blanket was wet with dew. I buried myself deeper in its thick folds and tried to get back to sleep, but sleep was useless.

My nightmare was but a dim memory compared to my waking misery. My neck was stiff, my back ached, all my joints worked reluctantly in the raw morning air.

The sun was beginning to shed real light; the red, misty camp was astir with sullen figures. A pair of mockingbirds were singing furiously in the folds of the peachtree over my head, but were nearly drowned out by the phlegmatic cacophony of men rising after spending the night on cold ground.

I never heard such spitting, hawking and hacking; I woke with it in the field every morning for four years and never got used to it. I came to realize there were men never wounded in battle who but suffered the rest of their lives from the weak lungs, frozen feet, arthritis and rheumatism they developed in the service of their country.

The smell of fresh coffee and frying bacon made my stomach grumble. Henry brought me a tin cup of searing hot coffee and an army sandwich of bacon stuffed between two hard, unsalted crackers. I gobbled the food and was carefully sipping the coffee when skinny Lieutenant Whitner came around, ordering the boys in his squeaky voice to pack up quick and be ready to commence the march to Greenville.

I rolled my blanket and secured it with leather straps, then reached into my haversack and pulled out a rubber water bottle father had filled with sour mash. I uncorked it and poured a dram of the popskull into my coffee. I have always been a moderate imbiber, but I swan I can see how a man could be lured into pursuing alcoholic dreams. The temptation is great, the flesh too often weak.

"Knauff! Captain wants to see you."

Henry and I found Manse and the Sitton boys outside Captain Sharpe's stained linen tent, the one he had used in Mexico. Nearby sat an old black man wearing a ragged felt hat and a homespun shirt. His bare feet were dusty white and he had a blanket roll wrapped clumsily around his right shoulder and tied off at his left hip. He looked downcast, the moth-eaten brim of his hat obscuring most of his leathery face.

Henry stopped dead in his tracks and his eyes narrowed as the old man slowly stood.

"Hepsibah! What do you mean by this?"

"Now don't curse me, Mr. Henry," the old man pleaded. "I gots to go, I just gots to. After you left, my Katherine wouldn't take me in.

What was I to do, Mr. Henry? You done the honorable thing, so I reckoned I could, too. I can cook, I can wash, I can mend, I can do anything them young bucks can."

"Who is minding my mother's house?"

"Miss Katherine, sir, and she is a good mistress. That's why she threw me out."

"Were you drinking?"

"No, sir, I swears not."

"How will you follow me, old man? This is a cavalry regiment. Are you going to run all the way to Virginia?"

Manse and the others were snickering, enjoying the morning's unexpected entertainment. Manse finally stood and waved for silence.

"Gentlemen, given our positions as Confederate warriors, I deem it ungentlemanly for us to soil our hands with the commonalities of everyday labor. I propose we form a mess of the six of us, with Hepsibah as our cook. Each day we'll pool our rations for the day's meals. Hepsibah will cut firewood, make the fires, wash the pans, and he will get his share of the forage."

Manse concluded, "We shall dine in the field as elegantly as our friends back home at the Benson House. That shall be our name, the Benson House Mess."

We formed that morning in more or less a military column, some of the boys whooping and yelling like red Indians. They were drunk, having found a whiskey drummer in town where they procured jugs of the O Be Joyful. Sharpe quickly bore down, smashing bottles and ordering five of the biggest drunks tied to their saddles.

"If they fall off, leave 'em," the captain snapped.

It was a pleasant ride to the city of Greenville and took up the better part of the day. Of the six of us in the Benson House Mess, only Manse and I had been more than twenty miles outside the Anderson District. We were a green, home-tied bunch of crackers, all right.

Greenville was a town of nearly seven thousand souls, a railroad center for the Upcountry. As we approached the railroad depots we saw soldiers, and great corrals full of horses and cattle being readied for shipment north. Later in the war the government could not afford the luxury of transportation for its livestock, so herds were driven overland by teamsters. The stock cars were needed for troops.

We had several hours wait for our train. Captain Sharpe ordered us to separate our personal baggage, haversacks and blankets only, from the rest of our horse equipments and turn our horses over to a group of black handlers. The boys grumbled plenty but it was clear there was no way around it. I fed Siegfried an apple I had saved and he nuzzled me gratefully. But he was agitated, as though sensing something was going to happen.

My heart ached at the thought of the poor creature taking its first rail trip packed in a stock car with seven strange horses. If I had known then what I found out days later, I would have cut him loose, or presented him to a reputable-looking citizen. Because the moment I left that handsome animal, feeling not a whit better than a traitor, I was seized with a dark foreboding I would never see him again.

I never did. He disappeared among the great stocks of horses the Confederacy was gathering, and though I later received fifty dollars in government payment for his loss, I cursed forever afterward my naivete trusting in the powers that be. I never had a better horse throughout the war.

Knowing the army, Siegfried probably ended up pulling artillery or hauling supply wagons. Even after all these years it burns my heart to think of my betrayal. I despised the government for stealing my horse but I should have known better.

The train, when it came, comprised only ten cars and half of those were stock cars for the ones unlucky enough to get on last. Manse and I shouldered our way aboard a sitting car and squeezed into one of the stiff-backed benches that passed for railroad comfort in those days. We shared our train with several companies of infantry recruits also going to Columbia for training. They were a boastful bunch, as cocky and sure of themselves as my brothers had been the year before.

Traveling by train in those days was hardly genteel or pleasant. Hot coals blown out with the black locomotive smoke discouraged riders from getting too close to the windows, and on long curves in the rail line, when the wind was right, we choked on the acrid clouds that filled the open cars. All that humanity made the train sluggish as a fat man; the cars pitched and yawed from side to side at the slightest curve.

On the open stretches, however, which became more common as we left the foothills of the Blue Ridge mountains behind us, we made a good twenty miles each hour. Figuring in stops for water and wood, where invariably groups of mothers and young ladies gathered to hand up to the boys baskets of sandwiches, cold fried chicken and ginger beer, it took us better than seven hours to reach the capital city.

If the sun had been out, my first view of Columbia would have been at dusk. But the city was sodden and dreary under a leaden sky. Rain had turned the city streets into ochre mud. We took the back streets marching from the depot to Camp Hampton, slogging through the dark, deserted city.

After several miles, footsore, backsore and hungry, we splashed down a muddy lane and through the arbor gate marking the entrance to the camp.

The camp was a newly cleared farm field, studded with freshly cut tree stumps; a long oval drill field was situated at the center, holding so much water it appeared to be a small lake. The drill field was flanked by a dozen long, unpainted sheds, planked with raw wood pungent of pine. A line of cooks stood beneath a crude canvas lean-to, stirring huge pots of army bean soup. The fragrant aroma made my mouth water. We ate our soup and hard crackers standing in the rain but there were few complaints.

Then Captain Sharpe marched the company off into a bare corner of the camp, where, amid shorn cornstalks and with rivulets of water coursing through the furrows, he ordered us to make camp. The boys grumbled in an ugly manner.

"What about them sheds?" demanded Ezra Sitton, careful to address J.B. Whitner and not Sharpe.

"Them's for horses," snapped Sharpe. "Get busy if you want a place to sleep tonight."

Most of us had about had it with the army then and there, but, bean soup or not, nobody was willing to challenge Elam Sharpe. We went about sullenly, collecting planks and fence rails for a hut floor, which Manse taught our mess how to build. We raised two poles and a crosspole and managed to fashion a tent from a rubber blanket and two woolen ones. The six of us squeezed inside like sheep; it would have been comical if we had not been so miserable.

I remember breathing the stench of wet wool and unwashed bodies, and passed around my whiskey so the boys could shake off their chills. Following a round of sincere cursing of the army and government, we began to settle in. Hepsibah snuck out and returned with an armful of straw he pilfered from the stables. We stuffed it beneath our wet coats and so made serviceable beds. Manse rigged a little fire, and while the sharp woodsmoke burned our eyes, we were grateful for the cheery sight of the flames.

Hepsibah boiled a pot of water and made sassafras tea. Soon, the army did not seem such a bad place to be after all. The patter of rain and Hepsibah's bass voice crooning in sing-song lulled me. I was weary but warm when sleep washed over me in a black wave.

None of us save Manse had any idea when we joined the cavalry that being a horseman in gray meant anything but dashing pursuit, the thrill of close combat and gay nights in camp under the stars.

Our first days in camp should have taught us differently. After a week of utter boredom and monotonous food, infantry drill and hours of fruitless picket duty (the nearest Yankee being at least one hundred miles away), the truth began to dawn on us.

At least we were not alone in our misery. Other companies from Laurensville, Greenwood, Seneca, Easley Station and Abbeville began coming in. We derived endless amusement from their shock and dejection at the camp conditions. It made us feel like veterans to show a select few of these fresh fish where to find materials to make their huts more comfortable, or how to steal extra straw and rations. The boys felt no guilt, either, of relieving them of useless equipments: canteens with built-in water filters, pillows, comforters, beaver hats, mackintoshes, rubber galoshes, even umbrellas. Food items from home were especially prized and worth their weight in gold, but they were jealously guarded and difficult to pilfer. Hepsibah found ways.

These companies and ours were part of a battalion of cavalry forming under Colonel John Logan Black, a Columbia engineer who, like Sharpe, had seen action against General Santa Anna in the Mexican War. Black was a tall, handsome man in his forties possessed of a pleasant personality and warm sense of humor. He was no Bible-banger and could cuss with the best of them, but only when provoked. Manse and I came to admire him greatly; he was a fighter, and we served under him throughout the war. His only vice was a disgusting fondness for chewing tobacco; but in those days men who demurred from tobacco use were in a decided minority.

Within two weeks, Black had gathered more than five hundred recruits into camp, organized into six companies; Captain Sharpe's was designated Company F of the 1st South Carolina Cavalry Battalion.

One morning after reveille, Black announced to us that our mounts had arrived. The boys cheered at first but their cheers turned to curses when it was discovered that half the original mounts were not among the shipment. I shed tears of rage and frustration at losing Siegfried, and wondered what I would tell father.

I mourned the loss of my horse for weeks; I swore I would never again trust the government. Manse got back his fine gray mare, Dixie, and I was assigned a sorrel mare with an even disposition whom I named Lettie, partly out of loyalty to my fickle sweetheart and partly out of annoyance that she had neglected to write me. In my first month at Camp Hampton I received only two letters, one from my father and one from my brothers in Virginia, which father had forwarded to me.

The day after the battalion's horses were unloaded at the Greenville and Columbia terminal and driven through the city to Camp Hampton, the state of South Carolina delivered to us horse equipments, uniforms and an uneven issue of weapons.

We lined up to receive gray jackets with no buttons—brass "S.C." buttons embossed with the Carolina palmetto were issued separately—woolen trousers, cotton shirts and linen underwear. We kept our own hats and those who needed shoes got infantry brogans. I retained the soft leather boots my father had ordered for me from Savannah. Stockings I did not need but Manse convinced me to take them as issued.

I must say that the short gray nine-button jacket preferred by the Confederate soldier made him the nattiest figure of the war. Even late in the war the commonest trooper, his clothing patched with field repairs, looked the part of a cavalier of Stuart's in his jacket.

The leather accouterments we were given were more spotty in quality. My cap and cartridge boxes were stiff as new leather can be; I oiled them religiously to soften the leather. I also picked up a cartridge box sling, fitted with a bright brass eagle plate positioned martially over my heart; later, as veterans, we threw them away. They made too good a target.

I could not find a waist belt to fit me but Manse said I did not need one. Only infantrymen required a belt, he insisted, to hold bayonet frog and cap box. "What about my cap box?" I asked.

"Dump it," Manse sneered. "Keep caps in your pocket."

I considered myself lucky. Some of the boys were issued equipment dating from the Mexican War, or militia items dredged from old state arsenals; the leather was mildewed, the brass fittings green with oxide. Is it any wonder that, in our first action, many completed their equipage by scavenging among the dead and wounded of the enemy?

A few used their own money to buy brass numerals and company letters for their caps and hats from the drummers or sutlers who came around, selling everything from fried pies and tinned meats to envelopes, stationary, candles, soap and matches, items often in short supply at the quartermaster's.

Company F was first in line when the time came to draw horse equipment, so we got the pick of bridles and bits, spurs, blankets and saddles. Most of the latter were Grimsley saddles made in Columbia but some were of the newer "Jennifer tree" type, said to be favored by Beauty Stuart himself. The boys who copped them soon complained of back pains after only a few hours in the saddle. At the first opportunity, all of us traded ours in for the Northern-made McClellan saddle, by far the best single piece of horse equipment developed during the war.

While the uniforms and equipment we received set our spirits soaring, our shining new firearms fairly took our breaths away. We drew several hundred muzzle-loading, .58-caliber musketoons—sawed-off versions of the standard infantry rifle-musket—solidly manufactured in Montgomery, Alabama, and specially stamped "1st S.C. Cav." on the walnut stock and butt plate.

Some of the boys, all old hunters, looked suspiciously at the musketoon and refused to give up their squirrel rifles and shotguns. But the musketoon was a serviceable arm: compact, easily slung behind a rider, and at close range delivered a killing wallop. It could be loaded on horseback if need be, but as the war progressed that situation rarely arose.

Truth be told, I ditched my musketoon the day an unfortunate Yankee's Sharps breechloading carbine came into my possession, .52-caliber and weighing eight pounds; it was beautiful. Only trouble I had with it was getting cartridges.

"I swan we could whip the whole Yankee cavalry by ourselves," gushed Ezra Sitton, hefting his musketoon.

We felt invincible, all right, though we had yet to so much as see an enemy soldier.

A word to the modern historian: Company F never received an issue of sabers. Other companies did, and now and again the boys would pick up Yankee sabers. Most of us never missed them, and would borrow one if needed to impress the girls or home folks on leave. I do not recall ever drawing my heavy Prussian saber in battle, only in review; by war's end, horsemen as sword fighters had become obsolete. After Gettysburg, we still went into action mounted at a rush, popping away with revolvers. But more and more we fought dismounted, as skirmishers or to hold a position like regular infantry, every fourth man in the rear holding his comrade's horses.

It was about this time that a squint-eyed photographer called Cornelius Flye visited Camp Hampton and set up a tent studio and darkroom outside the camp gates.

The boys lined up like cattle to have their likenesses made by Mr. Flye. He charged fifty cents for the cheaper tintype portraits and up to two dollars for the glass ambrotypes, which came inside handsome cases of velvet and japanned tin.

I borrowed Manse's Colt pistol and sat with my arm around Henry's shoulder while he gripped my Prussian saber upright on one knee, then we adopted the grimmest faces we could muster for the lens. We greatly admired Mr. Flye's work and gladly paid our money.

Henry sent his to Pietra Zenker, in spite of my admonition to let old Katherine keep the picture safe; mine went to father, of course.

Years later, long after father's death and while I was practicing law in east Texas, Newton sent me the dusty old likeness. I could not have imagined its effect. I had buried Manse and the war years long before, but the image brought it all back. Memories of the war began creeping into my deepest dreams, then invaded my waking thoughts. I had to tuck away the case until the day I could look on it only to reassure myself that we were ever once so young.

In May, Company F was assigned a regular drill sergeant. His name was Hurt Connally and he had seen action in a dozen fights with Stuart and Turner Ashby. Connally was a short, barrel-chested Virginian who limped from the leg wound that had taken him out of the war.

We learned infantry drill at first, on the theory that if a recruit could march well on foot, he should have no trouble learning the intricacies of drill on horseback.

We drilled in the morning and in the evening. In between we would stop for dinner, drill, take some time to write a letter home, then drill, drill and drill some more. Fridays, on top of regular drill, Colonel Black supervised battalion drill. We got better slowly, if only to keep Connally and Manse—now a true corporal—off our backs. But Connally in particular rode us unmercifully.

One afternoon that May, when the scent of honeysuckle was sweetening the air, Connally began riding a whey-faced private called Raleigh Syms, a gentleman from one of Anderson Court-house's wealthiest families. Syms was not well-liked because of his snooty manners and the colored manservant he retained to cook his meals and keep his custom-tailored uniform well-brushed. To his credit, he had refused the commission his father purchased for him, intending to stick it out as a common soldier. Connally locked onto poor Syms like a boar in rut.

Syms did not have the legs to execute the proper step required of the outside man on the forward rank when the command, "Company, right wheel, march!" was given. He was supposed to lengthen his stride and quicken his step, to keep the line dressed as it pivoted on the inside man, who marked time until the wheel was complete.

Try as he would, Syms could not keep up, and Connally was taking an inordinate amount of pleasure screaming in the boy's ear. But the sergeant went too far when he grasped Syms by the yoke of his jacket and tried to bodily make him keep pace with the rest of the company as he ordered us through right wheel after right wheel.

Syms stopped dead in his tracks and slapped Connally's hands away; his smooth-cheeked face was scarlet and trembling. Connally stood stock still, dumbfounded. Syms stalked back to camp.

The company shuffled uneasily in place, shocked into silence. Connally muttered something, spat, then ordered us once more around the drill field. As we turned and marched parallel to the company street, Connally stepped between the column and the camp, counting cadence.

"Connally, you are a dead man."

Skinny Raleigh Syms had stepped from behind a tent-hut and was coolly leveling the huge bore of a flintlock dueling pistol square at Connally's chest. The gun exploded, and the company scattered like a flock of starlings.

Connally had shifted his weight to his right foot just as the piece discharged and his agility no doubt saved his life. The ball tore into his upper left arm, breaking the bone, and Connally dropped as if he had been pole-axed.

Syms gazed for a moment at Connally's body, threw away the pistol with a gesture of distaste and walked back to his private tent.

"Bone's broken for sure," Manse whistled, examining Connally's wound.

"Get me to the sawbones," Connally croaked.

Our regimental surgeon was Dr. Walker T. Spurgeon, a recent graduate of South Carolina College who admitted he had only treated one gunshot wound thus far in his brief career. Thus far, Surgeon Spurgeon's primary purpose had been to treat those on sick call by handing out what the boys called "blue mass," which was for constipation, or "white fire," for diarrhea.

"This is bad, gentlemen, very bad," Surgeon Spurgeon announced following his examination. "The humerus is shattered." He looked down at Connally and said softly, "Sergeant, the arm has to come off. I have to do it now, if I am to save your life."

Connally was barely conscious but he managed to snarl, "Well what in hell are you waiting for?"

Surgeon Spurgeon worked with precision, pressing a soft, ether-filled sponge to Connally's face and monitoring the unconscious sergeant's breathing, then stanching off the upper arm with a tourniquet to slow the blood flow.

When the doctor stepped away to retrieve his scalpel and bone-saw, I excused myself. Manse stayed. He returned to the Benson House Mess in a thoughtful mood.

"Boys, if that ever happens to me," he said finally, "I want you to finish me off. I won't go through this life half a man." Colonel Black threatened Syms with a courts-martial, but, being a gentleman, he was allowed to leave camp without the customary drumming out ceremony designed to humiliate the wrong-doing soldier. Syms went home and reenlisted as a private in the 14th South Carolina Infantry. He got himself killed, honorably, at Spotsylvania Courthouse.

Connally nearly died when the inevitable infection set in, but that was not Dr. Spurgeon's fault. All wounds became septic in that war; some men lived, some did not. Connally survived, and the boys saw to it he had tobacco and a swallow of whiskey now and again while in hospital. In a month the sergeant was back on his feet, his empty sleeve swinging as he marched troops in cadence, mean as ever.

Our Benson House Mess prospered in spite of the hardships of camp life. Hepsibah was a marvelous cook, capable of making an edible meal of the wormiest salt beef. He was a healer as well. If one of us cut a hand chopping firewood, Hep knew to wrap tree moss around the wound in a poultice. He became renowned for his ability to "talk out fire," that is, relieve the pain of a wound, burn or strain through incantation and a laying on of hands. Hep also could fashion a drinkable tea from any number of swamp or forest plants and roots, obscure varieties for which he had his own names.

But there was little Hep could do for dysentery or typhoid and when the weather turned warmer, the sicknesses began and boys began to die.

First Henry got the fever. Hep tended him night and day until Henry became so weak we insisted on carrying him to the camp hospital. Hep stayed there with Henry, refusing to leave his side. One by one, Bob Sitton, Ezra Sitton, Manse and then I got the shits, Hep claimed from drinking the camp well water. That was the low point of our camp existence, lolling about the hut, grunting with every cramp, unable to keep down any solid food, barely able to muster the strength to stagger five, seven, ten times a day to the company sinks.

Manse was the strongest. He tended us the best he could but it was short comfort. Bob began to recover from his dysentery and was wobbly but getting stronger when the typhoid raging through the battalion hit him. In his weakened condition I thought he would die; Surgeon Spurgeon told us to take his last testament and write to Bob's folks, there was little that could be done for him. But Bob thumbed his nose at the grim reaper and got better on Hep's sassafras tea.

We were all lucky.

Each morning we watched the orderlies carry out the boys who had died in the night to the tent where the newly dead were stacked. Sometimes the shrouded corpses were carried by their comrades to the corner of the camp where a crude cemetery had been laid out; within two months of our arrival it held over one hundred graves. Sometimes a sad old gentleman or red-eyed lady dressed in mourning came to camp in a wagon. Stopping at the dead tent, their servants would clamber down, unload a simple pine coffin from the wagon and carry it inside. They emerged carrying what had been a beloved son, brother or husband. These vignettes soon became too common to notice.

That was the way it was. Before we ever got to Virginia, one hundred and fifty boys of the old regiment were promoted to glory and laid to rest in their native soil without seeing or tasting the smoke of battle.

At this time, Manse was one of eight corporals in Company F, which had shrunken to sixty-five effectives because of disease. He was becoming well-known in the battalion for his size, temperament and military experience. He was Captain Sharpe's right hand; Sharpe liked Manse's independence and his aggressive nature, something the Mexicans call "cojones."

One morning Manse whipped a fellow from another company who made a taunting remark about his red hair. Although stout enough, the taunter came out of the scrape unconscious, with a gouged eye, a busted hand and a cracked skull. After word spread, even the toughest men in the battalion gave Manse a wide berth. He was viewed as a dangerous man to cross.

Manse could be a brutal taskmaster on the drill field as well. He learned his cavalry drill quickly and had little patience with slow learners. His earnestness was justifiable, he claimed, because he was teaching the boys the best way to survive in combat: working together like a team of horses, obeying orders without thinking, your mind set wholly on the mission and on the group. Manse also knew that the better horse soldier he was, the more he was acknowledged a leader of men, the better his chance of making sergeant, his old rank in the infantry. That was his goal and he reached it that June, when we were told that our training—such as it was—was nearing its end.

We were fighting soldiers now.

CHAPTER 4

Scouring the Lowcountry

Word came from Captain Sharpe one steamy morning in June that we were moving out. All six companies of the 1st Battalion, South Carolina Cavalry, were to entrain for the swampy coastal country around Charleston, not to Richmond, the destination for which we had prayed. Major General John C. Pemberton needed troops on the coast and there we would go.

Manse was dangerously touchy for the next few days. He had resigned from the infantry at Sullivan's Island to see some real action in the cavalry, and now the army high command was shuttling him right back to where he started.

"Shitfire," was his terse comment to us.

I prayed for any Yankees Manse would meet on the coast; he would prove to be a terrible enemy.

Our horses went first to the coast, company by company, so that we were ensured to get our own mounts back. I had bonded with my sorrel mare, Lettie, who was as soft and feminine as Siegfried had been impulsive and fiery. I could not then have appreciated the full measure of her equine devotion, but this I would learn.

We marched to the Columbia depot in the blazing heat of a Carolina summer, abandoning Camp Hampton to the next class of unlucky recruits, and boarded a long train of flat cars bound for Charleston.

The Lowcountry rolled by in the hot hazy light of day, forests of pine, scrub oak and drooping cypress reflected in shallow lakes of brackish water or in sluggish brown streams that followed the railroad tracks for miles. There were big gators in those waters, the boys said. Red sandy roads crossed the tracks at rural freight stations where wagonloads of cotton and raw lumber were parked and barrels of turpentine and pitch stacked, waiting for shipment. Ragged groups of black men and women, young and old, occupied the stations, their children's bare feet as dusty red as the roads. They waved or sullenly stared as we passed.

When the train stopped to take on water or wood, we took the opportunity to step into the woods to relieve ourselves. We had been issued no rations, so when the colored children brought around sugared hoecakes, cornbread or fried pies to sell for pennies each they found us eager buyers. We had no way to boil coffee and depended on the barrels of rainwater furnished on every car to slake our thirst.

We never made it all the way to Charleston, which in Carolina we call the Holy City for its many famed and ancient churches. Instead, we were reunited with our mounts at a cavalry depot near Summerville, so close to the sea we could smell the salt air on the night breeze. The business of sorting out horses and waiting for our baggage and equipment took days, during which time we lived without tents in the woods, fighting mosquitoes and fearful of cottonmouths.

Four more companies, recruits like ourselves mostly from Florence, Cheraw and Darlington, joined the regiment at this time, bringing it up to its full strength of ten companies and nearly seven hundred men. Instead of serving as a unit, however, the regiment was dispersed, squad by squad, over a thin line of picket posts from Charleston south to the Edisto River, a distance of almost fifteen miles.

The Benson House Mess lived tolerably well in the shelter of a pine forest a few miles from Colonel Black's headquarters on Johns Island. Manse, as first sergeant of Company F, commanded our little picket post of a dozen horsemen. Manse was withdrawn and snappish much of the time. The boys interpreted this as a swelled head from his recent promotion, but I knew it was the nature of the duty that stuck in Manse's craw.

The four months we spent in the Lowcountry was like service in a foreign land to Upcountry boys used to green hills and fresh mountain air. Every morning our post sent out patrols to wander the endless stretches of marshland and salt-water inlets, sometimes trotting through acres of sea grass and across white sand dunes down to the ocean itself where we would watch the endless Atlantic horizon for Yankee sails.

We mostly patrolled the rivers that fed the sea; there were hundreds of them. Federal sloops and gunboats constantly probed the countless waterways and inlets, looking for blockade runners and scouting undefended areas for places in which to land troops. North of Charleston, at Georgetown, the Yankees landed and built forts strong enough to defy assault; when we were not vigilant, they sent their gunboats far inland to attack our river batteries.

For us, it was a frustrating sort of war because the action always seemed to be somewhere else. There were Federal incursions along the Combahee outside Beaufort, and along the Santee north of Charleston. In spite of riding from the scene of one Yankee raid to another, sometimes twenty miles in a night, we always arrived too late for the fight.

What made things worse was the news in the Charleston papers of the war that was exploding around Richmond. Beauty Stuart had marched his entire division of cavalry clear around McClellan's army, and early in July we began hearing about the great battles Johnston was fighting north of the James River.

One hot afternoon, an aide from Black's headquarters dropped off a bundle of letters and packages for our outpost, the first mail we had received in weeks. I remember cheering along with the rest of the boys, desperate for any diversion to relieve our boredom. I had two letters, one from father, the other from my old college chum, Parker Pope, postmarked in mid-May.

I eagerly opened my father's letter first.

My Dear Son Ansel

It is with great sorrow that I once again take pen in hand to write you of the awful news I have received. Your brothers Thomas and Newton were in battle in Virginia and heavily engaged for several days. Their brigade, that of Gen. R.H. Anderson, lost 800 men but won the field.

Near a town called Glendale, your brother Thomas was shot through the head and killed. I was told this by David Clinkscales, who also was wounded. He saw Thomas fall. He has since delivered to me a letter from their captain which confirmed how Thomas came to die.

Ansel——Newton, too, was hurt in the fight. He was wounded in the lower leg and now is in the military hospital at Chimborazo in Richmond. I think it is not bad. He has not written but Mr. Clinkscales assures me it is a good hospital. May God protect him and you as well, Ansel, my last healthy son.

It grieves me to bring you this news as you prepare to fight. Please to take care of yourself; be brave but not foolish and come home when you can. Things are dark here——the whole district is in mourning. Amos Sterling lost his two oldest boys and many others you know are dead or injured. Be loyal to your comrades. Try to temper your need for vengeance with Christian forgiveness. I know you will not make me ashamed of you in your grief.

Your loving Father,

Augustus Fries

I tried to imagine what Tom must have felt in the moment he was hit. Was he scared? Did he feel anything at all? Were there comrades nearby to comfort him, to hear his final words, if he was coherent, or note his final breath? Did he die quickly or suffer on the field for hours?

I felt a great emptiness, an inner ache of which I could not discern the center, but I did not cry. I told myself Tom's death and Newton's maiming were the result of a horrible accident, struck down randomly by the deadly, flying debris of a manmade cyclone.

It was weeks before I thought of the dream I had had in the peach orchard in Pickens, of Tom and Newton sinking into a bottomless creek. I had foreseen their fate, and the thought chilled me to my very marrow.

Newton was in the hospital for three months. One day in October he went home for good, his left leg gone a little below the knee.

Manse and the others tried to comfort me, speaking grimly of the revenge I would soon be able to wreak on the Yankee nation. I said nothing. All that talk of killing made no sense to me. Death was death; some would suffer it and others would not, regardless of whether they deserved it. It was a joke to me that any fool could imagine controlling the beast of war once it was let loose. I felt certain then it would devour us all.

Not long afterward I got sick again, and Captain Sharpe offered to send me home on furlough. I thanked him but declined. The Benson House Mess was my family now and I would not desert them.

As I recovered, Sharpe found clerking duties for me at his headquarters. He admired my education and handwriting and soon had me copying scouting reports, general orders, dispatches and monthly company returns on those present for duty, sick, or on detached duty.

Soon I became expert at army bureaucracy, and because a company clerk rated corporal's stripes, I was promoted.

It was days before I remembered Parker's letter and opened it. He had written me from a hotel in Charlestown, Virginia, where he was trying to organize a company of infantry. Parker's violent disagreements with his father over Lincoln and the war had finally come to a head and he vowed never again to return to his Fayette County home while his father lived.

"If ever I return, it will be at the head of a column of Federal troops," he wrote bitterly.

Virginia's counties west of the Alleghanies shared few sentiments with their secessionist cousins in the east; slavery was neither practical nor profitable in that mountainous country. More than two-thirds of the men who enlisted there marched off to war in Union regiments.

Parker continued:

ॐ

> It is such fun, Ansel, to think of going off to fight for this great Cause, knowing that victory is preordained because of the holiness of the things for which we fight, Union & Liberty! I know you have the sense to realize the South has no chance of winning this war, or of surviving with its institutions intact. The South is as extinct as a mastodon, old friend; all that remains is the collection of its bones for the museum. Stay out of it, Ansel, and do your best for your family. If you do decide to join up, come north and hitch yourself to my star. I can assuredly get you a commission.
>
> My best to your kind father. I remain,
> Your good Friend & Obdt. Servant,
>
> Parker W. Pope
>
> First Lieut., 2nd West Virg. Battn. (Prov.)

I was to hear from, and hear of, Parker through the war but did not see him again until near the end. By that time he was a major of Ohio infantry. He had become the sort of avenging Northern warrior of which old John Brown or General W.T. Sherman would have been proud. Because of circumstances that will be explained later, I thanked God he remained my friend.

Early on Saturday morning, July 16, 1862, while Company F was on headquarters guard duty on Johns Island, several regiments of Yankee infantry broke across Stono Inlet, protected by a lumbering gunboat, and tried to smash through our defenses. The generals called it reconnoitering in force.

We galloped down the road to the inlet following Captain Sharpe, my heavy cartridge box banging against my right buttock. We filed behind the battle line where Georgia infantrymen were popping away at the enemy from behind a line of sand dunes. We faced left, dismounted and were directed to the main line by an officer who begged us not to shoot his skirmishers in our front.

We peppered a line of low scrub pine trees three hundred yards distant, punctuated along its entire length by cottony puffs of smoke. The firing had a sharp patter to it, like a field of sugar cane being burned off. The Yankee bullets came in high, clipping green sprigs from the pine trees that shaded us. When they came in lower, they buzzed like deadly little bees. Now and then the slugs slammed into tree trunks with a dreadful thwack that made your bowels contract.

Henry quivered. "Jesus Christ in heaven, Ansel, I do not care for this one bit."

Manse ordered Henry to shut up and use his musket. The Sitton boys needed no urging; they were blazing away like madmen.

For a while it was all I could do to peek over the dune and watch the back of the brown-coated skirmisher fifty yards in my front; in the still, hot air I could clearly hear him cursing the Yankees as he worked the ramrod in and out of his muzzleloader. Suddenly, his sweat-streaked hat shot straight into the air and he disappeared among the sea grass as if a monstrous hand had snatched him and pulled him beneath the earth.

"No, I don't care for this at all," Henry whimpered, gripping his carbine and pressing his white face into the sand.

I got off my first round, after ruining two cartridges by nervously spilling the powder in the sand, and the musketoon exploded in my ear like a cannon.

Captain Sharpe paced up and down the line behind us, standing erect with sword drawn. Everybody was shouting.

"Easy, boys, easy," Sharpe urged calmly. "Shoot low. We must discourage them and you are the men to do it. Easy there." Here and there wounded men began climbing back over the dunes, gripping bloodied wrists or dragging themselves through the grass, shedding trails of bright blood like man-sized snails. Shortly thereafter our skirmishers came tumbling in, finding the Yankee firing too hot.

The Yankee gunboat, the Hamilton, was firing slow, ponderous shots from its eight-inch guns, loosing one round that roared over our heads like a train engine and erupted in a geyser of sand and tree branches fifty yards in our rear. It was their best shot of the day, killing and wounding several men in the 41st Georgia, to whom the skirmishers belonged.

Instead of mounting an all-out assault, the Yankee fire petered out bit by bit, and before noon we were ordered to stand down. We sat or stood about in idle groups, gripping our weapons and sharing canteens, staring at each other stupidly. Our faces were smeared with greasy black powder and gritty with sand.

Colonel Black cantered down the line and called out his congratulations to Captain Sharpe, who ordered us to mount. We passed the dead on our way back to Colonel Black's headquarters. They were laid out in a row, half a dozen heaps of brown and gray clothing covered with army blankets. Here and there a hand protruded; blood pooled in the road.

Most of the wounded were Georgians, pasty-faced young fellows who winced and groaned as comrades removed their clothing to ascertain the seriousness of their injuries. One young officer with a cornsilk mustache and wearing a homespun uniform babbled to the sky about home and mother, while a civilian wearing a straw hat tried delicately to staunch the blood that bubbled up from his groin wound.

We returned to camp, picketed our horses and stumbled to our messes like dead men walking. No one spoke. Hepsibah used a salve to tend the burns on Manse's hands caused by the overheated barrel of his firearm, then rubbed the same concoction on my back and Henry's shoulders; every muscle ached, I supposed from the simple tension of being under fire.

I borrowed Henry's hand mirror and looked at my face in the candlelight. I was appalled by what I saw: a grimy, haggard visage, speckled with a week's worth of whiskers and red pimples, eyes bloodshot from lack of sleep.

Looking around at all our faces, Hep said, "You done seen the elephant now for sure."

I do not remember falling asleep, but we awoke to hot tin cups full of Hep's salty bean soup, with mouthfuls of tart fried apples on the side. In moments it was as if the fight had never happened. Manse cracked a joke and we all laughed; it felt good to laugh.

Soldiers miss awfully many things in the field, chief among them the warmth of a real bed, the comfort of secure shelter and food.

We lived on white beans, fat bacon, hominy and hard crackers; coffee already was hard to get because of the blockade. Country folks sold the soldiers milk, butter, eggs, even ham and gingerbread, but their prices were steep. One tightfisted squire tried to charge us for the water from his well. But most citizens were openly friendly and generous, in spite of the fact that, after a month in the field, the troopers of the 1st South Carolina Cavalry began to resemble nothing so much as an organized group of armed field hands.

ॐ

July 29th 1862, on Johns Island S.C.

My Dearest Mary—

Once again I seat myself to pen a few lines to you, and to Mother, my Brothers and the rest. I do miss you all. I Confess I miss even the farm work this Summer, 'tis well There are enough still at home to make do, though I now hardships abound.

Today Saw I my first dead Yankey. We had a sharp fight on the Island with a heavy patrol of federal troops and they were not in a good mood I can tell you. We were two companies of dismounted horse-men and they were at least a Battn. of infantry. The Minee Balls flew thick and fast—they sound like nothing so much as angry Bees, but each one seems aimed directly & Person'lly at your Head. We had two fellows shot before we Ever saw the main body of Yankey troops, who rose out of the saw-grass in front of our Line and delivered a volley that staggered us. We fired at the smoke and ran like Hades back to the treeline.

Capt. Sharpe shored the company back up, slapping the boys into line. He ordered us to load and prime and go after them again. I thought him mad but he is a Game fellow. We went back in but the Yankeys all had run away leaving one of their wounded, an Officer, I saw him stretched out on the dune with a Hole big as my fist in his chest. He gasped and squirmed for some time like a fish out of water and finally died. I thought no more about him than if he were a dog. He and his Boys tried to kill me, you must remember. I Doubt they would stop to shed a tear had it been me lying there. It is hard, but that is war. You cannot imagine it & I hope you may never witness it....

As Always yr Loving Brother,

Manson S. Jolly

After the fight at Stono Inlet we began skirmishing with the enemy almost weekly. We learned the lay of the land, where the bridges and causeways were, where the ground was impassable after a rain. I felt like a real soldier, and began to appreciate more the rough camaraderie and prosaic routine of camp life, even came to find a certain comfort in the routine of reveille, sick call, roll call, mess call, fatigue duty and picket duty, which requires a minimum of effort and no brainwork; you do what you are told without questioning the wisdom of army logic. Still, some of the boys had a harder time adjusting.

In August, we witnessed how grim army discipline could be. Desertions had become a problem, and word had come down from the departmental commander that an example must be made, one severe enough to impress the rank and file.

That very week a private in Company I was caught in the swamps after deserting his picket post. The man protested he had only been out gigging frogs for his messmates, and left his musket and cartridge box behind to keep them dry; lots of hungry troopers did the same. If Colonel Black had gotten wind of it, that would have ended the matter. But this fellow had a reputation as a shirker; his captain cursed him as a coward for disappearing during the Stono fight. On this evidence he was condemned.

On a warm, overcast morning, more than half the regiment was drawn up in a three-sided square in a sandy field not far from Black's clapboard headquarters; the open end of the square was formed by a man-high ridge of sand dunes whose reverse sidesloped to the shoreline. We could hear the ocean breakers pounding on the distant beach.

The condemned, a man called Suggs, was marched through ranks to a point in front of the dune where a shallow grave had been dug; beside it was an open pine coffin. A lieutenant and sergeant from Suggs' company escorted him to the coffin, turned him about and secured his wrists with a line of rough hemp. Suggs was a heavy-browed man. He stared at the ground, then doubled over, his shoulders heaving. The boys next to me began to shift their feet uneasily, a few muttering under their breaths.

"Silence in the ranks!" commanded Lieutenant-Colonel Twiggs from atop his black stallion.

Suggs straightened up, a silvery strand of saliva clinging to his chin.

The sergeant wrapped a piece of burlap over Suggs' eyes, then guided him gently to the coffin's edge and sat him down. The condemned man's chest began to heave again; he was sobbing.

From behind the right wing of the square the firing party appeared, eleven men marching in two ranks. A captain halted them twenty-five paces in front the coffin, faced them right, then double-quicked to the flank of the squad. At his first order, the shooters leveled their muskets sluggishly, as if performing in a dream.

Then the muskets discharged, raggedly, and the reports bounded across the little field like slaps in the face; I jumped, as if I really had not expected them to fire.

The scrub trees along the shoreline erupted with seagulls taking flight, hundreds of them, wheeling and squalling. A soldier in the firing party threw down his weapon and covered his face. His captain watched for a moment, then ordered the squad to shoulder arms, right face and forward march at the double-quick.

Our officers came alive, shouting orders, marched us back to where our horses were tethered and from there we found our ways back to our various posts.

I looked back once and saw the emotionally distraught trooper being led away by an officer as three black teamsters slouched toward the grave and coffin, sand shovels yoked across their shoulders.

We toiled away in the Lowcountry through August and September, patrolling and skirmishing. Once we burned a wooden bridge and causeway virtually in the face of an approaching column of Yankee infantry. When the flames caught the pitch and the black smoke started boiling, we popped away in their general direction and dashed to safety under its cover, their videttes sending after us a ragged volley of frustrated lead.

The following week, Captain Sharpe received orders for Company F to rebuild that same bridge.

That was the army. And we were soldiers, in a regiment that was gaining a reputation for its hard service; we were also day laborers. We laid in wait along moss-shrouded banks to ambush Yankee gunboats, washed our ragged clothing, we fished and hunted the creeks and fields bare, we dug trenches and artillery redoubts, wrote complaining letters home, got scurvy, fought lice and chiggers.

During this time Manse had news that his oldest brother, Jesse Alfred, died of malaria in a Richmond army hospital. Manse took it stoically, and he seemed genuinely touched when some of the boys offered their condolences. But he never spoke of it.

One pleasant, golden day in mid-October, Colonel Black sent aides to all the company picket posts, where they read an order signed by Lee himself authorizing the regiment to move by rail to Richmond with all possible dispatch.

We were stunned, certain that we were fated never to leave South Carolina. But in four months we had progressed from foolish youths and green recruits to, as Lee himself had stated in his order, "veteran troops accustomed to severe picket duty." Lee's bloody Maryland campaign had assured our transfer to the Army of Northern Virginia; Stuart badly needed fresh troops to shore up his decimated horse brigades.

When our relief marched in, we bid farewell to the lonely picket outposts, packed the horses and retraced our steps to Summerville where the trains took us back to Columbia. This time, our horses followed us.

The depot in Columbia was jammed with wounded. They were the maimed and blinded from the Seven Day's fighting, well enough now to be sent home from Richmond, where the hospitals had been forced to make room for the masses of freshly injured coming in from South Mountain and Sharpsburg. They were armless or on stretchers, some without legs bearing crutches, and a few wearing hoods to mask ghastly face wounds, being led about by a kind comrade. It was not pleasant to think of war as such a relentless consumer of young men.

The ambulatory wounded grinned at us, called us fresh fodder for the Yankee cannon. One straw-haired fellow remarked loudly there was plenty of room for more graves on Virginia's bloody soil.

There was no Camp Hampton for us that night. Colonel Black's agents had gone before us and arranged for quarters in the city for every officer and private soldier. Company F drew an old warehouse converted into barracks, but the floor had been vigorously cleaned and fresh straw spread thickly over it; the stoves inside were stoked with new coal.

In the morning, we found that the quartermaster had scoured the city for fresh clothing for the regiment. We were in desperate need especially of underclothing, stockings and trousers. I had almost forgotten what a sensual pleasure it was to wear clean clothing, blessedly free of lice and other critters.

The ladies of the city prepared for us a breakfast of fresh eggs, fried ham and biscuits slathered with butter and honey. There was so much food that we—veteran campaigners now—stuffed extra biscuits into our pockets and haversacks.

That morning was glorious. We filled canteens with root beer or lemonade and boarded the flat cars whooping like Indians. We felt invincible. We felt like men of war.

Eight hours later, squeezed into small spaces atop the car, fighting for breathing room between prone bodies and heaps of equipment, we slapped away red hot cinders and got pelted by rain as the train navigated the interminable North Carolina piedmont. We stopped to take on water and wood at stations that appeared to be at the world's end, lacking firelight, food and friendly faces.

For three days we traveled. The nights were frosty but we could not make fires on the cars to warm ourselves or boil coffee. Those with thick woolen greatcoats were fortunate; the rest of us wrapped up in blankets and made ourselves comfortable the best we could.

We arrived outside Richmond at dusk on October 20, 1862, and were unceremoniously rousted from our cars eight miles from the city; we could see the lights of the capital twinkling from the bluffs overlooking the James River. That was as close as we were going to get. There was no welcome, no food, no parade.

Reunited with our horses, company by company we filed out onto the roads leading northwest to Culpeper Courthouse, the site of Lee's headquarters and of the great depot where Stuart was reorganizing and reequipping his division.

Already sore from three days of jouncing around on open railroad cars, we made our first long forced march: ten hours a day along dusty Virginia roads, stumbling over stones in the night and cursing the moonless darkness. For many it was too much. In spite of the exhortations of officers, men fell out right and left, leading lame horses and limping into the woods. Henry and his loyal Hepsibah were among the stragglers.

Six days and one hundred miles later, our march ended just before dawn in a green meadow shrouded with early morning mist. We were more dead men than soldiers by then.

Our officers marched out each company—Company F had dwindled to fewer than twenty-five riders—in an attempt to stake out something resembling a regimental camp. They failed miserably; we were sullen and stupid with exhaustion. We had no tents but we built fires in that dew-soaked field, picketed our horses and, without orders, wrapped ourselves in blankets and collapsed by the camp fires to sleep the sleep of the dead.

When the sun had risen high and burned the moisture off the clover, we slept still, so that the field must have looked to an observer like the scene of a great slaughter, only with breathing but inert bodies strewn about indiscriminately.

The officers literally kicked us out of our stupor about noon and put us to work setting up a proper camp. We fed, watered and groomed our horses, boiled coffee, gnawed hard crackers snatched from boxes marked "U.S. Army Bread," rubbed stinking horse liniment on sore muscles and tended blisters and boils.

Word soon spread that General Stuart had invited our regimental officers to his headquarters for a review of Brigadier General W.H.F. Rooney Lee's horse brigade, made up of the 9th, 10th and 13th Virginia Cavalry, regiments renowned to every horse soldier in the South.

The Benson House Mess, minus Henry, voted to sneak over and watch the fun; we were as curious as schoolboys about Beauty Stuart and the Army of Northern Virginia, and we were not disappointed. Those battle-hardened troopers appeared to us as exotic as Arabian knights, riding superbly prancing mounts, their brilliant regimental colors bedecked with battle honors snapping in the mountain breeze. We stood not far from Stuart himself, mounted on a chestnut mare beside his elegantly uniformed staff.

Stuart was an imposing man with a handsome, flowing beard and aquamarine eyes. He wore rich yellow leather gauntlets and demonstrated the manners of a chevalier at court. Even Manse admired his style.

But it also deflated us to see those dashing cavalrymen at the zenith of their legend. We felt like uninvited poor relations, crowding like rubes along the rail fences lining the parade field. But we were impressed, and we cheered ourselves hoarse.

I remember seeing Beauty Stuart glance over at us in an amused way, then say something to his staff which produced a ripple of laughter.

I have since often wondered what Stuart said that day. I would bet it was not very complimentary.

CHAPTER 5

Under J.E.B. Stuart

Now each cavalier who loves honor and right
Let him follow the feather of Stuart tonight.

—"Riding A Raid"

We were in the real war at last.

The regiment immediately joined Brigadier General Wade Hampton's brigade of cavalry, three thousand men organized into Colonel M.C. Butler's 2nd South Carolina Cavalry, Cobb's and Phillip's Georgia legions, Colonel Lawrence S. Baker's 1st North Carolina Cavalry and the Jeff Davis, or Mississippi, Legion. They were tough, lean troopers led by the cream of the West Point elite, an officer corps unmatched in American military history.

In my opinion, Colonel John Logan Black was among the best of them. He was West Point but was doomed to a certain obscurity in the clique of important commanders in the Army of Northern Virginia. Black was one of the few truly humble men I ever knew, endowed with the Christian quality of knowing that as long as a man always did his very best, win or lose, he had nothing of which to be ashamed, given the Almighty's inscrutable ways.

In spite of his profanity, Black was a devout man. In spite of his self-doubt, he was a fine commander. And while Manse and others frowned at the colonel's abhorrence of gambling and liquor, he and every man in the regiment respected his courage. Black was wounded three times in the war, and only another old warrior can know what that takes out of a man. God bless him, he deserved higher rank, but we were glad we kept him. He survived.

We had been in camp barely two weeks when orders came from General Lee himself for the regiment to march to Gordonsville, accompanied by the four guns of Captain R.M. Stribling's Virginia battery, the Fauquier Artillery. Several regiments of Yankee cavalry were making pests of themselves in the area after dogging the army's wagon trains and rear guard from Maryland. It meant more than a few hard days in the saddle.

Something happened outside Gordonsville that was to change many people's impression of Henry Knauff, something that permanently altered our friendship so that it would never again be quite the same.

Lettie was still in a nervous state following her long trip north. Henry looked ill as well, but there was something else. Since coming into camp he had developed a sullenness about him, a slouched shoulder attitude that made officers and non-coms lash out at him. Manse scolded Henry daily about his slovenly appearance, careless attitude and his dirty weapon.

"You trying to grow something in there?" Manse mocked upon inspecting the barrel of Henry's firearm, untended since the Stono fight. "Goddamnit, if you don't clean up that piece I am going to bend it around your neck, or give it to a man knows how to take care of it."

Manse further threatened to turn Henry into a cook or, worse, a hospital orderly.

Fortunately for Henry, Manse's lectures in the saddle never lasted long. Captain Sharpe would call him up to the front of the column and Manse would be cutting out cross-country on a scout.

I tried talking to Henry but it was no good. He was becoming generally disliked in the company; some thought him a shirker of the same general class as poor Suggs, who was shot for his bad attitude. I finally stopped defending Henry; it was hard to like him anymore.

Some nights, sleeping under the frosty autumn sky, I heard Henry moaning in his dream-sleep. Once I got up and crept over to his sleeping form. Clutched in his hand was a carte de vista portrait of a woman. I did not recognize her but knew that it was his long-dead mother; I picked my way back to my nest, chilled.

Not long after that, Henry told me he was going to die. I started to laugh but thought better of it. Soldier lore holds that some men know when their time is up.

Everybody in the regiment had heard the story of a fellow in Company K named McCormick who gave away all his worldly goods one night while we were at Johns Island. Jesus had visited him in a dream, told him the Kingdom was coming and that he was going to join Him in heaven, but not to worry because it would not hurt. McCormick was a good Baptist. He visited a preacher, made out his last will and gave it to his closest friend, and asked him to take care of his old woman. McCormick was found at his picket post the next morning, stone dead. He had been bitten numerous times by a water moccasin and his face was blue as the sky.

"He didn't look like he was seeing heaven," said one of the troopers who helped bury him.

I fear that all Henry wanted was sympathy. He was homesick, but so were we all. I became less and less patient with him.

Meanwhile, the army rumor mill said that General Burnside had succeeded General McClellan as commander of the Army of the Potomac. Those bright days in mid-November, as we galloped to Gordonsville, the rest of Lee's army was marching east to Fredericksburg to confront thirty thousand Union troops moving toward a crossing of the Rhappahannock River.

Gordonsville was a little town with a brick church at a country crossroads that looked like so many other Virginia towns through which we passed during the war. Orange County, Virginia, was a sun-dappled country, rich with a lingering warmth that in the late afternoon made the rolling landscape glow golden. Barns bulged with corn, apple orchards were heavy with fruit; farmers were rolling out stacks of hay for winter fodder.

The regiment's companies fanned out from Wares Crossroads on the Pamunkey River to Boswells Tavern, looking for Yankee videttes screening the larger columns of cavalry. Late one afternoon, Manse, Henry and I were on a scout and had stopped at a country farmstead on the road south of Gordonsville for water and conversation.

The whiskered farmer and his shy, barefoot daughter jawed with us at their well, where we watered our horses under the cooling shade of oak trees. Lettie had been stepping lame on her right fore-leg, so Manse and the farmer hitched her up to take a look. The sun was setting red behind the barn, and I hoped Manse was thinking what I was, that perhaps this good Virginian would take in three tired rebels for supper.

We heard the rider before we saw him, pumping hell bent for leather towards the farm from Gordonsville. The dark-clothed rider reined up fast when he saw our group at the barn, his lathered mount doing a pretty pirouette on its hind legs as he decided what to do.

He shouted something cheerily and then came ahead. As he got closer we could see he wore a dusty blue sack coat and patched sky-blue trousers. His boottops were rolled jauntily up to his knees in the European style.

Manse had slowly eased inside the shadow of the barn doors. Henry stood behind his horse, peering over his saddle at the rider. I was talking to the farmer and paying no attention to the situation; I supposed the rider was a neighbor. Suddenly, the old clodhopper swatted his child on her rear end and told her to scat. Then he turned and stepped quickly behind the barn.

I turned and saw the rider, very close now, as he cantered up, the brass buttons on his blouse flashing, his teeth gleaming, his eyes searching.

Henry fired, and I very distinctly saw the dust puff on the soldier's coat where the big slug hit. He went over backwards and hit the ground in a heap. A few chicken feathers settled atop the body, gently as snow flakes; the Yankee had tucked a dead hen into his belt. His handsome black mare was already dusting the road back to Gordonsville.

I screamed at the top of my lungs. "Jesus Christ Henry what in hell you do that for?"

Manse stepped out and holstered his Colt revolver. He smiled broadly at Henry, who was still peering over the barrel of his musketoon and soothing his horse with his left hand.

"That was fine shooting, Henry," said Manse. Then he looked at me. "My God, Ansel, I could tell that was a Yankee forager from ten rod away. Open your damn eyes."

Henry stared at me defiantly, feeding on Manse's praise. He had killed a man. I could not help the feeling of jealousy that welled up within me. I, too, wanted to hear Manse's praise. I cursed myself for my stupidity and inattention.

"How's it feel to get your first Yankee, Henry?" Manse asked as he rifled the dead man's body, taking not only his hen, but his wallet, pocket watch and change.

The Yankee had been a little fellow, spare and lean, like me, good for the cavalry. Henry's ball had gone straight through his heart and out the spine. Blood was curling in a thick, languid stream from beneath the corpse's shoulder. Its half-lidded, unfocused eyes seemed to be looking in opposite directions; the teeth were bared.

Manse said the dead boy's name was A.S. Gumpertz, a musician in the 8th Pennsylvania Cavalry. Manse appropriated a .22-caliber pinfire revolver he found in one of the boy's boots; Henry took his saber and belt.

"Let's get out of here," I croaked, unable to catch my breath. I felt sick.

Manse ignored me. He called for Mr. Sisk, who edged around the corner of the barn, his eyes wide. They spoke in low tones and shook hands. Manse went to Dixie and swung into the saddle.

"I'm going to fetch back that Yankee horse. You stay here and help Mr. Sisk clean up. We don't want to cause these good folks any trouble. Keep a sharp eye out, Henry."

We wrapped the corpse in a horse blanket, and Mr. Sisk covered the dark pool of blood with dirt and straw. Henry did what he could to erase the horse tracks around the barn. Manse soon returned, leading the black mare. We tied the dead man over his former mount and Manse bid farewell to Mr. Sisk, who watched us ride away with obvious relief.

We rode two or three miles to where a wooden bridge crossed a rushing creek and there Manse halted. While I held the horse's reins, Henry and Manse eased the body from the saddle, laid it parallel to the bridge rail and Manse, with a single kick, propelled it over the side into the water below. He threw the blanket over the black mare and ordered us to remount.

We rejoined the company, encamped in open country at a nameless crossroads, and that night we ate fried chicken. Henry got the breast because Henry was the hero of the hour; Hep and Manse made over him like suitors. Boys came from all over the regiment to congratulate him on his bag. Henry enjoyed pulls of brandy and whiskey from numerous canteens, and with each slug he told a more exaggerated version of the murder he had committed. I was conspicuous by my absence in Henry's receiving line.

"Come on, Ansel, you're acting like this ain't a shooting war," cajoled Manse. "Ain't anybody's fault that damn Yankee was so dumb. We could have captured him, sure, but I guess old Henry was in a killing mood." He spat and looked at me. "One less Yankee to deal with."

I muttered, "Henry didn't give him a chance to surrender. He shot a man who didn't know he was in danger."

Manse got mad. He looked like he was going to pound my head, but he stalked off instead and did not speak to me for two days. It was me who did the making up. After Fredericksburg, after seeing so much death in one place, one Yankee more or less did not come to matter much at all. I forgot all about Private Gumpertz.

   December 2nd, 1862
   At Culpeper, Va.
   1st S.C. Cav., Hampton's Brig., With Lee

   Good Old dear Mary....

   You must be my confessor, like the Catholics believe & I guess it is a
   good idea. It worrys me not that all my deepest Thoughts are contained in these words to you, I now you will keep them close. You cannot imagine how Grand it is to be a horseman & Cavalier of Stuart's.
   Could a man be any luckier? If I die tomorrow, that fact alone will survive my name. May God bless this war and our Cause, for fighting &
   killing Yankeys is truly a Glorious thing....I remain Respectfully

   Yr Loving Brother

   M.S. Jolly

For my regiment, the Fredericksburg campaign began when Colonel Black addressed all ten companies on morning parade and asked for volunteers to ride on a raid with General Hampton, to harass the

Federal rear north of the Rhappahannock. Manse, Henry and one hundred others stepped forward but I stayed with the company.

Next day, the depleted regiment jogged the length of Lee's army and took up positions on the extreme right flank, in front of D.H. Hill's division of infantry. Hill's troops had been in Port Royal only the day before and made an eighteen-mile forced march to reach the battlefield. They spent most of the engagement hugging the ground behind the ridge, exhausted, while Yankee shells soughed overhead and spent Minie balls dropped among them like a nasty sort of man-made hail.

Company F, drawn up beside an Alabama battery, was posted on a bluff that overlooked a gentle valley sloping to the gray ribbon of the Rhappahannock River below. The weather had turned bitterly cold; Indian summer was gone and those of us who had them were wearing greatcoats. Those without wore blankets like hoods over their hats, hoping their friends on Hampton's raid might return with caped, woolen Yankee greatcoats slung over the pommels of their saddles.

Morning dawned cold and foggy on December 13, 1862, the day of the great battle of Fredericksburg. A great haze rose in the cold air over both armies from the thousands of campfires scattered for miles along both sides of the river; adding to it was the smolder of the buildings still burning red in the ruined city three miles from our position. Union artillery had spent the previous two days reducing it to rubble, and in covering the crossing of their immense army. Its blue columns looked to us like a Biblical host of old, massive and unending. And yet we held sway over it.

There was a queer stillness in the air that morning, so that sounds were at once muffled and magnified. We could clearly hear Yankee officers on the plain below barking orders, the clink of canteens and tin cups, the neighing of horses and the heavy, measured tread of thousands of marching feet.

We huddled around our campfires and sipped bitter boiled coffee, waiting for the sun to burn away the haze. When Ezra Sitton called us to his post on the lip of the bluff, we ran like school boys. What we saw took our breath away, awed us into unaccustomed silence.

One hundred thousand Yankee soldiers were marching and wheeling on the plain below, division after division swinging into line, bands bravely playing, colors snapping in the stiff morning breeze, drums thrumming and the very air breaking with the throaty roar of the disciplined Yankee huzzah. Baz Hilliard pointed out the green smudge of the flag of the Irish brigade marshalling near the foot of Marye's Heights.

It took the blue host two hours to arrange its ranks for battle and when the great army was ready to advance, the bands stepping lively to the rear, it moved like a deadly but ponderous and uncoordinated snake in multiple lines of battle a mile long. But the infantry came ahead with muskets at right shoulder shift.

Batteries of Union artillery massed on both sides of the Rhappahannock belched white smoke. The reports at first were dull and muffled, but grew gradually into a roar that increased in volume as if a monstrous train was bearing down on the battlefield. The hot crackle of musketry began to rise over the bass thunder of the cannon. The wind pushed the acrid battle-smoke in our direction, blowing it in tattered clouds over our heads, carrying with it awful sounds from the field below. Silent sheets of fire marked the volleys from the Confederate trenches, raking the slope up which the blue infantry struggled like men facing into a fearsome wind. Seconds later, we heard the crashes of musketry, like breakers on an ocean beach, while countless other flashes stabbed the battle-fog. Dead and wounded men and horses, battered drums and broken flagstaffs, wrecked guns and their carriages lay piled upon one another in random heaps like the debris left by a hurricane.

I watched, enthralled. It was the greatest battle of the war up to that time and we had front row seats, safely removed from the heaviest action. At the battle's height, most of the field was obscured by banks of dirty gray smoke that even the breeze could not diminish; it rose in a death pall miles above the city into the winter sky. Occasionally the smoke cleared long enough to reveal the terrible canvas of human wreckage, one not witnessed since the days of Wellington and Waterloo.

As the battle raged at its fiercest, the Alabama gunners were alerted to give supporting fire to the right flank of General A.P. Hill's works, below us and to our left. They went into action lethargically at first, letting off a few desultory shots, the gunners ducking away from the bucking recoil of their 12-pounders then moving back to wheel the piece forward again, one man thumbing the barrel's vent while another swabbed the gleaming bronze tube and an officer directed the sighting.

As the crews gained the rhythm, their firing slowly became heavier and more regular; the concussive pounding increased. Some of the boys passed around balls of cotton, with which we plugged our ears. As the enemy return fire grew heavier we kneeled. Then we got on our bellies and soon we were hugging the frozen ground, which jiggled beneath us like jelly.

Black-faced and frantic, the Alabama gunners sweated and screamed like madmen as they worked their guns, the cords on their necks straining as taut as ship's ropes.

A Yankee shell burst overhead, killing and wounding several of the battery's horses. The wounded animals huddled together pathetically, trembling, strands of blood and foamy saliva dripping from their muzzles. It was too much for one young gunner, who fell to his knees and bawled when he saw the lead horse on his team thrown to the ground, disemboweled by iron shards of the shell. He howled through the storm, then dabbed his eyes, got to his feet and ran back to his gun.

We were fortunate, being near the top of the ridge, but a regiment of North Carolina infantry lying in reserve just below us was not so lucky. The hot Yankee iron came flying over our heads making whispering insect sounds, kicking up chunks of sod wherever it happened to fall. Even through our cotton ear plugs we could hear the Tarheels cursing like teamsters as stray Minies and jagged iron from the storm boiling on the battlefield dropped among them. Finally, their colonel got them up, put them through the manual of arms to calm them down and moved the regiment several hundred yards farther to the rear.

Our lieutenant, J.B. Whitner, spent the battle of Fredericksburg with our company horses in a copse of trees several hundred yards to the rear of the Alabama battery. No one noticed. Those of us on the line were too busy embracing Mother Earth while she convulsed and grumbled beneath us.

By late afternoon we no longer heard the Yankee cheer. Finally, before sunset, it got so quiet we pulled the cotton from our ears. My whole head seemed to have gone numb, so that every sound was strange, even that of my own voice. When we tried to stand, we had to use our carbines to lean on. Our legs were wobbly; we had no sense of balance.

Gunfire sputtered up and down the lines, but the battle was over. That was when J.B. rejoined the company, nervously chewing a thick wad of tobacco. He sidled up to Robert Sitton.

"No, sir," said Whitner with great sincerity, "I don't care for those big guns one damn bit."

Whitner's line became a standing joke within the Benson House Mess.

A deep freeze set in again that night. Nervous sentries continued popping off their weapons long after dark, shooting at looters raiding the Yankee dead and wounded. Parties of armed men carrying lanterns searched furtively among the thousands of bodies scattered over the field, looking for brothers, comrades, high-ranking officers.

The bitter weather was an added ordeal for the Yankee wounded. We heard them calling all through the frosty night, moaning for water, death, their mother. Many no doubt froze to death, and yet others I was told survived because the cold actually staunched the blood flow from their wounds.

I drew picket duty that night of all nights, shuffling my feet to stay warm. When Lieutenant Baz Hilliard came by my post on his rounds, he drew me aside to show me a packet of letters sent from his sister's Sunday school class in Brushy Creek, his home in the Anderson District. He read them to me, illuminating the pages with a lit candle stuck into the socket of a bayonet. But I believe he had already committed the tender passages to memory.

One, titled "The Soldier," began: "The Soldiers are fighting for our Country so I want them to win the fight but I don't want them to get hurt, and if they do I want them to get well. And I do not want to get hurt. Goodbye. Miss Sallie Sinkhorn." Another, laboriously scrawled, read, "I hope that you can't have no more war so the soldiers won't get hurt and shot and die. Your Friend Sandy Durrell."

"Ain't that something?" Baz smiled, stuffing the letters into his jacket and gazing into the starry night where the wounded were moaning in chorus. "Sandy is my little niece."

Next morning, the ground that sloped the ghastly half-mile from Marye's Heights to the river looked like a slaughter-house. Naked Yankee bodies, frozen and stiff, gleamed like white boulders in the sharp light of morning; our men had stripped them in the night, desperate for warm clothing.

"Thank God for this weather," Baz muttered.

Manse and Henry returned from their raid, which had been a small affair, after all, not loaded down with Yankee loot but haggard, hungry and shivering. Hep pumped them full of hot tea made from dried sassafras root and a watery, salty potato soup. When they felt better we got busy building a winter hut planked with pieces of cracker and munitions boxes, complete with a mud chimney but big enough to sleep six.

In the days following the battle we stayed snug in our hut, one of fifty or more that sprang up like mushrooms to become our regimental camp. Hep acted as our watch guard when we were called out on patrol for picket or other duties, such as wood detail or burial party.

On patrol we occasionally exchanged shots with Yankee cavalry across the Rhappahannock, but these were half-hearted affairs. More often we just stared hard at one another and then moved off, waving.

During one of these bloodless encounters Manse, feeling mischievous, rose in his saddle and loosed a tremendous blast of gas that resounded like a shotgun. We erupted with laughter when the horse of a Yankee trooper on the opposite bank suddenly heeled and kicked, throwing his rider into the water. Oh, how we hooted and jeered! When the insulted Yanks reached for their carbines, we spurred our mounts up the bank until we were safely out of range, shouting and cheering the whole way. Were we full of ourselves? I would say yes, shamelessly so.

The Army of the Potomac's winter quarters were spread south from Falmouth to Fredericksburg; we hunkered down on the other side of the river. When the weather was temperate and the Yanks were bored, they would send out their bands to play. Our boys, just as bored, would come out by the thousands to sit on the river's banks and listen. Somebody would yell out, "Play 'Dixie!'" and the Northern musicians would oblige. That was the signal for one of our bands to reply with a Union song. I recall that the Irish brigade had a particularly fine band, one the boys admired greatly. The best Confederate band I ever heard was that of the 26th North Carolina. They played "Home Sweet Home" in tones so melodious that it made men weep.

The Benson House became a true mess that winter. Six men, five white, one black, living in closer confinement than inmates in a prison for weeks at a time, get to know one another's moods, bodily stances, looks, each other's very smell. We learned the noises each of us made in the night, the names that were spoken, half-muffled, and the very essence of our friend's nightmares.

Ezra Sitton was our clown and storyteller. We loved to hear him tell of the time he saw Dan Rice's famous mud circus in Abbeville. The show's main attraction was Harry "Irish" McCarthy and his pet cockatoo, Junius, which danced and sang songs, recited Shakespeare and performed feats of derring-do. When the war started, Mr. McCarthy taught Junius to squawk, "Three cheers for Jeff Davis!" The act never failed to bring down the house.

Whenever Ezra told that story he made his lanky body look like a cockatoo, turning his arms into wings, throwing back his head and screeching at the top of his lungs.

Falling in every morning for roll call, Ezra was the one Captain Sharpe glanced at first. If Ezra was quiet and subdued, the company was in manageable shape that morning. If he was restless, elbowing his comrades and chittering like a sparrow, the captain would bawl out for him to shut his trap and be still, or be gagged.

Robert, Ezra's baby brother, was a stocky young man, smooth-muscled as an Indian but a head shorter than his brother, which made him an inch or two taller than me. Robert hardly ever said anything, neither in protest or to voice an opinion, nor to pass the time of day. Robert smiled when Ezra clowned, looked away when Ezra did something foolish. His mission in life was to keep his older brother out of trouble. Ezra was the juvenile and Robert was his truant officer. He was Ezra's keeper, his guardian, which everybody knew Ezra badly needed.

∾

December 20th, 1863
Camped Near Fredericksburg, Va., with Hampton's Brig.

Dear Father,

Many thanks for the gift—How it brightened our dreary mess! Tell Eastie the cake was superb, so Sweet! It reminded me of her. Tell her that, 'tho I know you will not.

Your generous gift of clothing, especially the Underwear, was warmly received by the boys. Clean clothes are always treated like Gold but no Man dares ware something new without getting first a good bath Or, de-lousing. Because we are so Filthy in the field, with no chance to wash or procure fresh Clothing. Graybacks are our constant comrades, and so Combs are in great demand. The boys take to making their own lice combs for Beards and head hair, but the battle is often lost before it begins.

Thank you Also for the canned oysters and Fruit, esp. the olives. Some of my friends had never seen one, Much less tasted a black olive. Only our Col.'s cook, Mario, who is Italian and from New Orleans, had seen such an Oddity! Mstr. Mario was very envious, and grateful.

Good Night Father. I must go. I think often of you & Home. Remember me to our Friends & give my love to Bro. Newton.

Your Loving Son,

Ansel W. Fries

P.S.—
Direct letters to:
1st S.C. Cav., Hampton's Brig., Stuart's Corps, ANV

CHAPTER 6

"I Fights Mit Sigel"

One cold morning before dawn the entire regiment received marching orders to intercept a column of General Franz Sigel's German corps as it tried to ford the Rhappahannock near Brandy Station and join the rest of Sigel's forces west of the Blue Ridge in the Shenandoah Valley.

The weather was soggy and cold, the roads muddy during the day and frozen solid at night. After an hour's ride our spirits were lagging; we missed the relative comfort of our little hut. Even the horses seemed moody and gloomy. No one was in a mood to fight Yankees.

Colonel Black drove us hard, constantly galloping up and down our column as we moved along the dreary turnpikes overhung with sodden stands of pine and bare, dripping hardwoods. Black fairly frothed at the mouth, calling upon his lengthy lexicon of profanity to keep the companies from separating. A misty freezing rain began to fall. We shed water and swallowed snot, shivering, for twenty-five miles before dismounting to a miserable night's bivouac.

Just after dawn on the second day of the march we reached by way of a twisting cowpath the top of a thickly-forested bluff overlooking a silver band of the Rhappahannock. A mile away we could see Sigel's column, a dark, sinuous band of infantry, artillery and wagons struggling to cross a shallow ford in the river.

I could see the muscles in Manse's face contracting and tightening, his brows knitting, the sinews in his bare forearms taut as he rolled up the sleeves of his jacket. Manse was getting himself into his killing mood. Those familiar with the sagas of the Irish hero Cuchulain may recall the warrior's similar ritual, rendered in the ancient lays as a "warp-spasm," which made him invulnerable to wounds.

When Captain Sharpe called a halt and shouted for volunteers to scout ahead, everybody knew he meant Manse. Manse loosened his revolver in the waistband of his trousers and spurred to the head of our column, which was obscured by the trees, the turns in the trail and the long line of horses from which steamy clouds of vapor rose.

We could hear the German teamsters a mile upriver, shouting and cursing in the language once so familiar in my house. The words were indistinct.

We dismounted and began cinching up our horses for a fight, loading and priming our weapons, tying blankets and heavy greatcoats behind our saddles. Some men tied their canteens and haversacks together and hid them along the cowpath. Robert and Ezra carefully loaded their double-barreled shotguns, primed the nipples with percussion caps and eased the hammers down on the caps. During winter quarters they had sawn off the barrels of both shotguns twenty inches from the breech, making them easier to handle on horseback and deadlier at close quarters.

I loaded and capped my short musket and slung it over my shoulder, determined to keep both my hands free. I had no revolver or pistol of any kind; my Prussian saber was tied to my saddle. I loosened the old blade inside its black sharkskin scabbard, but had no real intention of drawing it. I felt better knowing it was there.

Henry, just ahead of me in file, kept glancing at me as he worked over his mare, feeling her belly for burrs and tightening his cinches.

He caught my eye and gave me a look that put me in mind of a helpless puppy.

Ezra and Robert shared a canteen with me. We took turns drinking deeply, then Ezra grinned and belched. Robert took a pocket Bible from his haversack and tucked it into the breast pocket of his homespun shirt, so that it rested snugly over his heart. Up and down the column other men were doing the same, hoping that, if the Good Book did not stop a bullet, they would at least wake up in heaven.

Manse began picking his way back along the line, ignoring the questions of those who wanted to know what was going on. He said only, "Keep quiet. Yankees ahead. Lots of Yankees."

Manse reined up beside me and Robert, Ezra and Henry crowded around to listen.

"There's a shitload of Germans at the landing below," he said. "They've got a couple companies of infantry across and a few squads of cavalry. And wagons! The dumb bastards brought their wagons over first and they're parked there, maybe twenty of them."

Manse said Colonel Black's plan was to send six companies crashing down on the Yankees at the ford, scattering them and then cutting between the survivors and the river like a wedge, trapping every wagon and enemy soldier left on our side in a neat little package. Two companies, A and our F, were to turn east and drive back the troops still in the ford. Two companies were posted in reserve in case things went badly.

Manse said the Union infantry had placed pickets to guard the trail winding down to the landing, but they were lounging about, drying their wet boots and stockings over wood fires and boiling coffee. The regiment was to charge down the cut and onto the camp, using pistols and shotguns to create as much confusion as possible. The lead companies would slash through and then circle, destroying formations and cutting down soldiers wherever possible.

The sky had cleared and the air was crisp, fragrant with the scent of pine. We went forward by twos, every trooper leading his mount as we wound down the trail.

My heart leaped when the order came to remount. Then we heard Colonel Black's trumpeter, Corporal Villines, blowing the charge on the brass bugle he brought from Charleston. The boys in front began hollering the famous yip-yip-yip of the rebel yell and I joined in for all I was worth. The effort felt good, warmed me up, steadied my trembling hand.

We heard only scattered shooting ahead as the lead companies went in. Captain Sharpe pranced down the line on his charger with his saber drawn, his broad-brimmed hat pulled down tight, his long beard fluttering. When we heard the first crash of Yankee musketry aimed at us from across the river, we went in.

Our horses thundered down the muddy lane at breakneck speed, clods of mud flying in our faces, directly into and through a thick gray wall of smoke that pushed at us from the landing.

I lay low against Lettie's neck; the heavy butt of my musketoon banged against my kidneys. She passed by dark blue bodies as she flew over the uneven ground. Lead missiles were zipping through the air like unfriendly insects; each one that came near made my muscles constrict more tightly, as if flexed flesh and bone together could ward off the hurtling lead.

I do not remember hearing the captain's orders to dismount. Somebody grabbed my reins and we were off our horses, every fourth man taking hold of his three comrade's animals and leading them to the rear. We dove for the cover of a thin line of trees along the riverbank.

Dark forms in frock coats were wading through the icy water, running away from us, frantically calling to the troops on the other side of the river not to shoot them.

"Nicht schiessen! Nicht schiessen! Wir sind Freundin!"

Two wagons teetered on the rocky bed of the fast-flowing Rhappa-hannock, abandoned by their drivers who had cut the harnesses on their mules and were flying back to the Union shore with a hundred others.

Federal infantry was sending out a ragged covering fire from the protection of the shoreline. Cottony puffs of smoke were billowing from between the trees; bullets were chipping the tree trunks we pressed our bodies against. Clipped bark and branches dropped about us in a steady rain.

Captain Sharpe strode up and down our line, roaring like a wounded lion.

"Spread out there!" he commanded. "Shoot low and fast, boys. Keep it up, keep it up. Steady there, Mr. Bridges. Shit on a sheet! That was a close one."

I was small enough to hunker comfortably behind a big water oak, while Yankee slugs whacked into its trunk with sickening regularity. My hands were calm, though slick with sweat, and I had no trouble biting the paper cartridges, ramming the bullets home, capping the nipple, aiming in a quick, split-second lunge around the tree trunk and firing, then jumping back and digging once again into my car-tridge box for another round.

"Good, Mr. Fries," the captain nodded approvingly as he walked by. "Stay calm, that's my advice. You might also try aiming, sir. And shoot low, by God!"

Something crashed by me through the brush. I jumped back, star-tled, remembering the time as a boy that a huge whitetail buck hur-tled out at me from a cedar thicket.

But this was a Yankee soldier, a big man with bright blond hair that flew behind him as he ran. He clambered desperately down the steep bank, making for the river. He had gotten as far as the shallows when a pistol went off behind me, and the soldier pitched head first into the water.

I turned to see who the shooter was. It was Lieutenant J.B. Whitner, his pimply, angular face wearing a maniacal grin.

"Son of a bitch thought he was home free," Whitner cackled. "See that slug hit him? Did you see it?"

I backed against my tree and prayed for the shooting to stop. Just as I fumbled for one last cartridge, it did. The smoke and thunder of the combat gradually settled, and soon the firing from the Yankee side of the river petered out as well. There were men over there who continued to curse us in German, calling us shit-eaters and other unsavory names. I understood every word and, peeved, discharged my last round in their direction. I very distinctly heard the slug smack into a tree. Those Yanks shut up.

Because of the weather, the condition of the roads and the possibility of an enemy counterattack, Colonel Black decided to destroy all but six of the captured wagons, which he ordered loaded with most of the cargo from the others: munitions and rations for a brigade, hardtack in boxes, salted pork in barrels, beans, coffee, commissary whiskey, cheese, new leather harness and cases of fine ceramic bottles filled with German white wine.

"Oh, the Dutchies like their wine," went the joke in camp, after several cases somehow escaped the officer's grasp and ended up warming the bellies of the Benson House Mess.

We had killed or wounded a dozen of the enemy, teamsters included, and captured nearly one hundred. The prisoners were herded into a tight circle where they stood or sat, some defiant, but most in a dejected state, their faces bloodied or smudged black during the fight, uniforms muddy and disheveled. A few were barefoot or wearing only their trousers; they muttered to one another in guttural German. An old sergeant with graying mutton-chops calmly filled his clay pipe, lit it and studied us, as we were studying them, with admirable poise.

They were mostly soldiers of the German 29th New York, but we had also caught several men from my old friend, Parker W. Pope's,

2nd West Virginia Infantry. There were also a few Ohio cavalrymen, who looked around them as fearfully as grasshoppers at a trout convention.

Manse said these men had been pretty well used up at Second Manassas and had not been of much account since. The prisoners shared a hangdog look of profound shame and shock, like most soldiers after a losing fight. I walked up to a Yankee officer who was standing stoop-shouldered with his men as our boys gathered up their weapons and accouterments and piled them into the saved wagons. Other squads were quickly unloading the wagons to be burned, cutting free the horse and mule teams to herd back to our lines.

"Is Parker Pope here?" I called out.

The dark-haired West Virginia lieutenant turned to me. He wore gold-rimmed spectacles and had thick pouting lips.

"Parker's back yonder. He's no fool," said the lieutenant, his upper lip trembling. "He warned the colonel about sending the wagons over first. Parker was right, damn his eyes."

"Look, you'll be paroled soon," I said. "Tell Parker you saw Ansel Fries, will you?"

The officer snorted, "I won't get paroled. I am going to Libby prison and I expect there is where I shall rot."

I muttered, "Well, you go to hell then," or something akin to that but he did not hear me over the clatter of the captured wagons taking the main road to Brandy Station, under escort.

Colonel Black cantered up, sweating and grinning. He ordered our company orderly sergeant, Cater Post, to ride to the two reserve companies waiting on the bluff and tell them they were to act as the regiment's rear guard as we followed the wagons. Black dismounted, mopped his brow and enjoyed the jokes of his troopers as they gobbled Northern cheeses and eyed the prisoners with interest.

"Are any of y'all Americans?" Wilson Bridges asked, leaning on his carbine. "I mean, born in this country."

"Yah, sure, I vas," answered a burly New York corporal. "I vas on z' Hudson Riffer born." And he grinned.

Colonel Black guffawed and the boys joined in. Just as somebody handed the prisoner a canteen, a pistol shot exploded so close by that we felt the concussion of the discharge.

"Oh, Jesus," I heard Robert Sitton say.

J.B. Whitner was half-crouching over the body of the Union officer I had just spoken with. Whitner wore a silly, apologetic smile on his face, a smoking revolver in his right hand, a chain holding a gold watch dangling from his right.

The dead lieutenant had been thrown violently on his back by the impact of the slug that went in under his chin and exited behind his right ear. His glasses hung diagonally across his face, of no earthly use now to his half-lidded eyes. Blood washed over the face and seeped like red syrup into the cold ground.

"Wouldn't let me see his watch," Whitner said softly. "He dug in his vest and I thought he had a hideaway in there."

Colonel Black strode to Whitner, looking him straight in the eye, snatched the pistol from his grasp and handed it to Private Bridges. Another trooper searched the dead Yankee and looked up.

"Colonel, the Yank was not armed."

Black's eyes were bloodshot and bulging. "Lieutenant Whitner, upon our return to camp you will surrender yourself to the provost marshal. Until then you are under arrest and relieved of duty. I'm placing you in Captain Sharpe's custody."

Sharpe nodded, and Ezra Sitton and I hustled Whitner away. He squirmed like a schoolboy and shouted over his shoulder, "He was just a goddamn Yankee. I didn't do nothing wrong!"

Ezra made certain Whitner had no weapons hidden in his saddle or gear, then helped him mount. Whitner tried to look proud and defiant, but came across like a petulant, spoiled child who had not expected to be caught, much less whipped.

In Sharpe's official report, which I helped copy weeks later as his unofficial clerk, he informed the colonel that Whitner had been earlier accused of cowardice by his fellow troopers; Sharpe added that he had been watching Whitner for some time.

"He is the high-strung, nervous type," reported the captain. "I suppose he has gone and cracked."

Few in the company liked Whitner, but even fewer were going to shed tears over a dead enemy. Most thought just as Manse did.

"Since when's it wrong to kill a damn Yankee?" he asked.

Only Manse continued to treat with Whitner as he had before the wagon fight; he could not see the difference between killing a man in battle and murdering a prisoner. He was getting harder each day the war continued. But, then, we all were.

Just as with Raleigh Syms' shooting of Sergeant Connally, nothing came of the shooting of that helpless Yank lieutenant. J.B. Whitner never was court-martialed. He endured instead a bust through the ranks to private and a transfer to Company E, where his older brother served.

Buddy Dunn and Willie Grew were the company's second lieutenants. Dunn got J.B. Whitner's gold bar, joining Baz Hilliard as a first lieutenant, and Captain Sharpe put up Bill Noggle for Dunn's now vacant second lieutenancy. Later, Noggle easily won election.

We left the Yankee dead where they lay, and gave the wounded water; those who could walk we sent back across the river to bring their own surgeons, if they would come. We lost two men, both killed in the leading column. Several more were wounded but not badly. We had won a complete victory.

On the ride to Culpeper I found I had been wounded also: a spent Minie must have hit me during the fight, striking my right shoulder, though I never felt a thing until it swelled red and sore. When I showed it to Hep, he just snickered. That was all the sympathy I got. Some big joke.

Bill Noggle, our new second lieutenant, and Wilson Bridges were lifelong friends from an Anderson District community called Hopewell Church. It was pretty farm country, green and rolling; in the spring, the blossoming dogwoods made the hills look like cotton fields. Honeysuckle scented the air when the weather turned warmer. Wilson was a straw-headed farm boy who knew Manse and the Sitton boys because they liked to race their horses on Sunday afternoons down on the Rocky River shoals.

Noggle was a good-natured fellow with an unfortunate nose, which was shaped rather like the roof of a privy; it shaded the lower part of his smooth-shaven face like an awning. Noggle's eyes were quick and intelligent and guileless, however, and most everybody liked him. He wore a brown hat with a cut-down brim and a shallow, rounded crown we called a bee-gum style. It suited his smallish head but made him look like a schoolboy. He later tied a gold Yankee hat cord around the base of the crown to give the hat a more martial look, but he was so quiet and pleasant-faced that officers from other regiments often failed to recognize the rank on his collar, modest as it was.

Back at the Benson House Mess once again, I began having trouble sleeping. Nightmares of talking corpses and rivers of blood invaded my dreams. Hep mixed me up a bitter potion, made from boiling dried hemp flowers, to give me sweet dreams; sometimes the mixture worked.

In my waking hours I tried not to think about the killing. You learn that killing is nothing a civilized man gets used to. In the end, I was grateful to Whitner because he showed me the worst thing a man could become. That helped me keep my sanity, and retain my humanity, right to the end, when most everyone else seemed to have lost theirs.

It was about that time I gave up any idea of ever achieving high rank. Our officers were mostly good men who knew by and large what they were doing, and went about it in a fair manner. There were some soldiers always thought they knew more than their commanders, but not me. Having practiced small town law, I knew what could come of trying to fight a war by committee.

I respected the men I followed because I trusted them with my life. Could I ask another soldier to put his life in my hands? I reckon I would have made as good a leader as some, but, until the last few days of the war, when most of the old men were gone and those veterans still breathing had to take command, I successfully avoided the responsibility of rank.

But I never ran away; I stuck it out to the end.

We spent the winter of 1862-63 in our winter camp hut between Fredericksburg and Culpeper. The following spring and summer were to encompass our most trying duty and hottest work during our stay with the Army of Northern Virginia. But the winter that preceded was relatively quiet and uneventful, building up to Brandy Station and Gettysburg with an ominous serenity.

In mid-April, the whole of Hampton's brigade was detached from Stuart's division and sent south of the James River to recruit. That was how we missed the Chancellorsville campaign, which not many of the boys overly regretted. It would have been grand, though, to have seen old Jackson hammer away at the Yanks in his last fight.

We heard the news on a warm May afternoon while taking our ease at a country inn in Disputanta, Virginia. The sky was boiling black with a spring storm and fat drops of rain were beginning to pelt the dusty roads and countryside. Our bugler, Corporal Villines, who had been idling up at the railroad depot, burst in and cried out that the Richmond newspapers were saying Stonewall had been shot.

No one believed him, but over the next week the news proved to be all too true. Army scuttlebutt had it that skittish North Carolina pickets took the general's party for Yankees and let loose a volley that killed two officers. They hit Stonewall in three places, breaking his left arm which later was amputated. Old Jack died of chest fever not long afterward. The boys cursed Tarheels for days.

Regiments have a way of dwindling in winter quarters. Keep men active and campaigning and they will stay tolerably healthy, if fed regularly, for a period of weeks; even so, men will be lost to battle or accidents. And relentless weeks of marching and fighting will wear down the toughest men and turn their every thought to despair and desertion, as we saw in the last six months of the war.

But confine them to winter quarters for months at a time, standing monotonous picket duty in freezing weather, eating dreary army fare and exchanging illnesses in their crowded, stale-smelling huts, and a regiment will quickly waste away. Not counting those in hospital, on detached duty or away on furlough, Company F that spring mustered barely twenty-five men. Returns for the 1st South Carolina Cavalry showed twenty-four officers and two hundred twenty troopers present for duty.

Only men with the best reasons, usually officers, received thirty-day furloughs home. When Captain Sharpe's wife succumbed to consumption a week after Christmas, Hep accompanied the captain on his journey home to Pendleton. Upon their return late in January, Hep brought with him a box crammed with two pecan pies, a cake, dried meats, jars of pickles, molasses and sourwood honey, bread, fresh butter and bags of flour and sugar.

The captain had changed. His beard had begun to show flecks of gray, his eyes were less bright. He grew more reflective. On parade, his mind appeared to be wandering in regions unknown.

Other men who received furloughs elected not to return to the army; some were hauled back by comrades or officers, some were hunted by the Home Guard and arrested, but a good many stayed at home until war's end. I never felt any ill-will toward those fellows; they did their bit and served and suffered, more than many I could name.

We wandered from Amelia Courthouse east to Petersburg searching for recruits. The heavy losses of the 1862 campaigns required Lee's army to reinforce itself piece-meal through the winter in preparation for the spring campaign. For the cavalry it was crucial, not only for men but for horses. Every brigade in Stuart's division had a dismounted battalion made up of troopers waiting for replacement horses. All of Hampton's brigade mustered but fifteen hundred men and horses, half its paper strength, a month before the Chancellorsville campaign began.

The Virginia countryside was showing the effects of two years of war. Even sections in which there had been no actual fighting nevertheless had been marched over by both sides and stripped of food and forage by the ravenous armies. Her counties were being quickly bled dry of manpower as well, but the recruiting officers knew well that every month, somewhere, young men were turning seventeen who had not yet seen the hard face of war and who could not imagine a finer life.

And it was spring, as fine a season as I could remember in my life, so we could count on the fact that the blood in these young men's veins was pumping, hot and rich, so what could be more bully than prancing about on a smart mount with Stuart's troopers like knights on a violent but patriotic quest? It was easy for a glib sergeant like Manse to paint romantic pictures of the regiment charging with sabers flashing, crashing with irresistible momentum into Yankee ranks and wreaking unimaginable slaughter.

The yokels lapped it up, but they did not flock to the colors as in the old days; there was just not enough of them. We recruited every village and town, and even in the army hospitals where there were many soldiers recovering from minor wounds or sickness looking for a way out of the infantry. Some already had discharges in hand but did not want to go home; some, it turned out, were bonafide shirkers or outright deserters who for some reason thought that joining the cavalry was not at all like the army. Others hankered only for the $50 in Confederate scrip we were authorized to pay every man who enlisted.

We signed them all up. Manse never lied to these boys but neither did he tell the entire truth. I felt guilty; it was like luring children with promises of candy. But we needed men, so why could not these idle fellows, who were holding up ploughs or idling at inns and hospitals, stop a bullet as well as my poor body?

We soon learned the best place to set up our recruiting desk was outside a general store, since most small town stores at that time also had post offices and every citizen gravitated there at some point. All that was needed was a literate clerk (myself) and a cocky veteran or two to talk up the Cause (Manse and Ezra).

It was in this way one afternoon in May, while lounging outside J.T. Lankford's Dry Goods & General Notions store, that the Benson House Mess signed up two more men for Company F.

John Lamb and Ab Tucker were eighteen-year-old cousins from yeoman farming families, like Manse's, in Prince George County, Virginia. They heard cavalry recruiters were circulating so they jumped on their fat gray mule, Esmeralda, and rode to town to "jine the calvary."

"I am proud to serve," Ab said, bending to sign his name with a practiced hand.

Manse glanced at me and Ezra conspiratorially, handed Ab his Colt revolver and told him straight-faced that he would have to shoot his old mule, as no such animals were allowed in the regiment. Ab's mouth dropped open. Slowly, his jaw set. You could tell there was a battle going on in his mind over who to shoot, Manse or the mule.

"I will not do it, sir," Ab decided, handing Manse back his pistol, butt first. "And I damn any government that would."

His dark brows knitted with anxiety, Lamb busily stroked Esmeralda's neck. The mule was totally unconcerned.

It was a good joke and Manse and I laughed heartily, but Ezra must have felt a twinge of guilt at his part in the foolish deception. He explained and produced several captured Yankee cigars, which soothed the cousins' ruffled feathers.

By the end of May, the regiment had beefed up to more than four hundred officers and men; the brigade had swelled to over two thousand strong.

Early in June we returned to our winter camp in Culpeper to rejoin Stuart's division, which now consisted of six brigades of horse and six batteries of artillery, more than ten thousand men all told.

We were veterans enough to become immediately suspicious when the grub began to improve. We were getting fresh beef and soft bread, onions and potatoes on a fairly regular basis. Then came a shipment of jackets, trousers and even shoes. Manse proclaimed that the spring campaign was imminent.

It had been a beautiful spring. The weather was warm and delightful. Honeysuckle vines threaded the roadside rail fences. The Virginia forests were growing thick with verdant foliage; the rolling meadows were lush with clover.

It was good to be young and robust and in the saddle in the elite vanguard of a great army. We all were in good physical condition. My puny body had gained not a pound but I had firmed up considerably. My arms and shoulders and back felt strong; my grip was tight, my thighs were like springs from spending so much time on horseback. My hands and behind were equally calloused from living the cavalry life.

On June 8, 1863, Stuart's entire division paraded before General Lee on the plains between Culpeper and Brandy Station, one of the grandest sights I remember in the war.

We were deployed in line of brigades, the largest body of horsemen ever assembled at one place on the continent. Our brigade, Hampton's, held the position of honor on the extreme right, and the

1st South Carolina Cavalry was on the right of the brigade, more an accident of our camp situation than for any other reason.

But it was an indescribable feeling for us to lead that magnificent host. We broke into column of companies from the right and passed in review at a walk in front of General Lee, and we gave him a cheer as we passed. We passed a second time at a trot and then charged by squadrons, rallied and reformed our lines.

We heard later that Lee asked about those smart-looking, wiry fellows who had no sabers. General Hampton told him the army needed more such soldiers, or words to that effect.

As the review ended, the division's artillery, some twenty-four guns, opened up with volley after volley of blank charges, creating a thunderous climax to the spectacle. None of us understood at the time that the purpose of the mock cannonade had been to divert attention from the movement of General Ewell's corps, which at that moment was marching north toward a crossing of the Potomac River.

Union General Joe Hooker did not know it either, but when he heard our guns he intended to find out what the devil was going on. The probing force he unexpectedly sent against us the next morning started what we came to call the fight for Fleetwood Hill. The generals and historians named it the first battle of Brandy Station.

Before dawn on June 9, that old Yankee devil, John Buford, crossed the upper fords of the Rhappahannock River in force and drove our pickets all the way back to our camps at St. James Church. He came on with a division of rough-riding Federal cavalry and two brigades of infantry, and he meant business.

Each of our regiments already had their marching orders for the move north. The boys were feeling good and it had been a night of some merriment; I slept through it with untroubled dreams.

Manse and a few others were already up and warming themselves around the hazy fires when our pickets came galloping back, their horses lathered with sweat, the pop pop pop of the foremost Federal horsemen sputtering behind them, intermittent but worrisome.

Manse rolled me out of my blankets with a whoop and said a fight was brewing. I could hear the tinny blare of faroff bugles and the unmistakable crackle of musketry; my stomach tightened like a banjo string being tuned at the sound of the gunfire.

Sleepy-eyed men were rushing about, so I washed my face with the chilly morning dew and hunted my boots, stepping on a horse-shoe nail. It put me in a foul mood. I cursed and snapped and wrapped my sore foot tightly with a strip of linen.

We saddled, cinched and mounted, and did not wait for Captain Sharpe to give the order to fall in. We each knew our familiar place in the line: Manse and Henry in the rank to my front, Robert and Ezra on either flank. The horses caught the excitement of the men, snorted, reared and bucked.

I made sure that John Lamb and Ab Tucker had their shotguns primed and loaded. They were alert but their nervous faces were pale; the sound of the guns and the strange murmur of thousands of horsemen beating across the plains barely a quarter mile away made them shiver. I tried to think of some good advice that might keep them alive in their first fight.

"Whatever happens, stay with the company; follow Company F's guidon," I told them. "If one of you falls, do not stop. Stay with the troop."

The captain ordered, "Company! By the left flank, march!"

We spurred our mounts, doubling into column of fours as we turned. Our second squadron fell in behind the first and soon the entire regiment was galloping around the division's camps, heading for Stuart's headquarters atop Fleetwood Hill.

The countryside was alive with battalions of mounted troops, officers and aides, horse-drawn caissons with limbered guns jounc-ing into battle and others being wheeled into position. The leaden spring sky boiled with billowing banks of clouds, a background that richly complimented the drama of the scene.

The regiment, guarding the brigade's right flank, marched to a line of trees facing a broad field about three hundred yards from the foot of Fleetwood Hill. We wheeled by companies, entered the cover of the trees and dismounted.

Smoke rose eerily from the hilltop in the half-light of dawn; pulses of gunfire stabbed the haze making a muffled, grumbling sound. We were drawn up in two ranks in line of battle when Colonel Black cantered down the line, speaking softly to ease the fear of the recruits about to taste their first fight.

Robert Sitton pulled out a piece of leathery beef jerky and cut a huge bite; the tough jerky made his tense jaws work overtime. My poor foot throbbed and felt as if the nail were still embedded in it. Manse passed around a medicine bottle filled with whiskey and made sure that John, Ab and everybody in the Benson House Mess took a long swig. Henry raised the bottle high; I watched his adams apple bob, then he offered it to me. I savored the burning liquid as it went down, warming the cavities in my back teeth.

I noticed that Henry's linen canteen strap was nearly worn through, so I took out my pocketknife, cut the strap and retied it, then clapped him on the back. Henry smiled at me over his shoulder.

"Horses to the rear!" The holders, eager to be out of the line, led our animals away.

"Fall in!" Colonel Black bellowed. "Dress your ranks!"

Oh, I thought absently. We are going to fight on foot.

Suddenly, we were stepping forward in two loose skirmish lines, shouldering our way through the trees edging the field and plunging into the waist-high grass beyond, breasting our way toward Fleetwood Hill.

Our officers walked ahead of us, shouting encouragement. Buddy Dunn marched as if on parade, head erect, his sword blade tucked upright against his right shoulder. Captain Sharpe pointed his sword uphill and waved his revolver.

The Yankee troopers held the crest of the hill on our side and were shooting down on us, though our ranks were still out of range but pressing ever closer.

It was like walking into a thunderstorm that you watched coming at you from the near distance, flashing over the hills and fields, popping and crashing, until it was right overhead and the wind was scything around and against you. The air smelled thick and strange.

Colonel Black halted the regiment at the foot of the hill and we dressed our ranks. He told us the Yankees had caught us with our britches down and knocked two of Stuart's best regiments clean off Fleetwood Hill. It was our job to take it back.

The boys began giving out with the famous Rebel yip yip yip, and in that grand theater of battle it sounded fierce and bloodthirsty. The colonel waved his sword and we followed.

The heavier the Yankee fire got, the more the men would crouch or walk with their bodies half-turned, heads slightly bowed as if walking into a strong wind. It was an involuntary thing because there was no cover. The flesh on my spine crawled and quivered, and the hairs on my head seemed to stand up straight, each anticipating the impact of a soft lead Minie ball.

Men around me shouted unintelligible things in their fear and were jerky in their movements, as if every physical action required a force of will going against the natural human inclination to hit the ground, crawl, find a hole and hide. Others were utterly quiet, their faces pinched with the intensity of their concentration.

Manse strode forward like a hunter, expectant, confident, hungry for the slaughter. He talked to the boys as if we were back in our Benson House Mess hut, making jokes.

"Watch your britches, John," he called out in a fatherly tone. "General Lee can't buy pants for every man after his first fight. Look ahead there, Ab! Watch the man in front of you. And don't slouch so!"

Fleetwood Hill was studded with thorny brush and gray boulders, some as big as privies. The Yankees had gotten our range and were sending bullets zipping past our ears. Our battle line began to break up into ragged squads as we stepped around the bigger rocks, which were geysering with dust where the Yankee rounds were hitting.

Men began dropping out of sight into the brush. Wilson Bridges was in front of me when he kicked with both his legs and went down, grabbing his right leg and squealing like a shoat.

Manse kept us going. He had lost his forage cap and his red hair was blowing in the wind that was ushering in the dawn. Even his powerful voice was lost in the din.

The Yankees had corrected their shooting and were popping away at us at a lower angle, clipping the tops from the thorny heather. My foot no longer hurt; I could feel blood squishing around in my boot but I went on, following Manse's treelike form.

The sun was burning a smoky red on the horizon when John Lamb, still wearing his floppy farmer's hat, clutched his side, dropped his shotgun and sank forward, putting out his gun-arm to break his fall. I stepped over his heaving body and he looked up at me with a mystical smile. Then I heard someone shouting frantically through the pounding of the guns.

"Buddy Dunn's killed!"

"Keep going, boys!" Manse screamed. "Not so far, not so far now. There, goddamn 'em! Look at the Yankee shit-eaters run!"

We struggled the last few yards to the crest and saw it was true. Buford's troops, many of them unhorsed, were streaming down the other side of Fleetwood Hill. The morning wind blew away the smoke in ragged sheets and suddenly the dawn burst, full and dazzling, lighting the plains below us like a huge arc lamp illuminating an unimaginably grand stage.

Regiment after regiment of blue-coated troopers were drawn up on the plains below, some in reserve, others deploying and on the move, while a mile to our left a ferocious cavalry battle was raging between wheeling and charging squadrons of horsemen in true, old world style. Banks of dirty smoke rolled in again and from our position on the extreme right of Stuart's line we could catch only glimpses of the great fight: lightning-like flashes of drawn sabers and bobbing battle flags, accompanied by a wall of sound made of the drumming thunder of countless horse's hooves and the shouts of ten thousand combatants that crashed on our ears like ocean breakers against a shoreline.

Fleetwood Hill slopes gently on its eastern side and we could see fresh Yankee regiments arrayed in columns, cueing up to get into the fight. Others were reforming, rehorsing, refitting and refilling empty cartridge boxes, getting ready to go forward once again. Some were reforming on foot, to fight as we had. A battery of Yankee artillery came up and unlimbered, the gunners wheeling their bronze pieces about to bear on Fleetwood Hill. Still another battery clattered up to join them.

"Dig in!" screamed Manse, who went around smacking soldiers to their knees, forcing them to seek cover behind rocks and dead horses. "Dig in, or you're going to be goddamn sorry when that Yankee iron starts dropping on your heads."

The battery pounded us first with solid shot and then air bursts that scattered red hot shards of iron in a deadly rain.

"Here they come!"

Yankee troopers were clambering up the slope, men of the 8th Illinois Cavalry and the 3rd Indiana, tough Westerners. But they were unaccustomed to attacking on foot and we dropped them like blue-bellied doves. We soon ran low on ammunition, and when the blue lines pushed again up the hill we retired slowly, picking up our wounded on the way. John Lamb and Wilson Bridges were both still alive but dumb from shock and loss of blood.

We took Fleetwood Hill once more that day and then lost it again for the same reason we lost it the first time. By the time the sunset on June 9, we were once again in firm possession of the hill.

By nightfall, infantry from Longstreet's corps showed up to scare the rest of the attackers back across the Rhappahannock.

And I was in possession of a new firearm. Some Hoosier had cached his breechloading Sharps carbine under a boulder where I had scampered for protection, and obligingly left his cartridge box as well, crammed full of linen .52-caliber rounds. He also left bright drops of fresh blood on the box and carbine's stock, which were easily wiped away. Like a friendly packrat, I left my old musketoon in place of the Sharps.

At Brandy Station we killed and wounded more than five hundred of the enemy and captured five hundred more; our own division's losses were half that number, but many were officers not easily replaced.

Our brigade commander's brother, Colonel Frank Hampton, had been killed, and the general made no bones about placing blame on the 4th Virginia Cavalry, which cut and run at a critical moment, leaving Frank to the enemy's mercy. And a single Yankee shell took off Colonel M.C. Butler's right foot, went through his horse, took off the left leg of Captain W.D. Farley who was at Butler's side, then killed his horse. They carried Farley and Butler to the rear in horse troughs their aides found in our old camp. The colonel from Columbia survived to fight again; Farley did not. They buried him with his leg in a farmer's vineyard. Farley was not one of our regiment, but like Butler he was a South Carolinian, and a man of good family from Laurensville.

In doing its part the 1st South Carolina Cavalry lost three men killed and nine wounded. Two of the dead were officers in Company F, First Lieutenant Buddy Dunn of Pendleton and Second Lieutenant Willie Grew of Pickens.

Buddy was found just below the crest of Fleetwood Hill, lying on his back, one hand still clutching his sword. The slug that killed him had gone in at the bridge of his nose and taken off the back of his head.

Colonel Black wrote Buddy's family that their boy had died a mercifully quick death while leading his company in the front rank. In the letter, Black enclosed a thick lock of Buddy's matted brown hair and the blood-stained remnants of an unfinished letter home the dead boy had stashed in a pocket of his butternut blouse.

John Lamb had sustained a painful but glancing blow from a Yankee bullet that bounced off his ribs, tore a long gash in his gray jacket and raised a huge ugly welter along his side. Hep washed John with herbs and wrapped him tight with a long woolen bandage. John was stiff and sore but able to stay in the saddle.

Wilson Bridges was not so lucky; the surgeons sawed off his right foot at the ankle. The last we saw of Wilson he was being painfully jounced around in the back of an ambulance wagon that was taking him to one of the army field hospitals in Culpeper.

A week later, the regiment joined the rest of Hampton's brigade in a hurried march north to Warrenton, then farther north still, skirting the Bull Run mountains on our right, screening the long columns of Lee's army as it wound its ponderous way up the green and fertile Shenandoah Valley, headed toward Maryland and unspoiled Pennsylvania. No orders saying so ever came down but we all knew what was happening. Bobby Lee was snapping his fingers at Joe Hooker and daring the Army of the Potomac to come find him, if it could.

We were going to the land of milk and honey.

CHAPTER 7

Every Yankee In Creation

Castles are sacked in war;
Chieftains are scattered far.
Truth is a fixed star, Eileen Aroon.

I do not recall the spring and summer of 1863 with much fondness.

Too much happened, most of it bad, though it helped that things were clear cut. A man chose his side, hunkered down and took what was coming to him. I rode with my friends and tried to stay alive and unhurt.

What was bad was the killing and the unending destruction and the great waste of it all in lives, animals and property, and the ten million hurts and tears that came from all battles, great or small, and sent ripples down through time for generations. I began to feel that with every fight we were scarring the face of God Almighty and there was nothing could ever heal it.

I had a recurring dream in which I was again on Fleetwood Hill, tired, footsore and bleeding, my head dulled to stupidity by the concussion of guns, weeping inwardly for my dead friends and maimed comrades. The world revolved about me on that smoky hilltop and the exhilaration I felt at winning, and surviving, was darkened by the fear that one wrong step would plunge me again into the nightmare of combat below, where dead men were fighting.

I walked this tightrope, hid within the camaraderie of the company and determined to live, even though at Gettysburg and after the world seemed to fall about my ears like the gradual but inevitable collapse of a derelict house—first in dustings of plaster, then in hunks and finally entire walls.

There were omens. Hepsibah saw them. The Benson House Mess had come to respect Hep's understanding of things natural and unnatural. When Hep hung a dead snake in the lower branches of a tree to bring rain, more often than not it rained. When he used incantations to talk out the fire in a wound, it did ease the pain and help the healing.

It was Hep who told me the story of Buddy Dunn's homecoming. How he heard of it, he never would say.

The day Buddy was killed at Brandy Station, his family reported seeing him, youthful and handsome in his butternut jacket and cavalry boots, swinging his arms as was his habit, striding up the long lane leading to the Dunn home in Pendleton.

Old Isiah Dunn was standing on the veranda of the house and he fell to his knees, thanking God for the safe return of his son. Buddy's mother, his brother, Winston, and an uncle rushed out, waving and weeping in their joy. All saw him. Buddy looked neither right nor left but walked straight into the trunk of an old oak tree and disappeared. His mother fainted dead away. Ten days later, the news reached them that Buddy had died on that same day, that very hour of the morning, on a lonely hillside in faroff Virginia.

Of course, the Dunn family already knew the worst. Buddy brought the news himself, in the only way that he could.

Old man Dunn and fourteen-year-old Winston made the long trip north to Richmond by train, then bought a wagon and mule team which took them to Culpeper. They stopped to visit Wilson Bridges at the army hospital, then hired a Negro to guide them to the Brandy Station battlefield.

They found Buddy's grave right where Wilson Bridges told them it would be, a bare mound of dirt beneath a tall cedar tree. One of Buddy's hands stuck up out of the shallow grave and they recognized a scar on the palm by which they identified the corpse. They had the body embalmed at an undertaker's in Culpeper which had done a booming business following the battle. I could not imagine there was much left of Buddy to embalm, but the Dunn family all said the man did an admirable job.

Buddy's father and brother brought him home to Pendleton and buried him under the spreading oak tree where the family had seen their young hero plain as day for the last time. I am told that the tree under which he rests is still alive, enfolding forever in its gentle roots a sublime secret.

After the war, whenever I talked with veterans and told them I had served with J.E.B. Stuart, I endured the same question over and over, in varying stages of mockery according to how much liquor the questioner had imbibed.

"Where was you boys at Gettysburg?"

Old infantrymen in particular delighted in that question. I answered, usually with good humor, "Getting my skinny white arse shot at. Where was you?"

Honest truth was, I did not know half the time during those hot and bloody weeks whether we were in Virginia or West Virginia, Maryland or Pennsylvania, always being poor in geography and depending for news solely on what rumors drifted back to my place in the company from the long lines of dusty horsemen ahead. Mostly I was too hungry and backsore to care.

As Stuart's brigades screened Lee's long columns of marching infantry, we ran into nasty little fights with General Pleasanton's cavalry division, first around Aldie, then at Middleburg and Upperville a few days later. Every valley in those mountains was cut by gaps to be guarded or crossroads to be taken and held. While we beat the Yankees at this game most of the time, it was clear to everyone their cavalry was much improved; they were finally getting the hang of horse-fighting.

Toward the end of June, Pleasanton's columns forced us back through Ashby's Gap but we came out again through the Shenandoah Valley like rabbits through an escape hole. We broke off from the trail of Lee's army to embark on a roundabout raid east into Union-held territory, loading wagons with badly-needed forage for our horses. It took us a week to cut back across northern Virginia. We forded the Potomac River twenty miles above Washington City and crossed into Maryland just before dusk on June 27.

The history books tell us that General Stuart made a bad mistake in losing touch with the main body of Lee's army. All I know is we did a lot of hard riding across some right pretty farm country, green hillsides dotted with stone barns and criss-crossed by stone walls. We ate well, filled our canteens with buttermilk and applejack, and got back to the army, as the books relate, in time to tangle with every Yankee trooper in creation on the bloody afternoon of July 3, 1863.

The problem was that once we broke off from Lee, we played hell finding him again. The Army of the Potomac was stretched out for miles between us and the vanguard of Lee's army in southern Pennsylvania. No matter which way we turned and twisted, we always ran up against Yankees by the thousands between us and the Army of Northern Virginia.

We captured a long Federal wagon train at Rockville and took two hundred prisoners, who were promptly disarmed and paroled. We dragged that damn train with us across Maryland and into Pennsylvania, hoping to find our troops in every town we passed through. At Hanover and at York and at Carlisle, we were riding out of town on one side just as Yankee militia was coming in on the other. Our boys were always in the next town. We had to fight past pesky militia and blue-coated cavalry to get there, only to find that our infantry had left the day before.

We were like blind men pursuing a butterfly. After two weeks of hard riding and running fights, men and horses were nearly done in. We were dead tired, frustrated and awful sick of hauling that useless Yankee wagon train. It weighed us down like a dragline of boulders.

Outside of Carlisle, Pennsylvania, on July 1 Stuart got word that Lee had concentrated his forces at Gettysburg and had in fact been fighting there all day.

At dawn the next morning we set out. There was no cheering, I can tell you, and damn little enthusiasm. We were as sullen and irritable as troops can be. For it was a thirty mile ride that was ahead of us, and my poor old Lettie was getting wobbly on her legs. My legs were fine but my behind felt as numb and sore as if it had been skinned. Every mile proved to be an agony. Robert Sitton and I agreed that if either saw the other swaying in the saddle, he would do his best to keep his pard from tumbling to earth.

If I had known then what I know now, I am not so sure I would have kept to it. I might have done like others I knew who slipped away from the column in the night, taking their chances getting caught by Federal patrols or trigger-happy militia boys, and gone home.

Damn my soul, I did not do it. What a fool.

We rode hard all morning and arrived on the outskirts of Gettysburg shortly after dusk on July 2. We smelled the stink of the battlefield long before we ever laid eyes on it.

The heat was oppressive. Above the steamy, still air hung the indescribable stench of the rapidly decomposing dead. We had seen them as we came in, pathetic clumps of bodies lying in every conceivable attitude of death, many with their arms raised in rigor, their mouths frozen open, faces swollen and black. Many bore the cruel, amputating wounds made only by artillery firing rounds of double canister at point-blank range. A single round of canister turned a 12-pound field piece into an immense shotgun, spewing 27 iron shot with every discharge.

Where the dead lay the ground was littered with the wreckage of war: splintered caissons, putrefying horses still in harness, haversacks and shredded bits of uniform, pistols, rifle-muskets, bayonets, shattered drums, cartridge boxes and paper cartridges of every caliber, canteens bent by some sudden, lethal blow, identifiable body parts and chunks of human flesh flung randomly about the fields of trampled corn and wheat. Dead soldier's letters fluttered like dying birds in the rare breeze that stirred over the sun-baked earth.

Robert retched as the column picked its way through the carnage, and he threw up with me hanging onto his belt to keep him in the saddle.

We made good time the last mile, pounding down the Chambersburg Pike and passing around to the left flank of Lee's army, where we halted behind the cover of Ewell's lines. My saddle had gnawed a painful blister into my right thigh, but I was groggy enough to literally drop off Lettie's back into the first comfortable-looking ditch and fall instantly asleep.

I woke up to Henry Knauff pouring warm, metallic-tasting water from his canteen over my face. His face was dirty and sweat-stained, his eyes bloodshot.

"Wake up, Ansel. Time to get up."

My limbs felt as heavy as lead but I stood up unsteadily like a drunken man. Lettie was gone; details had taken the horses to a muddy stream nearby. We were resting under cover of a thickly-foliaged forest, but even in the shade the air was dense as steam. Nobody had the energy to light a fire. The boys were wearily munching captured hardtack. Henry brought me a cracker and we did the same, no one talking, staring at nothing in a lethargic daze.

An ominous stillness had fallen over the battlefield. The patter of musket fire was growing faint, like the sounds of a receding rainstorm.

I never in my life felt less like fighting a battle than on that third day at Gettysburg. All of us were badly winded and nursing minor hurts. Robert still stood strong but his face had aged beyond his years. His brother Ezra looked like a man in the final stages of a fatal case of jaundice, sallow and fatigued in body and mind. John Lamb was just there. Henry had cut his thumb chopping firewood with Manse's Bowie knife; the joint swelled red with infection. Hep treated it the best he could, but Henry was in pain, irritable and having trouble holding his horse's reins.

My body ached all over; I wanted nothing so much as to find a bed of cool clover to lie down in and forget about the army and the war. But when Manse came up, looked us over with narrowed eyes and squatted on his haunches, the Benson House Mess gathered round to hear what he had to say.

Stuart's badly-thinned out four brigades were to create a diversion to keep the Yankee cavalry busy along the Baltimore Pike, while Longstreet's corps tried to crack the Union center. As plans go it was not a bad one, but anybody who knows war knows that battles are never fought according to plan. I must admit, though, this battle-plan was more poorly executed than most.

Manse had weathered the hardships of the campaign well; he just kept getting leaner and rangier, his skin browned to the consistency of old cowhide. He had no jokes left in him.

We watched from the cover of the trees as skirmishers from Jenkins' Virginia brigade fanned out to envelope a farmstead of four stone buildings half a mile to our front, the Rummel farm. The Yankees were situated atop a wooded ridge half a mile beyond the farm, which occupied a cleared valley between our woods and the ridge.

It was not long before the Yanks dismounted a regiment of horsemen and sent them out in a long ragged line, popping away, to drive off our skirmishers. A hot fire soon developed; pretty white puffs of smoke dotted the green valley and hung in the stale air like low-scudding clouds. Soon, we felt beneath our feet the bass rumble of a great artillery battle roaring not too many miles away.

"Longstreet," said Manse.

The distant thunder rolled on, gathering intensity, until it was joined by the thud thud thud of a battery that opened up from a bald knoll behind us.

Odd the thoughts that go through one's head before going into a fight. I sat with my back against a tree and chanced to glance up through the leaves into a blue patch of sky. I saw what was probably a round from some poor fellow's ignited cartridge box. It fizzed white smoke and shot straight into the air like a rocket, then blew up in a shower of red sparks. It was grim and beautiful and for a brief instant it took me home.

As a boy, I liked to hide in an old feed bin in my father's barn. It was a good place to crawl into when I did not want to be found, cool and dark and musty-smelling. My older brother Tom would climb into the loft above me for the same reason. He liked to lie in the hay, smoke his pipe and gaze out a wide crack in the siding at the blue mountains humped like whale's backs in the distance. He would tamp his pipe gently now and then on the outside of the barn, to prevent any danger of starting a fire, so that the embers in the bowl sparked briefly on their arcing descent to the hard clay floor of the barnyard. At dusk, the embers were as bright and graceful as falling stars. Tom would fast hide his pipe and greasy tobacco bag in a cranny of the loft when he heard father calling....

"Ansel, will you look for me if I come up missing?"

It was Ezra. His voice was faint, and it was not because of the noise of the fighting that was rolling toward us and gathering weight like that of an approaching storm.

"I've got a terrible feeling that if we go out there today I'm going to get myself killed."

"I read to him from the good book," said Robert. "But he wants you to ask Hep for a charm."

I stood up, dug into the oily haversack tied to my saddle and pulled out a muslin poke-bag, tied at the neck, which Hep had pressed upon me before our first fight on the Stono Inlet. I never wore it; it smelled like there was something dead inside.

"Here," I said. "It's kept me alive for almost a year, so I reckon it's good for one more fight."

Ezra thanked me, looking so relieved I thought he might cry. But the more I thought of it, the edgier I got. What if that foul-smelling thing had been protecting me? What had I done?

Manse shouted down the line, "Mount up, boys."

I swung up onto Lettie and eased a folded piece of woolen blanket under my thigh to cushion the rub of that painful boil against the saddle. Poor Lettie snorted at my sudden weight, demanding some consideration. I had neglected her through no fault of my own. She needed a fat bag of oats, cool spring water, a liniment rubdown and a week's rest, but it would have to wait. I stroked her mane and thought it will be a miracle if either one of us comes out of this fight alive.

I carefully loaded my precious Sharps and checked the cartridge box: seven rounds left. Then I slung it stock up over my left shoulder, barrel on my right hip. I told myself again to look into getting a pistol; after all, this business was beginning to get serious. Smiling silently at my joke, I felt for father's Prussian saber. Its time had come.

Manse on Dixie pranced through the mounted company like a knight of old astride his charger. Manse's eyes gleamed with anticipation. His cavalry jacket had sprung its seams at both shoulders and his patched trousers were stained and dusty. But his Colt revolver was stuck into the waistband of his pants and an Enfield carbine was loaded and primed and ready to draw from an oilcloth case at Dixie's side. Manse's red fringe of beard was tangled and awry, his square face streaked with sweat. Manson Sherrill Jolly looked every inch the Confederate warrior.

There is a man, I thought. He knew a big fight was brewing and that he was going to be in the middle of it, but he gave not a thought to dying. He cantered up to me and drew up short.

"Stay behind me, Ansel. I'll need you to watch my back."

Then Manse drew out his Enfield and pushed it at me.

"Carry this for me and give me your old sword. It's a fair trade. You'll get it back."

He drew the old saber from its scabbard and brandished it about his head, yipping like a wild Indian. The blade made an ugly, zipping sound as it cut the muggy air.

Manse pushed his way into line in front of me, shouting at troopers to close up, straighten their backs and check the priming on their revolvers. The boys responded like men in a dream, moving in the dense heat as if it was an atmosphere of molasses not air. Battle was swirling in the valley around the Rummel farm, but I heard it as through wads of cotton, distant and dull. The Enfield was an unwanted weight as I held it across my saddle. What would I do with it after loosing its single shot? My head ached.

The lead squadrons of Hampton's and Fitzhugh Lee's brigades cantered out of the woods a rod or so ahead of us in column of fours, gripping their bright sabers upright against their right shoulders, their battle flags unfurled but limp in the airless afternoon. We were going in, and my greatest desire was to curl up under a shade tree and sleep, long and deep.

Then we were moving, part of two parallel columns four thousand strong snaking across a long open meadow flanked by hills layered in smoke. Soon the valley floor was littered with dead and dying men and horses, and wounded crawling desperately out of our path. We covered five hundred yards before the Yankees, occupied with the North Carolinians and Georgians on our right, saw us coming and turned to meet the assault. The Federal batteries quickly began to shift their alignment, and at the sight of the blue-coated gunners wheeling their gap-mouthed pieces by hand my stomach rolled like a crawfish on a hook.

Bugles blared and their skirmishers went streaming back to the cover of their lines. We were galloping now; Lettie's big heart was pounding like an engine. Manse was hunched low in his saddle, the blade of my saber resting on his shoulder. Ezra and Robert rode so close to me that we bumped several times crossing the uneven terrain. Henry Knauff was a horse length ahead, staying close to Manse's side.

The column bunched into a mass of men and horses shaped like an arrowhead, the red regimental flags tossing about, the color bearers each trying to surge ahead of the others, and General Hampton and Colonel Black forming the arrowhead's human apex. The men were making an ungodly din with their voices, the sort of roar of hosts that must have been heard at Toulon and Agincourt. And when the Yankee batteries opened, a great groan rose from our ranks, as of air being forced all at once from four thousand throats.

The command began to spread out, men trying to avoid running over the screaming horses and troopers knocked over by the artillery's first blasts of canister. Horses killed outright piled up five or six of the riders close behind them in a squirming, kicking collision of equine and human bodies. Just as at the Stono Inlet I saw a hat shoot straight into the air and float lazily to earth as we pounded by. I could have almost grabbed it.

Guns were exploding with ragged intensity, the canister making dreadful bee-like noises as it cut through our ranks. The iron balls thudded like dropped melons when they struck human and horse flesh.

Ahead on the jarring horizon, gray with a heavy curtain of smoke, appeared a vision of men on horses not one hundred yards distant, their striped banner beautiful but indistinct, thundering towards us through a shimmering pane of heat.

Manse looked over his shoulder but not to me. He pointed his heavy saber at the oncoming columns of Yankee cavalry and shouted something in the way of a battle cry.

We were perhaps fifty yards from the lead guns of the Yankee battery pounding us on our left when Fitzhugh Lee's Virginians jumped in among the guns and began shooting down and sabering the gunners.

I turned for a moment to look and saw a pint-sized Yankee with no shirt, his bare arms black with powder, his white chest streaming blood, go down before a butternut horseman. As he fell, that scrappy Yankee jerked the lanyard of his gun and its ugly iron mouth blossomed white, the purest, most indescribable white I ever saw, like a huge and growing ball of cotton, ever expanding, and in that instant Ezra clutched his throat and his horse skidded to its knees. Something whispered over my head and I felt a savage blow whipped by a gale of hot wind buffet my left side. Lettie grunted, and she kneeled abruptly, as if she had taken it in her mind to stop in the middle of battle to pray. I went over her, Manse's Enfield unfired in my hand, the hot wind choked out of my lungs.

Then the sun guttered out, a candle unexpectedly extinguished.

Consciousness returned in stages. Black sun burned red inside lidded eyes. Head terrible hurt. Skull cracked like a crock. A cough, a flinch, any movement sent out spasming jolts of pain making the stomach revolt and bitter bile come rushing up.

I lay on my back, pricked by tough stems of vegetation. I had one consuming desire: water. Flowing streams of water, cold, clear, purifying. I dreamed I was wading in the fishing holes I had known as a boy. But when I tried to move, lips crusted, eyes tightly shut, my headed expanded painfully and my guts rolled.

I lay there dreaming, hot and sick. Once a horse galloped by, not very far away, but I could not stir. A heavy weight pressed against my left side. When I pushed weakly at it, it gave slightly then fell back against me. Slowly, I forced an eye open enough to see the broad blue back of a dead Yankee trooper; wisps of light brown hair were blowing over his sweat-stained collar.

A hot breeze wafted over the field, bringing with it the acrid stink of gunsmoke and the coppery smell of fresh blood. There was another odor, too, a privy smell. I pushed the dead man over on his face; the seat of his breeches was stained dark, the final indignity heaped upon men in their last moment on earth.

My left leg was soaked with blood, drying brown in the sun. I tested it slowly, easing up the knee, rotating the ankle. I remembered the cannon going off and Lettie sighing like a balloon being bled of its air. It was her blood that drenched me.

I raised myself on my elbows and looked around through half-lidded eyes. The haze of heat made the meadow seem to undulate gently, but its greenery was now a garbage pit, humped with still forms, the bodies of horses and men. A lone saber spitted the ground at an odd angle.

Then I saw Lettie.

She was stretched out on her belly a few yards from where I lay, her forelegs twisted beneath her. Her soft muzzle rested gently in the grass, leaking blood; her eyes, covered with a death-film, seemed to study me. Files swarmed over her gore-streaked body. Something caught in my throat and I choked and wept.

A moan answered me, very human and not very far away. I crawled toward the sound; the victim seemed to be gargling. I could see a man's chest heaving convulsively, hidden behind the mutilated corpse of a horse. I recognized Ezra a few crawling feet before I reached his lanky form.

Ezra appeared to have been dipped in a vat of blood. The left shoulder and side of his jacket had been shredded by the cannon's blast. His bare chest, left shoulder, arm, ribs and left cheek were peppered with little black holes; with every beat of his heart, blood pumped from a larger hole in his chest.

"Water, please," he gargled. "Water, please. Water."

I crawled back to where Lettie lay. My wool-covered canteen was still tied to the pommel of the saddle, only now it bore a neat round hole about the size of a quarter just below its pewter spout.

I carried the punctured canteen back to Ezra and held it to his parched lips. With each fevered sip, I could see the water oozing out of the hole in his chest. Ezra sipped and wheezed, sipped and wheezed. He was choking on his own blood and could not catch his breath. He had a ragged throat wound as well, but it was not mortal. He was drowning.

"I'm a dead man," Ezra rasped. In his delerium, he muttered about being buried where mam and pap could find him. He cursed the war. He asked me to look after Robert. I washed the dried blood from his face with warm water from the canteen and then drank deeply myself.

"There, there."

I brushed back Ezra's hair, shielded his face with my hat and tried to keep the flies off him.

"There, there."

Helpless to do anything else, I waited for my friend to die.

The hand that woke me felt in my feverish dream like the grip of an iron vice.

It was dusk but I soon made out Manse's lean face in the deepening twilight. I started and reached for Ezra; I had fallen asleep with my hand in his. He squeezed, weakly, and I knew he was alive.

Manse whispered, "Quiet, Ansel. Yankee pickets are just a few rods away." He pinched my cheeks, poured warm, metal-tasting water on my face. "Come on. You'll have to help me."

I dozed stupidly while Manse crept about the darkening meadow, collecting things. When he returned he carried two muskets and a pile of clothing.

"Here, put this on. Then help me with Ezra."

He tossed me a smelly wool jacket and I did as he said but in a dream-like daze. Manse quickly rigged a stretcher using the muskets and buttoned cavalry tunics. We eased Ezra onto the makeshift carrier; he groaned softly. Manse led me—already puffing with the exertion, for Ezra was no small man—into an indistinct, smoky darkness pricked by flickering points of light. We could hear men shouting and occasional gunshots, now nearer, now farther off. We were soon challenged from out of the gloomy darkness.

"Who goes there? Answer quick with the countersign."

Manse replied briskly, "Stretcher party with a wounded officer."

Manse did not have the faintest idea what the password was but the pickets passed us through anyway. They were as dog tired as we, and happy to help two weary comrades on a mission of mercy. We hunched ahead in the near blackness, having crossed into the outlying camps of the Army of the Potomac.

Manse had stripped the Union dead and clothed the three of us in blue uniforms so we could pass through their lines. A vague inkling of what was in his mind suddenly began to dawn on me; its outright ballsiness was awe-inspiring.

We carried Ezra through the muggy darkness, passing dozens of Yankee troopers laying about their campfires. They looked like drugged men, staring absently into their fires with no fire of victory about them, no noise resembling celebration. Conversation was muted, as if spoken in church. Manse paused several times to ask directions from those awake and ambulatory.

Once we stumbled into a line of picketed horses and the startled animals raised a ruckus. But no one hailed us or followed. We finally trudged up a lane lined with the remnants of a rail fence; soldier's campfires lit the way to a huge stone barn. It may have been the Rummel farm, around which the day's battle had raged, but I have no corroborative knowledge of that.

Lanterns dimly lit the barnyard and surrounding grounds where countless wall tents had been pitched, along with every sort of shelter imaginable to shade the wounded, including low, crude soldier's shebangs, made of tent halves buttoned together and held up by inverted muskets driven into the earth.

Bodies of men lay sprawled everywhere in poorly aligned rows, many of them moving or writhing, and from them rose a soft, almost dreamy murmur of moans, cut by the syncopated snatches of speech of men in delirium. Inside, the barn was no better illuminated, but we could see the shadows of men lounging about the open doors, some smoking, some grimly watching the operations being performed inside. A high, piercing scream rent the air as we approached.

Manse turned aside at the door to where an open-ended wall tent loomed. Inside was a table saturated with dark blood; men were bending over it.

"Put him down here," Manse said, a little louder than he needed to, and sauntered up to the tent. "Major!" he demanded. "Major, if you please!"

A goateed face looked up from the table in annoyance, then nodded silently to an orderly by way of saying, "See what the sergeant wants."

"Son, this here is Captain Sitton," Manse explained to the nurse. "He's been shot through the lungs."

The nurse, a slight, stoop-shouldered man, seemed to sniff at Manse. "What regiment?"

"First Michigan," replied Manse without batting an eye. He stared the Yankee lackey down and like a crab the nurse sidled quickly back to the operating table.

The goateed doctor quickly waved away the others at the table and motioned for Ezra to be brought in. Four men lifted the body from the butcher's block and carried it out, its uncovered head lolling like a rag doll's and trailing blood.

"How long has this officer lain unattended?" snapped the surgeon. "The man is in a damn bad way. He should have been brought in immediately. Strip his blouse. Give me that probe."

I watched Manse's eyes narrow with disgust but he did not reply. Those Yankee surgeons handled Ezra as gently as a new born baby, cutting away the captain's coat he wore. The surgeon-major took a common shaving razor from its soak in a jar of clear liquid and enlarged the big wound in Ezra's throat. When he did a huge clot of jellified blood oozed from the wound. Immediately, Ezra's gasping breaths eased into a more normal rhythm.

Manse shouldered me out of the tent. When I started to protest he gripped the back of my neck with one iron hand and pushed me ahead.

"Ezra's got the best care we can give him," Manse whispered in my ear. "But that's all we can do for him now. Let's go."

Manse wisely decided to go out by a different picket post. We walked up to a campfire on the outer picket line, which the weary men kept burning to keep their coffee hot, and bummed two tin cups of that heady brew, the first real coffee I had tasted in months. My head began to slowly clear breathing the aromatic steam from the boiling pot. I felt that at last I was waking from a brutish night-mare to the familiar smells of breakfast back home.

Manse jawed with the soldiers about his brother, whom he said had gotten shot during the battle, and how he couldn't stand the thought of him alone on that bloody field, dying without the com-fort of a kind hand or word to succor him. Those troopers grew sym-pathetic, looked at one another and allowed, as we were from their brigade, that no man deserved to lie on the field unattended if he had family and friends willing to look for him. They passed us through.

On our way across the broad meadow, Manse and I shucking our blue uniforms along the way, the sky began to rain: thick, fat drops that were soon pouring down in a veritable waterfall. Manse had left

Dixie and two other mounts tied at a clump of trees growing from a stone outcropping in the ground.

In the storm we found the outcropping with great difficulty, but, once mounted, immediately began looking for the regiment. We ran into so many troops on the move that we were challenged by more Confederate pickets than we had been by Yankees.

Manse concluded that the army was retreating. But no one knew where Stuart was, much less the 1st South Carolina Cavalry. A tired foot soldier from the old Palmetto State told us the regiment was guarding the wagon train of wounded that was beginning to wind its way out of Gettysburg, south toward comparative safety in Maryland. If Manse had any idea where we were going, he said nothing and I did not ask.

That blessed cup of Yankee coffee helped me follow Manse's slouching form doggedly through the stormy night until we caught up with the tail of a lurching ambulance train carrying our wounded. An officer halted us on our approach, a hulking figure in the darkness. His voice was as deep and threatening as a mauled bear's.

"Sergeant Manse Jolly and Private Fries, 1st South Carolina," Manse announced. "Reporting for duty."

The horseman cantered toward us and I saw a glint of metal from a leveled pistol barrel. The rider bore a flowing brace of drooping mustaches beneath a wide-brimmed officer's hat; his slick poncho defined a pair of broad shoulders. We instantly recognized the figure. It was our colonel, John Logan Black.

"Sergeant, the regiment is ahead but you can do valuable service here," Black said. "Report to Colonel Imboden of the 18th Virginia. He will find a place for you both."

As we passed, I noticed the gallant old man was sagging in his saddle, favoring his left side. I learned later he had suffered a severe wound to his left shoulder in the fight at Rummel farm but had refused treatment. Black helped organize the army's unwounded stragglers into a rear guard to protect the wagon train with its wounded, and he stayed at his post until we crossed over the Potomac and back into Virginia. Then our colonel collapsed from weakness and loss of blood and had to be transported with the men he helped save. He survived his wound, only to be injured twice more in action with the enemy.

Manse and I fell in with a soggy column of gray-coated cavalry and spent the next week in the saddle, riding fifteen hours a day, body-sore, hungry and sick, our ears filled daily with the cries, the ghastly music, of our wounded. Along the way, those who died were taken out and left by the side of the road, unless they were officers and had kin or a man-servant to accompany the body home. The poor enlisted boys were not even covered up; their blankets were needed by those still living.

It rained, rained, rained until the sky could weep no more.

CHAPTER 8

We Was Played Out

July the 16th, 1863
Near Upperville, Virg.

Dear & Esteemed Mother——

You will by now have received news of the fight at Gettysburg. Many good Men was lost, and more wounded, in body and mind, by the Events we took part in & witnessed. I Promise to send you all the particulars but wanted to Write this note to let you now I was all right and still kicking, tho' not so hard or quick as I used to. Butler Burrell is dead, killed in Hampton's charge on the 3rd inst. So is Tom Barrineau, Cater Post, J.D. Whitley, and many more I can't even name. Soon I won't recall their faces either. Also Dead are many Yankees, of which I Accounted for at least three for certain and maybe more. The Yankee cavalry has improved considerably since those Early Days; I suppose we should have learned that at Brandy Station.

My Friend Ansel Fries is still alive, but peaked. He has dropped weight and stays at the sinks most of the day. That is because of the bad rations we've had. In Penn. we had butter, soft bread, apples and crullers. Now we break our health on captured hardtack and bad pork.

How is Mary? Tell her that I desire a letter from her. I lost all my letters somewhere at Gettysburg—it Burns me that some Yankee may be reading them—along with my new rubber blanket, and I dearly would like to replace both. You can not imagine how sanguine are my thoughts when I read news from home, no matter how old. It sets my tired spirit free. So Please, prevail upon my good Sister to write me, and often.

Mother send me something good to Eat, or anything to eat. Some nights I dream of your summer Pickles put up in jars.

Direct to: Army of Northern Virginia, Stuart's Corps, Hampton's Brigade, 1st S.C. Cav., Co. F.

Promise Mary that I Will get it.

It was more than two years before I again saw Ezra Sitton. His brother Robert learned from the war department that Ezra somehow survived his wound. Although our crude battlefield deception was quickly recognized, those Yankee surgeons saved his life. They saved him, then shipped him to that Union hell at the prison camp in Elmira, New York. Ezra came home a shadow of his former self.

He expressed his gratitude to Manse and me in later years, but our relationship was forever after strained. A part of him could never quite forgive us for delivering him to the Yankees. He lived as a bachelor with his aged mother the last thirty years of his life. Because of his wound he remained celibate, the shame of his disfigurement causing him to shun female company. Ezra breathed through a pipe stem he would hold to the hole in his throat, covering it again by a loose flap of skin when he wished to speak. Another scar on the face of God.

The regiment reassembled over a period of weeks around Rhappahannock Station, Virginia. There I found out who had and had not made it back. To my dismay, Hep was among the missing; no one had seen him after we formed for the charge in the Rummel meadow. But Henry was there, and John Lamb and Ab Tucker, whose cheek bore a scabbed-over saber wound. And Robert Sitton, who took the news of his brother with stoic courage. He thanked us for our efforts.

After Gettysburg we spent a lot of time skirmishing with Yankee cavalry; there was no doubt now they were good and getting better. It helped that they were armed with Sharps breechloaders, Spencer repeaters and the lever-action Henry rifle, in my opinion the handsomest and finest firearm the war produced.

There was little heavy fighting through the summer and autumn, only nasty firefights that took the names of river fords and railroad crossings nobody save the generals and the families of the fellows killed there remember. The armies had been too badly beaten up at Gettysburg. Losses were so heavy in both armies that the survivors of several wrecked regiments were commonly incorporated into one, or the units disbanded entirely. The Army of Northern Virginia underwent two major reorganizations as it rebuilt, one late that summer and again in December.

In spite of the express concern of General Lee, who wrote a letter of protest to President Jefferson Davis, our regiment was lifted from its old brigade, Hampton's, and thrust amid the 9th, 10th and 13th Virginia Cavalry of General W.H.F. Lee's brigade. Come December, however, we rejoined our old comrades in Wade Hampton's command, though not before we had been through several stiff fights alongside the Virginians.

The biggest of those engagements was at Kellys Ford on the Rhappahannock River the last day of July, 1863; some remember it as the second battle of Brandy Station. A number of fights were made in and around Kellys Ford during the war, but in this particular one I received my first wound.

The Yankees came brawling across the river with two divisions of infantry and cavalry; behind the advance elements companies of Union engineers deployed and busily began constructing pontoon bridges. That meant but one thing: assault support troops were on their way.

As at Brandy Station, our pickets were surprised and then overwhelmed by sheer numbers. Our new brigade was nearby and when its columns approached, the battle was fanning out through the forested hills around the ford like a brush fire, smoking and thudding.

From the first moments, we were fighting as dismounted infantry, and were in fact facing the blue-coated infantry of John Sedgewick's Sixth Army Corps, men who wore flannel Greek crosses on their hats and blouses.

It was in this fight that Colonel Black, dismounted and in the front line as always, was hit again, this time in the left forearm. He had only just reported back for duty after recovering from his Gettysburg wound. Luckily, the slug passed between the two bones of the forearm, breaking neither.

I got hit right off.

That was a mercy, because we had been knocked back on our heels. The Yankees brought a section of artillery over on their pontoons and gave us a canister pasting.

I had picked up an infantryman's .58-caliber Enfield rifle-musket. Still had my Sharps, just no cartridges for it. The Enfield was clumsy to load and carry after the breechloading Sharps, but it was an accurate killing weapon at long or short range.

How I came to get hit was this: I was crouching in some tall brush while the fight crashed about me, thinking myself well hidden. I loaded and primed my Enfield. Henry was behind a tree not far from me; he had just yelled for me to get my skinny butt behind some cover. I stood and turned to my left to break for Henry's tree, and that was when I got hit.

The impact of the slug fairly pushed me face down into the earth and I came up sucking for air. The bullet hit just above my left elbow, knocked it silly, then clipped my belt—I felt a violent tug—nearly cutting the leather in two. My arm felt as though a man had smacked the funny bone with a ten-pound maul. From shoulder to finger tips my arm went numb.

I kicked my belt and accouterments from around my ankles and stumbled fifty feet to the rear, holding my arm although I could not feel it. There was weight there, and bleeding flesh, I knew, but it might have been another man's limb that I gripped. My knees suddenly turned watery on me, then buckled, and I went under.

Henry Knauff came looking for me.

He had seen me grab my arm and weave for the rear. Thoughts of amputation and red searing pain were racing through my head when Henry pulled me to my feet and got me to walk. My legs did not want to comply. I was angry at Henry; I felt no real pain yet and saw no use in rushing it. But I might have died of shock that day if not for Henry. Lots of men died of shock in that war.

Henry walked me back from the fighting. We rested briefly in the shade of a grove of trees where other wounded had congregated. I asked Henry to leave me there with a canteen. My arm was beginning to hurt: a dull, head-racking throb. Blood had washed my entire forearm and left hand, and when I felt my elbow again it was clear the exposed tissue was stringy and raggedy, like badly cut corduroy. I felt dimly that I was missing something but I could not figure out just what.

Henry persisted. He hiked me up and half carried me for a mile or more. I started crying because my arm hurt so much. We came to a large farm house with a wide dirt yard shaded by thickly foliaged oak trees. Henry lugged me to the porch of the house and laid me flat in the shade on the bottom step, then went to the well for water.

A man stepped out onto the porch. He wore a yellowed linen vest over a tightly-buttoned flannel shirt. His trousers were baggy and his pinched face was flushed pink as sea coral. He had no teeth, but a briar pipe was clenched between his gums. He exhaled sweet-smelling tobacco smoke as he clumped down the porch steps and peered in my face with watery blue eyes totally objective in their blankness.

"This is my friend," Henry said. The woolen cover of his canteen was soaked dark with cool, fresh well water.

"His name is Ansel Fries, Captain Fries," Henry continued. "He's been wounded and he needs care. His daddy is a rich man in South Carolina; runs a cotton plantation and owns lots of Negroes. He'd be very grateful to you for helping his son."

Henry dribbled some of the cool water on my lips and washed the blood from my arm, which sent a sudden jolt of pain through me. He left the canteen in the crook of my good arm and then told me these people would look after me. He added quickly, "I've got to go," and was gone.

The aging farmer, a worn-looking man in his fifties, studied me deliberately. He was thinking. I began to tremble; waves of pain, cold and nausea were washing over me. I became suddenly, violently sick, and threw up all over myself and my new benefactor's muddy boots.

I spent a month in the house built with the money and slaves of Eli Hamrick, a prosperous tobacco farmer of Culpeper County. Old man Hamrick did not much care for me after that incident of our first meeting. But he was a pompous and cold-blooded old fart, who nearly let me bleed to death while he calculated what I might be worth to him in cold cash or business influence because of Henry's inspired and outrageous lie.

What mattered was that his wife, Mrs. Aurora Hamrick, was a good Christian woman, and a mother whose only son, a young officer, had been killed the summer before at Malvern Hill. Aurora Hamrick was a plump, handsome woman who wielded ferociously the protective nature of her sex when it came to nurturing and nursing, especially ailing waifs left at her very doorstep.

It was quickly apparent to me who ran the Hamrick homestead. No one, not Mr. Hamrick, his white overseer or black servants male or female, dared cross paths with the lady of this house. Aurora Hamrick's conviction was that her view was right. During my weeks within her household, I never once heard Eli Hamrick correct or question his wife; indeed, I believe he took great care to stay out of her way.

Yes, she held sway over her husband with an iron hand, while with the other babied me as if I was her beloved lost son. I lapped up her pampering like a puppy.

Eli bitched about me constantly but never in front of his wife. One afternoon I overheard him complaining to Lithia, the Hamrick's unparalleled cook, "For a scrawny beanpole of a boy I never seen anybody could eat so much ham and biscuits. I intend to dun the government in Richmond for his provender, I'll tell you that."

Lithia's cooking, overseen by Mrs. Hamrick, was magically bountiful, simple yet lush to a soldier used to a tiresome diet. The Hamrick's kept bee hives that yielded combs of amber-dark honey. Their evening table swayed with cold meats, sweet pickles, butter, dried apples, glazed ham, bacon, chops and real bread, not army issue hard crackers. Every week Lithia filled ceramic jars with molasses or ginger cookies. We had flapjacks for breakfast, and hot peach or apple cobbler sweetened with heavy cream in the cool of the evening after supper. God help me, the very memory makes me salivate.

Is it any wonder that I stayed on a good two weeks after my arm had begun to heal. The wound was an ugly one; that Yankee ball had permanently removed a considerable piece of muscle and gristle and forever left a scarred crater, along with occasional weakness and neuralgia.

So I spent August of 1863, and, looking back, it was the best time in the war for me. Did I neglect to mention that Eli had four daughters, as well as the dead hero son he had lost?

They were akin to a coven of quail in their likeness to their mother, were the Hamrick girls: pretty, plump, smiling and gracious. All four wore hair pendants, brooches or bracelets meticulously fashioned from brother Ross's living locks. Quite cruelly, it occurred to me the poor fellow must have endured quite a shearing before he went off to the war.

The oldest, Amantha, paled at any mention of the war. Besides the death of her brother, she lately had news that her fiancée, Captain Edward Henshaw Bates, died in Pennsylvania of a wound he received at Gettysburg. All the Hamrick women dressed in black to signify they were in mourning; when Amantha left the house she always wore a veil.

Amantha struck me as brave and noble, a woman who bore up well in the face of the unthinkable; only once did she break down in my presence. She came to my bedside and gently shaved me, using her father's basin and his best English razor and scented soap. I wore only my cavalry breeches, which had been lovingly repaired by the youngest Hamrick girl, Elizabeth.

Unexpectedly, Amantha asked me to tell her about the battle.

I assumed at first she meant Kellys Ford, where I was wounded, but she quickly corrected me.

"You were at Gettysburg, were you not, Captain Fries?" she asked without looking at me. "Tell me about it. I should like to know what it was like."

The last thing I wanted to do was talk about that horror, but she pressed me and I told her frankly all that I had seen. I only lied when I said that the dead on both sides were given decent burial by the Union army and local citizens, and identified whenever possible, especially if they were officers. She seemed satisfied, even grateful, and rose effortlessly from the stool on which she had been sitting as if to leave the room. But she paused, and, on impulse, leaned close until I could smell her lavender perfume and pressed my head into her soft shoulder and breast. Then she ran to the door.

"Miss Amantha, in which part of the field was your fiancée wounded?"

She turned. "His mother wrote to me. A comrade of Hensh's told her that he was shot down at a place called the Rummel farm, by a rebel colonel with a flowing mustache." She looked at me as if trying to read my thoughts. I offered my deepest sympathy and Amantha soundlessly opened the door and closed it behind her.

The moment she was gone I kicked myself for a blind fool. It was clear that Captain Bates had been a Union officer, and that he had been struck down by my own commander, Colonel John Logan Black, a man I loved and respected.

Needless to say, Eli Hamrick was overjoyed to hear the news in early September that my arm was sufficiently healed and I would soon be leaving to rejoin my regiment. The day of my leaving was a sad occasion for me. It was a warm, hazy morning and everybody in the family, from Miss Elizabeth to her mother, were misty-eyed, myself included. Only Eli was dry-eyed, and unable to suppress a grin. I will say this for the man: He gave me a red mule to ride back to the army. It was an aging animal, hardly suited for campaigning, but old Jeff was transportation more dependable than my legs.

I promised all that I would write soon, kissed Mrs. Hamrick's hand gratefully and respectfully, and told old Eli I would remember him and his gracious family to my father in South Carolina. I bitterly regretted leaving that sanctuary of security, rest and superb food. Elizabeth shyly asked permission to clip a lock of my hair. She promised she would tie it round with a red ribbon and pin it next to my autograph in her diary. I had written, "For fair Elizabeth, fragrant as a wildflower, from your friend, A.W. Fries, 1st South Carolina Cavalry, Sept. 7, 1863—'To thine own self be true.'"

I waved goodbye, kicked my heels into Jeff's bony sides and headed back to the war.

I made my way on old Jeff across the dry streambed of Mountain Run, down through the hamlet of Stevensburg, and crossed the Rapidan River at Mortons Ford, where I passed through the advance pickets of the Confederate army. It was from these men, rough-hewn but high-spirited Tennesseeans, that I learned of the reorganization of the army the month before. After directing a few unkind jibes at my loyal mule, they directed me to where W.H.F. Lee's brigade was encamped, a few miles west on the army's left flank, just north of Clarkes Mountain.

Just before sunset I cantered into the chaos of wagons, picketed horses and tents that was the brigade camp. Hundreds of campfires wreathed the mountain in wisps of white smoke. I drank in the sweet familiar scent of the woodsmoke.

Manse was squatting at a fire, hefting an iron frying pan in one hand and with the other fanning smoke away from his face; the cuffs of his trousers were ripped and raggedy. Nearby sat a forlorn Robert Sitton, a starved Henry Knauff, a stocky man I did not recognize, who wore his forked beard black and long, and a shriveled-looking Hepsibah who was lying with his legs crossed like an opium user, taking his ease with a pipe.

My left arm was still sore, and I dreaded the idea of returning to a diet of hardtack, coarse cornbread and sorghum syrup. But my heart went into my mouth at the sight of my comrades, my friends, my brothers in arms. I had missed them terribly, missed being with them. Two lean troopers turned toward me—Ab Tucker and John Lamb—and when they recognized my clean-shaven face, theirs broke into grins.

"By God, it's Ansel. Where you been, boy?"

They crowded about me, peppering me with questions, inspected my nearly healed wound and wondering aloud how I came by Jeff. I replied I just might ride him until the war ended.

"See what a good provider ol' Jeff is," I announced, and with a flourish of my good arm untied a poke sack from the mule's saddle and dumped its contents onto a gum blanket spread by the fire: tinned jam and meats, molasses, butter, three loaves of relatively fresh bread, bacon and biscuits wrapped in greasy brown paper and a thick round of cheddar cheese.

"Praise the Lord!" Hep shouted, and all the boys dug in.

"Ansel," Manse called, "Come here and meet Walt."

Manse presented the bearded stranger to me. He regarded me suspiciously for a moment. He was about my height but heavier, and yet at closer glance I could see he was younger than me. He was not in uniform but was well-dressed; his boots were well oiled and handsome. He stuck out his hand.

"Name's Walter Largent," was all he said. Manse recruited him after Kellys Ford.

"We weren't sure you were coming back," said Manse.

I was uneasy. There was something about the man that I disliked immediately. I could not put my finger on it. He looked like a shirker, a "coffee boiler" we called them; men who managed to fade away before every fight, reappearing when it was again safe with marvelous stories of privation and escape. I thought, times must be bad for the regiment to need men like this.

That fall there began a gradual transformation in the character of Manson Sherrill Jolly. His demeanor ran vinegar or molasses, and most days you never knew which tap was on. The boys laid this to the fact that Manse, more than any man in the regiment, liked action; he liked killing Yankees. Manse had his reasons.

By that time in the war the Jolly family already had lost three sons. Manse's older brother, Joseph, had been drilled through the head by a Minie ball at Sharpsburg. Jesse Alfred Jolly died of malaria the same year in a Richmond hospital. Manse's other two older brothers, John and James, were to die as well before it was all over: John in a nameless skirmish with Federal raiders on the Carolina coast, and James at the battle of Peachtree Creek in Georgia.

James had fallen within Union lines and was buried in a mass grave. It was not until years after Appomattox that the Jolly family received confirmation of his death. When the United Daughters of the Confederacy erected a monument on the battlefield, an Atlanta newspaper reporter studying the ground found a badly corroded brass disk that James had worn around his neck, stamped with his name and regiment. The reporter wrote a story about it, a family friend read the story and sent a clipping to Manse's sister, Mary, who replied to the newspaper, claiming her brother's property. The disk was returned to her.

But it was the death of the youngest Jolly boy, William Enos, that the boys said set Manse over the edge. William had enlisted at sixteen in the spring of 1863, the last Jolly boy to leave home for the army. Freeman wanted to go but he was clumsy and slow-witted and the army would not take him, not even after conscription began. He helped his father keep the farm going and often spent days at a time roaming the pine-covered hills, hunting for game.

William's regiment joined Braxton Bragg's army, and late that September, reinforced by Longstreet's corps sent west by Lee, it collided with the Union Army of the Cumberland along Chickamauga Creek. In the tangled, smoky thickets of those mountains William was killed. There was no earthly way to bring his body home, but a comrade of the dead youth carried his pocket Bible and his final, unfinished letter to his mother.

Manse received a letter from Mary soon after, detailing what they had learned of William in his last hours. Manse went kind of crazy. He ran off half-naked into the woods, living on grubs and berries, covering himself in coats of mud and dirt, the very way Thomas Mallory described Lancelot du Lac's state of mind after he was scornfully rejected by Guinevere, who believed him unfaithful. Manse was gone for three days, then came out of the woods one night and took his place at the campfire—beard caked with mud, his eyes glazed, a sweet smile on his face—as if nothing out of the ordinary had happened.

Largent let him alone that night. No one but Hep had the courage to approach. Hep covered Manse's bare shoulders with a blanket, gave him a cup of something to help him sleep and made him a comfortable bed at the fire, then eased the big man to his rest. Manse did not protest. He slept all night and late into the evening next day.

When he finally awoke, we saw the old Manse was back, or most of him at any rate.

Soon after, Manse began his private forays. At first he would step over to Colonel Black's tent and ask permission. But then he began going out on his own; his night raids became legend in the regiment and throughout the brigade. Even Stuart, it was said, inquired about Manse's nightly "bag." Our pickets had standing orders to pass him through the lines.

On dark, moonless nights Manse would stop at a creek and rub his face and forearms with black, foul-smelling mud, then mount Dixie, armed only with his Bowie knife and a pistol. He usually reappeared at dawn, sometimes with a brace of handsome horses trailing behind him, or a new firearm or a bloodied saber he would have to carry to the creek to wash.

Business on the Virginia front picked up in October, when the regiment went through several sharp fights, first at James City and later near Weaverville.

In the James City engagement, the 1st South Carolina Cavalry, led temporarily by Lieutenant Colonel J.D. Twiggs, who took command when Colonel Black was forced to leave the line after suffering yet another wound, charged a regiment of Federal infantry and, according to Twiggs' report, "dispersed it." Later that day, dismounted, we hunkered down behind a sturdy stone wall to protect Captain Griffin's Virginia battery, repulsing a stiff and determined counter-attack by columns of charging cavalry.

Weaverville was much the same thing. Fighting as dismounted infantry, a tactic that was becoming our specialty, we surprised a battalion of Yankee infantry creeping down a culvert to take our command in flank. I had just replenished my Sharps cartridge box with captured rounds and I used them freely. For a small action, I never heard such shooting, or saw heavier casualties suffered by a unit on such a small plot of ground. We left that culvert carpeted with Federal dead and wounded.

The very next night, Manse, along with a Private William Bolick of Company K and a man named Curtis with the 9th Virginia Cavalry, took some blouses off three Yankee prisoners "and strolled whistling into the Yankee lines," Lieutenant Colonel Twiggs reported. Manse and his friends captured six Union soldiers and their mounts, part of a cattle guard.

"They regretted only that the cattle could not be recovered," Twiggs wrote.

All three men were praised by name in dispatches that went up through the echelons to J.E.B. Stuart and General Lee.

I later met Private Bolick in person. When I told him I was a friend of Manse's, he drew back a little.

"Manse is a game fellow. There isn't anyone I'd rather have beside me in a tight spot," Bolick said. "But…."

He pulled me aside. "I hate Yankees as much as the next man, but I'm not going to kill a helpless prisoner." Bolick looked at me as if trying to gauge how deeply Manse had his hooks into me. "Manse wanted to kill the prisoners we brought in. He damn sure did. Curt and I had to draw our pistols and throw down on him. He was like a madman."

When I got back to the mess, Manse was out on another raid. Only Largent was there, licking tinned molasses from the blade of his knife. He grinned at me, his lips and teeth black with the syrup. I shuddered and rolled up in my army blankets but I did not sleep well. I dreamed of Manse.

We spent the winter south of the Rapidan River, inside a mean little hovel that did not live up to the glamour of the word. It looked mean, smelled mean and made meaner the men who lived in it. Food and even firewood were becoming scarce. When we could not go foraging to hunt extra food, we went without. Nothing makes a man meaner than an empty, grumbling belly.

For weeks, if we were lucky, we lived on rock hard hardtack and wormy saltpork doled out of barrels by commissary men who had to hold their noses to stand the smell. Fried, it made a rancid grease that one would crumble his hardtack into. Salt, black pepper and hot pepper sauce were in high demand, because any seasoning helped disguise the taste of these dishes. Is it any wonder that the winter sicknesses soon began? Diarrhea and dysentery hit everybody. Our gums turned black with scurvy and our teeth began to fall out. We looked like old men.

One day Robert, inspired, took down our old Benson House Mess sign and put up another: "Sons of Bitches Within."

I begged Captain Sharpe to give me a thirty-day furlough so I could go home, get fattened up and bring back a wagonload of provender for my friends. The captain was sympathetic but firm; he relented only to offer a week's pass. The opportunity set my mind clicking.

On a crisp winter's day I mounted old Jeff, who had taken a positive liking to army life and put on a thick red winter's coat, and cautiously recrossed the Rapidan to hunt up my old friends, the Hamricks.

Eli was horrified to see my face once again at his doorstep, but he quickly ushered me inside. Probably, he was fearful of the Yankee patrols that combed the region north of the Rapidan, looking for wayward Johnny Rebs, and stragglers and deserters from their own army.

"Captain Fries!" bellowed Aurora Hamrick. "What has happened to you? You look like a scarecrow."

She called her daughters and, for a moment, I regretted coming. I wondered how they would react, Elizabeth especially, to seeing me in the physical condition I was in. I nearly wept when they hugged me like a brother, in spite of my odiferous clothing and unkempt beard.

They set out a bowl of chicken broth and biscuits, which I devoured with unashamed relish.

Mrs. Hamrick allowed that her larder had been much affected by the Yankee occupation. Still, the fact her oldest daughter had been engaged to a hero who died for the Union counted for much with the Yankee troopers who passed through now and again. There were many Secesh families in Culpeper County who suffered far more than the Hamricks, and who had contributed less to the cause.

It was a week spent in paradise. Amantha, although three years my senior, seemed to grow more beautiful and mysterious, and even more unattainable, each time I was privileged to gaze upon her.

I returned to camp carrying all sorts of treats for my friends. Most prized were the oranges Amantha had given me as a Christmas gift. I gave two to Henry, as he was suffering the worst from scurvy. We savored the jarred tomato preserves, the okra and onions Aurora Hamrick had pressed upon me. That wonderful food kept us going in mind and spirit.

It was a quiet winter. A mighty religious revival swept the army; soldiers by the thousands were being saved daily in the spirit. They crowded under open tents in the snow, praying and singing and shivering. Robert Sitton and Hepsibah were caught up in the religious fervor, too, but I stayed away. All that religion seemed to me a bad omen. Only defeated men prayed in such numbers.

As I have related, the 1st South Carolina Cavalry was sent back to its old brigade after Christmas. Hampton had moved up to command our division, and brigade command passed to General P.M.B. Young, a Georgian who had commanded Cobbs Legion. He and the old brigade threw our regiment a welcome home party that featured roasted wild hog, and pans of hot gingerbread and molasses. It was a heart-warming scene, which some of the boys livened with canteens of Yankee popskull.

Hampton decided in January that the depleted companies in his South Carolina regiments, our 1st, the 2nd and his old Legion, should be refitted with new recruits. It was evident to all that the regiment was badly thinned out. Our effective strength had sunk to one hundred seventy-five men; Company F's muster roll listed only eighteen more or less healthy troopers, not counting cooks, teamsters and servants like Hepsibah.

The colder the weather, the less scarce the food and the longer the sick lists grew. Finally, in March of 1864 both the 1st and 2nd South Carolina Cavalry regiments were ordered to report "without delay" to General P.G.T. Beauregard, then in command of the military district of South Carolina. Men and baggage were to make their way south by railroad, if possible; the regiment's horses were to be put in charge of mounted detachments of herders which would move by the open turnpikes.

I can tell you that when we broke camp from winter quarters and prepared to move south, the men Colonel Black chose to herd the horses—mostly shirkers and chronic complainers—protested vehemently. Black arrested several troopers who absolutely refused the duty. One fellow sat down in the mud, crossed his arms and swore it would take a team of oxen to move him. As it was, a provost guard of soldiers with bayoneted rifle-muskets did the job nicely. We got a good laugh out of it and felt no guilt about going home by train.

We figured we deserved it. We had been two years in the service of our country, had been shot at and shot, wounded, starved, frozen and gut-sick, lived on shitty food and no food and yet survived to whip the Yanks to a standstill. We had been, most of us, without furloughs home in those two years. We had earned a rest.

Truth be known, we was played out. Everybody, that is, but Manse, who was already getting itchy because the spring campaigns were only two months away. He had become obsessed with the idea of killing, as if the more Yankees he killed the easier his dead brothers would rest. We mollified him with promises of the good life, that he would get to see his mother and sister Mary again.

Mary idolized her older brother. She had kept a steady flow of letters going from the Jolly hearth to Manse for two years. And Manse adored his little sister; his eyes turned moist at the mention of her name.

When Manse finally decided the move was a good thing, I determined to watch him more carefully than ever, for my sake as well as his.

CHAPTER 9

The Road Home

There is no holier spot of ground
Than where defeated valor lies

—Henry Timrod

Home was the cool green hills of the Upcountry, carpeted with pine and cedar, where the green swell of the Savannah River pushed its foaming way over sandstone shoals to the sea. Home was a place where the trains ran on time and a man might still get a homecooked if plain meal for a wad of Confederate currency. It was a place where there were no bugle calls to wake to, no lonesome hours of picket duty, no killing marches in the dead of night, a lush, wilderness country untouched by the armies, where the sound of a summer thunderhead did not trouble people's spirit with its mimicry of distant cannon. Home was where a train carrying lean, bearded soldiers chugged slowly over the muddy Saluda River on a trestle of pine logs, passing a family group of Cherokee Indians, dark and taciturn in the shade of late afternoon: women carrying children on their backs and swarthy, defiant men in white men's clothes.

The regiment, what was left of it, went home by the same route it had taken to the Virginia front in 1862. Like us, the railroads had been worn down by their war service. Yankee raiders had destroyed sections of tracks over many miles in some parts of Virginia. Dispatchers shuffled us between rail lines when possible; when it wasn't possible, we got out and walked. Being cavalry, our feet were tender, our narrow-soled boots not being much fit for long marches. We bitched and complained at the ignominy of being turned into infantry, but when we walked, all walked: merchants, farmers, women in hoops and bonnets leading young children. Only the most chronic shirkers could complain at so democratic an inconvenience.

Anyone could see the marks war had left on us. We had lost weight and were hungry all the time. Our woolen uniforms, field patched at knees and elbows, crawled with lice. Our teeth were loose in our gums, which often bled from months of a diet devoid of fresh vegetables, fruit, beef, bread, fresh anything. I was twenty-four, lean, jaded and jumpy as a terrier at any sudden sound, but still cocky when properly fed. Robert Sitton was a handsome nineteen and resembled the newspaper lithographs of a young Robert E. Lee. Only his somberness detracted from that beauty; his demeanor was Baptist sober, steady as a church deacon. Henry Knauff was twenty-one, a pimply-faced, immature whiner whom neither hell nor high water mark could seemingly change. Manse was my age but looked ten years older. His face, browned by two years of unrelenting campaigning, resembled an eroded farmfield.

Manse's mental state worried me. Manse did not rant or rave but withdrew into himself. He sulkily refused to speak to anyone, wearing his brittle temper on his sleeve. The boys avoided him. Robert said, "Make a living out of killing and you must surrender unto the devil his due."

Colonel Black ordered us to remount and refit ourselves as best we could, get fed and rested, pick up as many recruits as possible and reassemble in Columbia within a fortnight. He went on to his own home there to begin gathering the horses and equipment he would need to outfit the five hundred recruits he expected to swear in and train before the spring campaign.

The nearer the train carried us to Anderson Courthouse, the more anxious Manse got. He fretted over the buttons on his coat, the loose strings hanging from his threadbare vest. We all were painfully aware of how we looked: dirty, skinny and stinking, ill at ease at the thought of being in polite company until we could bathe, shave and don clean clothing.

When we arrived, Manse, Robert and I set out on foot from the Anderson station after saying goodbye to Henry and Hepsibah, who reluctantly proceeded to Henry's late mother's house for the inevitable confrontation with the formidable Katherine.

The weather was bright and cool. Manse, Robert and I—three old comrades—talked and laughed easily stepping along the muddy road that led north and west to the Lebanon community, and Pendleton; it felt good to walk unafraid on a country pike.

The Upcountry winter had been a wet one; rail fences blossomed with the fragrant white and yellow flowers of the honeysuckle vine. Manse began slowly unwinding, like a tightly coiled spring, as we trudged through the familiar countryside. He commented on the state of neighbor's peach orchards and corn. He was becoming a farmer again.

In early evening we arrived at the Jolly homestead, a two-story log house over which whitewashed planking had been carefully laid, set amid a haphazard complex of outbuildings scattered among clumps of pine trees. A single yellow light burned in a lower room. Manse strode ahead and halted at the entrance to the lane.

"You are both welcome to stay the night," he said. "I want you to meet my mother, my sister and brother. We'll eat and have a smoke of real tobacco and a swallow or two of popskull and sleep tonight in goosedown beds."

Robert was tempted, but it was another eight miles to his home in Pendleton. He thought if he kept a good pace he might make it home before midnight, wished us a good night and we waved him off down the road, the setting sun turning the road and trees before him a rich ruby red.

Manse and I walked down the muddy path, breathing the sweet, pine-scented air in deep lungfuls. We saw the orange pinprick glow of a pipe long before the figure of the man sitting with his boots off on a shadowed step of the front porch. The dogs came out, woofing; when they got a whiff of Manse, they leaped, yipping with canine joy.

"Cleotus, you old egg-sucker," Manse laughed, kneading one hound's velvet ears. "Well, I guess I still smell the same. Clove, is that you? It's Manse, and I brung a friend."

Manse's young cousin Clove rose soundlessly and shook my hand as Manse introduced me. He was tall and wiry and only seventeen, but was I supposed doing a man's work on the farm while Manse and his brothers were away.

Manse's frame filled the open front door. Inside, his mother and sister were sewing by the light of a single tallow candle. They looked up, then their mouths opened and quickly shut. Mary flew at her brother like a wildcat. Manse kissed her pale forehead and hugged and half-carried her to his mother, who stared at her soldier-son with moist, disbelieving eyes.

Manse kissed her sparely on the cheek and bellowed, "How about supper for two hungry rebels?"

Mary quickly set a simple table, averting her reddened eyes from my gaze. She brought a pot of cold beans, tin plates piled with sweet cornbread and strips of fried fat pork and a pitcher of sorghum syrup. There was no butter or coffee, but for dessert there was a heavy pan of gingerbread, Manse's favorite, made with sorghum instead of sugar, and homemade elderberry wine. Manse liked to sop his gingerbread in wine, gobbling the sweet cake while the wine dribbled into his tangled red beard.

"Where's Freeman?" Manse asked between mouthfuls, soaking a hunk of the gingerbread in a painted ceramic bowl brimming with wine. At that moment, Clove hollered something outside and Manse's brother Freeman shouldered his way through the door, a double-barreled shotgun in one hand and a string of dead doves dangling from the other.

Freeman was shorter than Manse but broader across the shoulders, sharing the same strength of face (my father's kindest euphemism) as all the Jolly boys. Freeman's unkempt black hair obscured his bushy eyebrows; his lower jaw hung slack like a gate in need of repair. When he saw Manse his eyes caught fire and he shambled over to his older brother, a dancing bear delighted beyond expression. They hugged; Manse grinned and complimented Freeman on his bag; Mrs. Jolly and Mary wept.

Manse dug in his pocket and produced a spent Yankee Minie ball he had saved as a souvenir.

"It hit me in the knee at Kellys Ford; raised a lump big as a hen's egg," he said. "Must be some good luck in it."

Freeman regarded the token with reverence.

"Freeman was in the army, you know," said Mrs. Jolly. "He was discharged on account of being somewhat, light-headed."

"He is a bit slow," added the loyal Mary, brushing field debris from Freeman's coat. "But a kinder man you will never meet."

Mary was a sturdily-built, plain-faced girl with an overlarge jaw. She tied back her light brown hair in a bun so severe the straining locks above her delicate ears looked painted on. But she owned a generous smile and her eyes when animated were like liquid drops of sapphire. She bore herself with a quiet dignity and country intelligence that became her yeoman ancestry.

But the warmth of her attention was turned fully upon Manse. Of course it would be; I was a stranger there. After we had eaten, Manse regaled his family with stories of the war. He talked in detail and at great length, as if he had been an impartial observer, about the night after Gettysburg we carried Ezra straight into a Yankee field hospital. When Manse explained how I had been wounded at Kellys Ford, I flushed with embarrassment.

Mary's bright eyes turned to me, expectant as a squirrel's. I don't care to say what thoughts I read there. You may call it a young man's dream or an old man's fancy, but the moment sent my heart soaring.

Freeman and Clove asked to see the wound. Mrs. Jolly remonstrated with them, but I showed them willingly, taking off my woolen jacket, fragrant with the woodsmoke of a thousand campfires, and rolling up my shirt sleeve. Eight months of healing had left only a star-shaped scar and soft depression in the flesh of my arm above the elbow, where a considerable piece of me once resided.

Clove whistled. Mary, who was just sixteen, seemed disappointed. I quickly covered it up, but was grateful to Manse for mentioning it.

After the story-telling, Mrs. Jolly insisted that everyone get down on their knees on the rough-hewn floorboards of the parlor to pray. We clasped hands, even a red-faced Manse, who grasped my left while Mary took my right—my heart swelled at the touch of her soft, moist hand in mine—and we amened while old Mrs. Jolly thanked God for returning at least one son to her whole and unhurt. When I detected a slight tremor in Mary's delicate limb, I looked out of the corner of my eye to catch the full glow of her frank smile.

I dreamed about Mary that night, I'm ashamed to say, in a less than Christian manner.

The entire family turned out to bid me fare-thee-well early the next morning. Freeman even lent me his old mule, Tolly, to carry me home to Townville, still a good fifteen miles away. I protested but not too strongly, because it occurred to me that returning the animal would be a good excuse to see Mary again. As I spurred the old mule down the lane, waving back over its fly-infested rump, Mary rushed up and pressed upon me a heavy batch of fresh apple crullers, still hot and fragrant, wrapped in a gingham cloth.

"I'll see you at the Benson House," Manse called. "Come into town Wednesday and we'll tip a jug."

Anna Jolly gave her boy a look that could have soured milk, but Manse just grinned, bent down and pecked his mother on the cheek.

Each jouncing step of the mule reminded me of the morning two years before when Manse and I set out for the Pickens courthouse to enlist for the war. The air was fresh after the rain and smelled richly of green growing things. I ate the crullers Mary gave me and felt a familiar strength suffuse me, spirit and flesh. It was the strength of earth and home, of knowing that I was among family and friends in our own country, and that everything—at least for a little while—was going to be all right. The morning dampness caused my maimed elbow to stiffen and ache, a reminder of what awaited me when my furlough ended. I banished the army and war from my mind and thought of Mary.

I rode into Townville shortly after the dinner hour and felt both pleasure and a twinge of annoyance that, unlike me, it had not changed. No, it had changed: It looked smaller and more commonplace. The Sterling's country house, which to my boy's mind had once seemed so grand and elegant with its long veranda and oak-shaded driveway, now appeared shrunken, seedy and badly in need of a fresh coat of whitewash. Johnny Sterling's old yellow hound was languidly stretched out to its full length on the front steps as if it had not stirred from the spot in two years. The Baptist church, by contrast, glistened with fresh whitewash that flecked its single tinted window, yet it too looked small and unalterably country. As I turned the corner of the first block in town, my stomach gave a twist at the familiar sight of the green-painted clapboard of Augustus Fries & Sons, Dry Goods, Ltd.

I was home.

The store windows were dirty and cluttered with unsold merchandise. The cane chairs on the front steps were empty. Cato Smalls, my father's itinerant handyman, moped on the bottom step, chin in one hand, but when he caught sight of me he stood up slowly, shading his eyes with his ancient beaver hat. He reached for the reins and his eyes narrowed disapprovingly.

"Go to war on your daddy's fine horse, come back on a mule," he said. "Welcome home, Mr. Ansel."

"It's fine to see you, Cato. The years have not improved your temper any."

"Oh, I'm the same man, Mr. Ansel. I will allow I has changed. I'm too old to fuss and fights anymore. Leave that to the young men, I say."

"Where is my father?"

"They is up at the funeral."

"Who died?"

"Mr. Moses Sterling, sir, Mr. Amos's father, don't you know. He was close to ninety, I reckon, but folks say he'd of lived to a hundred if not for the war and him losing three grandsons and all."

"I didn't know. Johnny? And Edwin, too?"

Cato nodded. "Both in one terrible week, up in Pennsylvania. Young Mr. Langdon, too, and the Post boy, and the Barrineau boy, don't you know."

I walked to the church, self-consciously buttoning my dirty cavalry jacket. I did not see a soul but two black women at their mistress's wash. I passed through the glistening picket fence and followed a rambling dirt path that led beneath low-hanging pine boughs to the churchyard. The stern voice of the Rev. Hogeboom wafted through the trees, growing louder as I approached the somber group of mourners gathered about a fresh mound of red dirt.

My brother Newton saw me first. Wearing his infantry frock coat, he scrutinized me carefully before his face spread in a smile of recognition. I thought, "My God, have I changed that much?"

Newton stepped back on his crutches, the brown flap of his left trouser leg swinging loosely. He tugged at my father's elbow. The old man's beard flowed down the front of his checkered flannel shirt, a broad-brimmed slouch hat gripped in both his hands. He looked first at Newton and then followed his gaze to me. His eyes narrowed against the midday sunlight for a moment before they focused and the realization sunk in.

We stood together, respectfully still, until the service was over. Father shook hands with Amos Sterling and his poor wife, all the while studying me as if regarding a stranger. For an uncomfortable moment I thought he was angry, but I was mistaken. He grabbed me roughly and hugged me hard and long, smelling so strongly of tobacco that my eyes watered. Newton grinned.

We stayed awhile in the churchyard, greeting old friends and visiting my mother's grave. Next to her simple limestone marker father had erected a handsome memorial to Tom made of the finest Elberton, Georgia, granite shipped up the Savannah River.

Of course, Tom was not there. Newton had not been in any condition to search for his brother after the fight at Fraysers Farm. Probably Tom was buried in one of the many pits I saw dug during the war, into which the pathetic dead were unceremoniously tumbled and quickly covered over, like victims of some horrendous and shameful accident.

Father's inscription read: "In Loving Memory of Thomas Augustus Fries, Company C, Palmetto Sharpshooters, CSA. Born January 8, 1832, Killed in Battle near Richmond, Va., on the 30th day of June, 1862, Aged 30 years, 5 months and 24 days. Beloved son and brother, asleep in Jesus."

"Sprout, I declare you've grown some," said Newton, clumping on his crutches up the dusty front steps of father's store. "The army's done you some good, boy. Look, Pa, he's even got the makings of a beard."

I kneaded my chin self-consciously, half-surprised at the uneven growth of whiskers there, then tentatively searched my upper lip. Goose down still.

"You can shave after dinner," said Father. He had gone to the extraordinary expense of hiring away the Sterling's prized cook, Bessie, to fatten me up. I ate as I had not in months.

"You've lost considerable flesh since you left home," Father noted disapprovingly. "Doesn't the army feed you properly? What happens to all the beef cattle and hard bread we see on the railroad cars going to the front, I want to know?"

"I can tell you we don't see much of it," I said between mouthfuls of fried chicken and biscuits slathered with sourwood honey.

"Pa, all that meat goes to feed the damn generals and politicians in Richmond, and their families and even their goddamned slaves," grumbled Newton. "Shit-fire, I saw fresh beef just once the whole time I was enlisted."

I choked down my food and wiped my mouth. "I am damned sorry about your leg, Newton."

"'Cain't be helped," he said tightly. Then, a little softer, "'Ansel, just be damn careful when you go back. I figure this family has paid its dues to the Confederacy, in aces. Come on, now, tell us what you've seen. I want to hear about the fight at Gettysburg. That's where Langdon Sterling got killed. You knew that."

Father filled his pipe. I crumbled up several more biscuits, laced them with ribbons of honey, and over that and a second cup of coffee I recreated the tales Manse and I told the night before. I stuck to as many as the funny times as I could remember, but when I came to that black night after Gettysburg and then the fight at Kellys Ford, I simply stopped talking. We sat in silence for several minutes.

"Those were good people who took care of you, Ansel," said Father, sucking on his unlit pipe. "I should maybe write to them."

Newton stared across the table at nothing. "You got it right, Ansel," he said, an absent look on his acne-ravaged face. "Getting hit is like being smacked with a maul. You just feel kind of numb and tingly. Then the cold sweats come creeping up your body and your bowels loosen—" Suddenly pale, Newton got up from the table and stumped to the pie safe where Father kept his jug of corn whiskey. Newton filled his coffee cup and downed it in a swallow. Offered me some, but I declined. Father watched.

"I'm sorry, Pa," Newton said, pouring more whiskey into his cup. "Ansel, you and Manse did the right thing carrying Ezra to that Yankee hospital. Our doctors, shit, they ain't doctors 't'all. They're butchers." He finished his whiskey, said a terse good night and swung his way up the stairs. He paused on the steps.

"Pa, I'm nearly out of laudanum. Will you see Mr. McNabb tomorrow?"

Father nodded, then inhaled deeply while Newton clumped up the stairs. The pipe stem left Father's mouth and stabbed the air.

"Every night he goes up to his room and drinks that vile medicine. Ansel, he says his leg still hurts him. The one they cut off! He groans in his sleep, asks to have his leg rubbed; talks about wiggling his toes, or the work we used to do when he was still a whole man. In his mind, in the opium dreams, he still rides, runs, dances just the way he used to."

Father sat up, his whiskered cheeks flushed with anger. "Those goddamned politicians! I wish they had to stay up one night with my son. I wish they could see his pain. I wish they could see what this war has cost me. But to this government there is no appeal. 'Just give us your money, your horses and your sons. Maybe we'll send them back to you—maimed, or dead, or maybe not at all.' It's a rich man's war, Ansel, and a poor man's fight. In the end, we will all be dead, or rooting like animals in the forest."

We sat for a moment in silence. I had never heard my father talk before with such passion and conviction. It was the longest speech the taciturn old German ever made. I knew I should embrace him. I reached across the table, grabbed his rough hand and squeezed. I yearned to lie down in my old goose-down bed, stretch, snuggle, sleep and forget.

"Ach," Father said, so abruptly I thought he had gas. "I nearly forgot."

He went into the store room and fumbled behind the oaken desk where he worked on his books, then pulled out a fat, much abused letter and laid it on the table in front of me. I recognized the cultured handwriting immediately as the hand of my Yankee officer friend, Parker W. Pope.

I did not open Parker's letter that day or the next. There was something disturbing about its presence in my house; it reeked of enemy army camps and blood-soaked battlefields and in it, it held obligations I was loath to honor. On the one hand, I was anxious to hear how Parker had fared. I told my father, "Knowing him, he is probably a damned general by now." On the other, there had been something about his last letter—the tone, perhaps—that made me wish he had not written again, in blatant contravention of both our army's rules of fraternization with the enemy. The simple existence of such a letter might inspire a charge of treason and a courts martial.

One morning over coffee, while Father jawed with Mr. Owsley, a corn factor, and Loy Harrison, the clerk who handled Townville's postal duties from the store, I mustered the courage to open the letter. There was no postmark or canceled stamp, just the legend: Winchester, Virginia, February something or other, 1864. Already two months old.

"Dear Ansel, I sincerely hope this finds you in good health though no Honorable Man can say the same for your 'Kingdom of Secession.' The end of the Confederacy is now only a matter of time, as I predicted long ago. Did you receive my last letter? It cost me no small amount of trouble and coin. I sent it secretly through the lines by a horse trader whom I know; he is familiar with the Savannah River country and over the years has made many Friends of both persuasions. I know the mails are as tricky a proposition as a Red Indian's politics, so I did not allow my feelings to be hurt when you chose not to reply. But I still consider you a friend and hope that you have not become as others in the South, root-hog-or-die types. Southerners will certainly do plenty of both before all is done. You have the sense and education to know better. I hope it will please you to write me in your own time. I get few enough letters as it is. My sister Eleanor writes me when she can. She is still in mourning for her husband, Ian, who was killed at Chancellorsville. He was a good man enlisted in a bad cause. Happily for Eleanor, her little boy, Willie, bears her husband's own fine image.

"You know how it is with my father. I have not spoken to him or received a letter from him since the day I enlisted. Eleanor tells me he has forbidden the mention of my name in our once happy home; I daresay he mourned for poor Ian far more than he ever would for me. I can only suppose how this has affected my dear mother, who, I am certain, still loves me. Yet she always quaked before the Old Man. She never had the courage to defy him, even for the sake of her only son.

"You may send letters to the Hotel Briscombe here in Winchester. My lady friend, Miss T—, will send them on to me in the army. Don't risk sending it through your lines, though I would sincerely kill to hear from you."

Parker's letter rambled on for pages, relating how he had been wounded and nearly captured in a brush with some of Mosby's command, and had witnessed the hangings of several of those same troopers; his dislike of his general, Sigel, the same fellow my regiment had whipped in the fight at the ford two years before; and his distrust of officers in general. Excepting himself, of course.

"I received my commission as major and adjutant of the 2nd West Virginia a week ago, Ansel. I may yet get command of a regiment before this war is over. I am angling for a job in the cavalry, though; this infantry work is not for me. I have made some enemies in my own army by my honesty and unwillingness to call a nag a thoroughbred. I hope you never need it, Ansel, but remember that my influence is at your disposal, whenever you may require it.

"With my warmest regards to your good father, I remain…."

Parker's letter left me feeling there was something unsaid and ominous between us. Parker never did anything without a purpose. Was he hedging his bets, so to speak, if his confidence in Union victory proved premature? If so, what possible good would be the testimony of an unconnected private soldier in the ranks? I had not communicated with him in almost four years; he could not know my position. Knowing Parker, he probably assumed I had used my education to elbow my way up through the ranks as he had.

Like a good company clerk, I tucked the letter deep in my haversack and pondered a reply, but knew somehow I would not.

A year later I would wonder what made me keep Parker's letter. That simple, reflex action caused me untold problems. It also saved my life.

Anxious to keep my date in town with Manse, I hitched a ride to Anderson Courthouse with Amos Sterling on his feed wagon. Barely a mile out of Townville, Amos reached under the wood plank seat on which we jounced and brought up a wicker-covered ceramic jug sloshing with whiskey.

Amos was a big, rugged man of about fifty who had thickened about his middle but still looked as though he could lick his weight in wildcats. Before the war he had been a good Baptist and teetotaler, but the deaths of three sons and his father in as many years had stripped him of his past, his future and his will to live. He compensated by pouring into himself as much spirits as he could get his big hands on. I watched him warily as he drank, never offering me a drop. Gradually, I managed to take the reins from him. Twice he nearly fell out of the wagon when it lurched over deep ruts in the road. But on he drank in determined silence, occasionally barking incoherent phrases from some internal debate out of the side of his mouth. Seeing the set of his jaw, I wondered what was coming.

Anderson's courthouse square was crowded with mud—covered wagons and teams of mules, children darting between the imperturbable teams, farm women in plain print dresses and men in homespun jeans. The square smelled of roasted peanuts from two street vendors, mixing richly with the rank scent of horse and mule dung. Amos directed me to pull up in front of the Benson House, where he stumbled out and stashed his nearly empty jug beneath the wagon seat. I followed him in. Manse and Henry Knauff were sitting near the back of the saloon, where a morose black man sat playing "Pop Goes the Weasel" on a battered upright piano. Their boots muddying the tabletop, Manse and Henry were singing along lustily; they sent up a whoop when they saw me. Amos went straight to the bar and demanded a bottle of whiskey.

Henry and Manse wore their cavalry shell jackets jauntily, with only the brass button at the throat fastened so their coats swept back to show off Manse's vest of polished cotton, or, in Henry's case, leather galluses and a new flannel shirt. Henry also had a small caliber Starr pistol tucked into his waistband. Manse carried a huge, home-forged knife with a D-guard that had been cut down from an old militia sword. Wearing sensible corduroy trousers and a cool cotton shirt, I thought, "It must be damned uncomfortable carrying all that steel."

The boys had been drinking all morning and were still on the giddy end of their drunk, before the alcohol wore off and left a surly sullenness. In spite of my unease, it felt good sitting and being seen with them. We were comrades. They teased me unmercifully for being out of uniform, and played out a loud and rather silly mock court martial. The barkeep, J.J. Lionel, smiled at the horseplay and drew for me a glass of warm beer. Amos eyed us balefully from the bar, but the other customers seemed tolerant and amused by my friend's antics.

When Manse began teasing Henry about being a virgin, Henry, being very young and very drunk, did not take the teasing too well. Manse had proposed taking Henry to Amanda Creel's famous house on the Savannah River for some "horizontal refreshment," when Amos Sterling began to make his personal miseries loudly heard. He was cursing, something I had never heard him do, cursing Jefferson Davis, Alexander Stephens, Edmund Ruffin and every prominent Confederate he could think of, wishing them blood and misfortune for having killed his sons. Amos cursed himself for a drunken fool because he had urged Johnny, his oldest and handsomest boy, to enlist for the cause.

Amos was abusing himself as strongly as the Confederacy, but Manse could not see that. As soon as Amos mentioned Jeff Davis, Manse got to his feet, Henry muttering for him to "fix that drunken fool's wagon."

I grabbed Manse's rawboned wrist but he shook me off and walked to the bar. Mr. Lionel sent a boy running for the sheriff.

"Mister, you are going to take back what you said about Jeff Davis."

Amos regarded Manse with half-lidded eyes, turned back to his jug, then hunched his shoulders, bellowed like a bull and charged, grasping the jug in his beefy right hand.

Surprised by the big man's quickness, Manse ducked as the jug whizzed past his ear. He recovered quickly, hugged Amos's broad shoulders, stopped his charge with one braking leg and lifted him up off his feet, then with a roar of exhaled air twisted him sideways onto his back.

Amos thudded into the hard dirt floor and flopped like a fish on a line, sucking air. Manse's neck cords were straining, his eyes wild. He had his big knife in one hand and was studying Amos's carcass for a place to stick it.

That's when I jumped in, grabbing Manse's knife hand and trying to talk some sense to him. Manse roared and lifted me up with that arm as if I had been a child playing jump-the-moon. He may have hit me, but all I remember is crashing into the solid, immovable wall of the bar and blacking out.

I woke up to see Amos's swollen face and the flowing mustachios of Sheriff John Porter.

"You all right, boy?" The sheriff hauled me up and steadied me as I gingerly felt for the parts I knew should be there.

"All right, no broken bones. Just bruised and abused. Now you two get your tails out of town before I haul you over to the court-house and toss you in the clink. Go on, pay your bill and get out."

Drunken Amos started to protest, but the sheriff stared him down until we meekly left, pushing our way through the crowd of grinning patrons and disgusted matrons gathered on the boardwalk outside. The sudden blast of sunlight made my head hurt even more. Manse and Henry had long since skedaddled. My head ached the entire ride home.

We stopped at a roadside spring outside Townville to douse our heads and gently wash the dried blood from our faces.

"Some lowdown son of a bitch threw a glass at me," Amos growled, almost smiling, pink reconstituted blood washing down his jowls. "Maybe I needed a fight to set me straight, Ansel."

"You crazy bastard, you know who that was? Mr. Manse Jolly, in the flesh. I seen him kill a dozen Yankees with that knife."

Amos grinned. "I know him."

So ends the tale of my one and only adventure on leave. My telling of the story tickled Newton no end over supper that evening. Father seethed. He said not a word, but from the way his beard bristled, I knew he was furious. He did not speak to me for two days. I can't blame him. I was old enough to know better. But so was Amos.

Each morning on furlough I slept a little later. I no longer awoke by habit at dawn but slept longer and heavier and seemed to get less rest. And as the days grew shorter and shorter between breakfast and supper, I grew grumpy and listless, having less and less to do to fill the hours in between. Father spoiled me, coddled me, catered to me as he had Newton, his ruined boy, apologized to customers that I was still convalescing from my wound. Perhaps I was. The wounds of memory were being slowly salved by the dull, unchanging routine of home, a home that seemed more alien each day.

I no longer knew anyone there. My male friends from school days were all dead or in the army, the girls all married or recently widowed. I thought frequently of visiting Mary Jolly, but neither did I care to sit in stuffy parlors with haughty, vacant-headed females. I knew Mary was not like that, but it was something else that tugged at me, made me restless and short.

Like an adolescent immersed in Sir Walter Scott, I dreamed about the war; my every waking hour was filled with it. I saw it, smelled it, lived it: the sharp tang of wood smoke in the open air, enjoying a rough laugh with the boys, jumping into the saddle and careening down a country lane with a thousand mounted men, horse's hooves thundering like a summer storm, wind sweet in your face as you entered the ghostly clouds of burnt powder billowing over the battlefield and felt the familiar, queer twist of your stomach as the deadly bullet-bees began to hum overhead, past your ear, all around.

"Daddy, I've got to go."

Newton's face, pinched all the time now as if in constant pain.

"Don't go back, Ansel."

Father said nothing, did not even look up, just sighed long and low. I shook my head, said, "Leaving tomorrow," and went upstairs to bed.

When I woke next morning, my gray shell jacket had been laid over the chair next to the chiffarobe, cleaned and brushed, its tears and rips expertly patched, its gold-plated palmetto buttons polished to a bright sheen. A pair of wool trousers hung over the arm of the chair, newly made from a bolt of gray broadcloth Father had bought wholesale in 1861—when he still had three whole sons—and stashed away. There was a new set of cotton underclothing, a used vest of brown polished cotton with hardwood buttons, newly-made leather-soled brogans and a black felt slouch hat with the type of low, rounded crown I preferred.

I gathered up the garments and held them tight, rubbed the soft broadcloth on my cheek, smelled its newness, felt its weight and texture. My heart swelled with the love these clothes contained. I smiled, noticing that even lye soap could not rid my jacket of its cooked-in fragrance of wood smoke. I dressed slowly, reverently, as if about to attend a solemn ceremony.

When I came downstairs, Father and Newton stood. "Give me your hat," Newton said. He reached into his pocket and took out a shiny pair of brass crossed swords, the regulation insignia for cavalry. "I been carrying this awhile, Ansel. Found it in a Yankee camp." He twisted the backing wires through the felt and tied them until the gold sabers pressed flush against the black crown.

Father stepped back to inspect me. For a moment, he was an old soldier on parade, shoulders back, chin beard jutting.

"Will you sit for Mr. Moorhead?" he asked. "I don't have a likeness of you, Ansel."

They drove me in the old buggy to the Blue Ridge Railroad station at Anderson Courthouse; Sally, Father's old mare, knew the turnpike by heart. Between my legs I straddled a huge wax paper box stuffed with ham biscuits and sugar cookies, an apologetic farewell gift from Amos Sterling's wife. We parked the buggy at the station, then trooped up to Sam Moorhead's photographic studio on the second floor over the Farmer's Bank.

I stood stiffly and somewhat gloomily for the portrait, one hand resting on a Bible set upon a small table, the other tucked between two open buttons of my vest, trying not to move during the forty-five second exposure or breathe too deeply of the noxious chemical fumes that pervaded the studio. Mr. Moorhead had beautiful, dazzling morning light there, from a meticulously cleaned glass skylight set in the slanted roof. All that light made you feel worshipful, even a little light-headed, like you were in a cathedral receiving grace.

I boarded the Blue Ridge train for Belton carrying my boxed lunch, a bedroll and a haversack father had filled with a new shirt, clean socks, precious writing paper and two pencils.

"Now," he said, "you write more often."

They waved me off, Newton gaily stabbing the air with the end of his crutch as he leaned against Father.

In Belton, I bummed a ride with a wagon train of teamsters carrying lumber to Laurensville, and there the station master gave me soldier's passage on the Greenville and Columbia for the ride to Columbia. I shared some ham biscuits with a stern old Mennonite traveling with his seven-year-old grandson. The boy could not take his eyes off my brass buttons, which annoyed his pacifist grandfather no end and prompted him to express his opinion that the war was started by rich slaveowners who were now reaping the fruits of the evil they had sown.

"And it's the poor common boys who get killed," he said with some heat, ignoring the sharp stare he drew from an elderly gentleman seated across the aisle. "I respect your courage, young man, but the truth is as plain as the nose on my face."

I was weary of politics. I nodded absently and looked out the open window; the sky was overcast and sullen. Hot cinders from the smoke stack were blowing in, stinging foolishly exposed skin. When I turned back, the boy was staring at me with his guileless, liquid eyes. He and his Grandpa rose to leave at the Clinton station and I took the boy's thin, pale hand to shake and pressed into his palm an extra Palmetto button I kept in my pocket. The boy was clever enough not to betray our secret by exclamation or gesture. He did not even smile.

We reached Columbia in a drenching spring thunderstorm. As I stepped off the car, there was Manse and Henry standing in a mire of bubbling red mud next to the platform, the driving rain pouring off the captured Yankee rubber ponchos they wore. The ponchos, glistening black in the glare of the conductor's lamp, made my friends look like tall, patient seals. They had been waiting two hours in the rain because the depot floor was crowded with litters of wounded soldiers from the Virginia front.

I shook hands with Henry and Manse in turn, not a word passing between us, and felt as I did a strange tingling shoot up my right arm, as if an electric charge or some positive energy was being passed. Everything was going to be all right.

Manse unrolled an extra poncho for me, Henry took my overloaded haversack and we walked in the rain through the dim, sodden streets of Columbia to the smoking cavalry camp laid out in a muddy cornfield a mile outside the city.

As I walked, my step got livelier and, though they were taller and had to work less than I with every pace, Manse and Henry settled unconsciously into the comfortable cadence. We turned down a deserted company street swept with sheets of rain and stopped before a ramshackle cabin over which a Sibley tent had been raised for a roof. A crude sign over the entrance read: Benson House Mess.

I felt I had come home.

CHAPTER 10

Like A Steadily Rising Wind

I'll be damned if I ever love another country.

—Rebel veteran of Hood's army

It was the Confederate practice to take established regiments depleted by the attrition of war and fill up its companies with recruits, so that the new soldiers might benefit from the experience, judgment and coolness of the veterans.

This system worked especially well when the regiment had to go into combat with large numbers of "fresh fish" in its ranks. In the noise and confusion of a fight, the simple presence of men who had been in battle seemed to have a steadying influence on recruits, or so went the official thinking.

The veteran's thinking was that a certain number of recruits were doomed anyway, so it was useless to waste time or risk on them. The front was a place where Mr. Darwin's rule applied with a vengeance.

Still, a kind of instruction went on. Veterans hunted their holes at the first inkling a fight was brewing. Eventually, it dawned upon recruits that if they were to survive, they had to mimic the veterans and develop this sense. Thereafter, whenever a veteran slowed or stepped up his pace on a march, lay low in his saddle, looked sideways or even crouched suddenly on his way to the company sinks, half a dozen recruits were doing the same.

When the Yankees needed more men they simply created new regiments, so that even late in the war most of the divisions in the Army of the Potomac had several regiments of raw troops commanded by officers newly commissioned from the ranks of veteran outfits. Our way just made more sense. It preserved regimental pride and tradition and kept our armies together long after they might otherwise have disintegrated.

Colonel Black brought the regiment's strength back up to seven hundred troopers, more than half of whom had never been in a fight; another hundred and fifty or so had mustered out from regular infantry regiments or militia units and so had put in at least some military service.

A much bigger problem was finding animals on which to mount them. The colonel had promised General Hampton that he could mount everyone in three weeks and he managed to beg, borrow and steal horses from army depots, contractors, farms, private businesses and plantations. Even so, some of the boys rode mules until they had a chance to find proper mounts. I would not give up old Jeff, my red mule; I had grown too fond of him. But I needed a horse. Jeff did not have the size or muscle to keep up with a column of hard-pressed horsemen. I feared that the next campaign would kill him, and I intended to return him to the Hamricks if I could.

Captain Sharpe knew my predicament. One morning his black manservant showed up at the door of the Benson House Mess leading a sleek, jet-black mare with an irregular white patch on its chest.

"Compliments of the captain, sah," the man said. "Picked her out hisself, sah."

I cannot speak for Patch, as I came to call her, but for me it was love at first sight. I had never seen such intelligence in an animal as I seemed to see in Patch's agate brown eyes. She nuzzled me as if I was her colt, as if to say, "You'll do." Patch was to prove as steady and loyal a comrade to me as any man I served with.

It was during this time that Henry Knauff was promoted to corporal. Manse was made first sergeant of Company F, finally becoming in rank what he had been in practice through the war: Captain Sharpe's right-hand man.

I will say something good about the recruits, of which there were nearly forty in our company alone. They added a spirit, a zest, that had been absent from the regiment since Gettysburg. It was as though the veterans had not been able to get their second wind after that fight. But these youths, ignorant of the elephant, were spoiling for action, proud to be part of a fighting regiment that served with the legendary Stuart.

So it was with soaring spirits that we heard in mid-May we were to pack up and move north again, to join Lee for the spring campaign already raging in earnest near the old killing grounds around Richmond.

Manse was elated. We spent the night helping the new boys stow their gear, showing them what to throw away and what to keep. You cannot imagine the junk some intended to take to war: unnecessary clothing, books, wash basins, umbrellas, armor plate, even cumbersome musical instruments. An Irish lad named Ragan owned a gold-gilt harp that his mother had taught him to play with rare finesse. We tried to convince him that a week in the field would ruin the delicate instrument, but the boy stubbornly strapped the harp to his back.

"If I'm to die, so shall Oisin," he declared in his sweet Limerick dialect. "We shan't otherwise be separated."

Just before midnight, a rumor raced through camp that we were not going to Virginia at all but east to Charleston, back to the sort of swamp fighting on which we had cut our teeth two years before.

Incensed, Manse sought out Captain Sharpe, one of the few men I knew who never showed deference to Jolly nor backed away from him a single step.

"It's true, sergeant. General Lee himself wrote the order, asked for us special. The colonel'll post it in the morning."

Manse made it clear he thought we were being relegated to the backwaters of the war, like the second squad of a ball team, then stormed out.

We found out later that what happened was this: J.E.B. Stuart had been shot and mortally wounded in a nasty horse-fight near Yellow Tavern, Virginia, on May 11. Wade Hampton, our brawny division commander, replaced the "Cavalier of the Confederacy," but he had to hurry from his home in Columbia back to the front, followed by General M.C. Butler's division of horsemen which, like us, had been home recruiting but in the Lowcountry, guarding the coast. Someone had to replace the troops pulling out of the works around Charleston and going north with Butler.

General Lee's order, which I read myself, recommended the 1st South Carolina Cavalry because we "were veteran troops accustomed to severe picket duty." We were honored to have earned the old gentleman's trust, but most were also secretly relieved. We were no longer eager to rush into big fights, not after Brandy Station and Gettysburg. One fight like those generally satisfies a man's curiosity about battle for a lifetime.

At our mess campfire, a seething Manse spat tobacco juice into the flames.

"Back to shoveling shit with the alligators and cottonmouths," he snarled.

The day before we left Columbia, our Benson House Mess admitted another member, a freckle-faced fellow named Ambrose Clinkscales.

'Brose had enlisted at the first call and served with my brothers, Tom and Newton, in the Palmetto Riflemen. He, too, was wounded at Frayser's Farm, standing in line of battle not twenty feet from Tom when my brother received his death-shot, and near to where Newton had his leg swept out from beneath him.

But 'Brose, who was shot in the shin, went home on a hospital train while Newton, wounded only minutes later, was not found by a stretcher detail until the next day. By that time his wound was so badly infested with blow flies that the blood was poisoned and the limb had to be amputated to save his life.

"I went to see Newton while I was at home," 'Brose told me. "We knew each other in school and we had become pretty good friends in camp. Back at home we didn't have all that much to say to one another. I think he was peeved I was able to get to a surgeon first. I kept my leg because of that. I don't blame him one damn bit."

'Brose did not have to go back into the army, but he did so willingly when he heard our regiment was recruiting. He argued bitterly with his father and mother, who said they needed him at home. But 'Brose packed his haversack, endured a storm of wailing and limped to the train station. He sought out Company F, which he knew from Newton was mine and Manse's outfit.

"I always wanted to be in the calvary," 'Brose grinned.

We roared with laughter, to 'Brose's befuddlement. He did not know that Captain Sharpe winced when he heard someone mistake a horse-mounted outfit for the sacred place where Jesus Christ died, so we quickly tutored him on the proper pronunciation.

I later drew 'Brose aside and gave him a twist of tobacco I had been carrying for months. Then I asked him straight out how Tom had died. He did not spare my feelings any, but looked me squarely in the eye.

"We were crossing a cleared field in line of battle and had come almost abreast of a rail fence from where our skirmishers had been shooting," 'Brose said. "We faced another field overgrown with brush and beyond that was a line of trees where the Yankees were hiding.

"On our right flank was a Louisiana regiment that had come apart crossing the field. They were fresh fish, still wearing that damn Louisiana blue instead of Confederate gray or butternut. They were milling about like cattle. Well, this colonel brings in another regiment quick on their right and those boys—Virginians, I think—saw the blue coats of those Pelican companies and thought they must have gotten in among the Yankees. They swung back their line quick like it was a hinged gate and cut loose with a volley.

"They shot too high, missing the Louisianans, but the rounds caught our right flank companies in enfilade, killing a few boys outright. Tom was one. The ball struck him in his right temple and passed through his head. He fell face down where he stood. Colonel Archbright galloped up to the Virginians and cursed them for their stupidity, but in all the excitement—the Yankees were shooting at us, too—it must have been some time before Newton even noticed Tom was missing.

"Tom never felt a thing, Ansel, I swear."

"Damn," was all I could say. "Damn, damn, damn."

I made 'Brose promise he would never tell my father what he had told me. His tale filled me with a dark melancholy, because now I was certain that it was the Yankees who buried Tom, more than likely in a nameless mass grave long overgrown and already forgotten.

Upon our arrival in Charleston, the regiment was detailed to garrison old Fort Johnson on James Island, the same outpost in which Manse had served when he was in the state militia back in '61. This development depressed him still further. He turned his energies to harassing the men for their laxness, organizing and supervising work crews, utilizing his verbal prowess and his status as first sergeant to the fullest.

We in the Benson House Mess were fortunately exempt from most of the tongue lashings, but the new men were fair meat. Manse was merciless in supervising the reconstruction work on the parapets of the fort, and on this project the entire company sweated and labored for weeks in the steamy Lowcountry heat.

Fort Johnson was a strong earthwork built of sand and fill dirt buttressed by palmetto logs. It guarded the southern flank of Charleston bay near the mouth of the Ashley River. From our picket posts in the fort's twenty-five foot high walls we could see Fort Sumter, by then little more than a pile of loose masonry and rubble, situated more than a mile east of us in the center of the harbor. Across the harbor at Cummings Point sat Battery Wagner, abandoned the previous year and now invested by the Yankees. Union ships of war studded the harbor entrances in a concentric battle line.

In the area of this earthwork were situated no fewer than nine Confederate batteries, each facing as many Union strong points. The three-square-mile harbor area bristled with guns, troops and warships, including the ten-inch Columbiad siege guns mounted on the walls of Fort Johnson. The gunners who serviced these pieces claimed they could brush a seagull off the main mast of a Yankee man-of-war three miles out. That was hard to swallow, but we had to admit the Union ships kept a respectable distance.

ॐ

May the 21st, 1864
Back in Old "S.C."—Ft. Johnson, near Charleston, So. Car.

Dearest Mother & Mary,

Received yours of the 7th inst., that most awful of news that my brothers were dead. I have thought of little else since the letter came to me. You would not wish to now my thoughts but can be assured I have made the Yankeys Pay at every Opportunt'y, and Will continue to do so.

How are you bearing up, Mother? Mary I count on you to keep every
Body's spirits up. Our blood is strong from long trials But the human
Spirit can endure only so much.

I have sent all my pay and I now it is not enough. But just do your best
to keep a Garden and Uncle Ez's cow and you will do well. Better than
us, I should say. Our Rations have been thin. Many of the Boys are sick.
We need fresh vegitables and clean clothing, and a Healthy climate
with good air. These damable swamps kill more men than the Yankeys.
In my dreams I see the green hills of the Anderson District and
breathe its pure Air. I smell and taste the juice of our Peaches, have
you kept up Pa's trees? I would give anything to taste Mother's cobbler,
or her peaches put-up with sugar syrup.

My Heart is too full too write more. Now forever that you are my
Loves. Yours Until—,

M.S. Jolly

On May 27, 1864, a bright hot Friday, our reconstituted regiment
took part in its first stiff fight as garrison troops when the Yankees
assaulted the batteries around Fort Johnson by land and sea. We
watched as the blue-clad regiments struggled across the sand dunes
from the direction of Battery Wagner. Other troops rounded the
point by water, sitting stiffly and uncomfortably in longboats navigated by sailors and marines who knew the sea's rhythm.

The landward attack crashed like a wave upon the first of two lines
of entrenchments set at one hundred yard intervals east of the fort's
works, manned by veteran Georgia and North Carolina troops. The
noise of the firing was terrific; thick curtains of smoke soon hung
over the dunes, obscuring our view of the land fight. The enemy
wasted its strength on these impregnable defenses; their infantry
simply melted away after a few minutes of horrific punishment.

In the meantime, five federal steamers tried to run up the
Ashepoo River under the very noses of our guns. Without orders,
Manse mounted Companies A, D and F, led us down the causeway to

Chapman's Fort and deployed us along the south riverbank just ahead of the Yankee flotilla.

As they rounded a wide bend in the muddy tidal river, we opened a merciless fire on the slow-moving targets. Within five minutes our rifle fire alone disabled one steamer's paddlewheel. The boat stopped dead in the water, turning slowly seaward with the river current as Confederate shells raised spouts of white water around its dingy hull. Our carbine balls thudded into its wooden superstructure, kicking up clouds of dust and splinters so that the entire craft seemed to be shuddering in its death throes. Panicky sailors abandoned the craft, jumping overboard for the nearest shore.

The dying steamer caught fire, flaring like a Roman candle and then exploded in a shower of sparks and smoking debris. As the ship struck a sandbar and gave up its ghost, an unearthly shriek like the scream of a living thing, shrill and gut-wrenching to hear, rent the air. The regiment's accurate shooting also disabled a second steamer, whose crew swam to the far shoreline. The hulk of the destroyed boats burned all night, their tar caulking steaming in the gently lapping salt water. The glowing corpses cast a firebrand of light on the water that only dimmed toward dawn.

At daybreak, parts of the wreckage beached just below the fort and we climbed over the parapet to pick over the remains for souvenirs. Henry Knauff crinkled his nose.

"What's that stink?"

It was the undeniable stench of burned meat. Aboard the steamer lay the charred, fused corpses of seventy or eighty horses, their blackened legs sticking grotesquely into the air, indistinguishable from the settling ribs of the wrecked hull.

"It's a goddamn shame," said Manse. "Those animals didn't have no politics. We might have saved them if the Yankee cowards had not abandoned their ship."

"It was their screaming that we heard," said Robert Sitton.

'Brose picked up a stick and dug out a human skull from the char-coal mess that filled the hulk like ancient, congealed tar. But no one that day spoke of the human dead; we were thinking of those poor horses. In spite of my horror at the sight, my unChristian stomach grumbled at the scent of cooked and spoiling meat that hung in the air over that beach.

We had seen precious little in the way of fresh provisions since coming to the Lowcountry; food was becoming scarce because of the Yankee blockade. We lived on wormy fatback and hardtack, fought the mosquitoes and stood guard in torrential summer rains.

In July, we beat back another Yankee attack. Colonel Black had taken deathly ill before the first Fort Johnson fight and went home to Columbia to recuperate. Lieutenant Colonel J.D. Twiggs, who took command in Black's absence, praised Manse in dispatches for his conduct in both fights, citing his "efficient services and gallantry." Twiggs suspected the Yankees had been trying to sneak several com-panies of cavalry behind our lines, to disrupt communications and strike the railroad connecting Charleston and Columbia.

We sweltered through the summer, our morale sinking as the food and the war news grew worse with each passing day. In September, Sherman took Atlanta and began rampaging through Georgia with his army of seventy thousand bummers, pushing Joe Hardee's boys around like whirl-a-gig toys. The Georgia troops garrisoned with us were uneasy; it was their homes the Yankees were burning and their families who were being abused. They began to desert, drifting home at first one at a time, then by twos and threes, then entire squads.

"They got the right idea," Henry said one dreary morning as we huddled in our cheerless bombproof shelter. "In a few weeks Sher-man will be burning our own homes. I'm thinking that's where we should be, not sitting on our butts here, scratching mosquito bites."

Manse came in then, and the way the conversation suddenly died made him instantly suspicious. Each of us looked away as he studied our faces, all but Henry.

"You go on, Corporal Knauff," the first sergeant said with quiet menace. "But if I catch you, and the colonel orders me to pull a rope on you, I'll do it with a smile."

That put an end to talk of desertion in our mess, though the newer men disappeared in handfuls. A few of those recaptured were summarily shot, but the numbers became such that execution was impractical. Most officers were losing their stomach for the business. A blind man could see the Confederacy was coming apart at the seams.

By early November, the situation around Charleston was desperate; the Yankee incursions were becoming bolder, each thrust stronger and more difficult to resist. Bit by bit, the troops and guns defending the city were being stripped away and sent to Lee in Virginia, or to Braxton Bragg then in command inNorth Carolina.

Christmas that winter was the most cheerless in my memory. Our bellies were shrunken, our spirits dry as dust. There was no good news from home. I know many felt as I did, that we were nothing better than condemned men.

Our duties were mostly dull and monotonous, which was good because the men were lethargic from a lack of sufficient and fresh provender. We were short on powder and ball, rations, soap, candles, fresh clothing, forage for our horses, every conceivable thing an army needs in the field. All the boys dropped weight and appeared shockingly haggard and lean, even to my eyes. The fish, shrimp, blue crabs and shellfish on which we had feasted two years before had disappeared. In my dreams I sampled dishes both plain and exotic. Once a fellow hauled in a sea turtle and the entire company gorged itself on turtle stew, but that was a memorably rare occasion. We paid for our pleasure by spending most of the night at the company sinks, our bellies unused to such sudden rich fare.

After the second assault against Fort Johnson we experienced little combat. Skirmishes even became rare. The Yankees were content to shell Fort Sumter and the once-grand city of Charleston into dust, as they had Battery Wagner. Our troops abandoned the works after a month of pounding by the heaviest naval ordinance of the time. The Yankees dragged the guns over miles of sand dunes, and the bodies of countless friends, to take those works.

A squadron of the regiment was detached (not Company F's) and sent south to Savannah when Sherman's hordes appeared at its very gates. Helpless to do anything except make their presence known, our friends were back within a fortnight, and Sherman's four army corps were only days behind them.

The world was coming down about our ears. General Wade Hampton returned from Virginia to take command of the cavalry defending his home state against Sherman. But Sherman did not aim for Charleston. Within a few days it became clear he was marching to Columbia on parallel turnpikes, sweeping aside any resistance put before him.

We had been a part of General William B. Taliaferro's brigade, thinly spread company by company over most of the Lowcountry. We became part first of Stephen Elliott's brigade, which was made up of cadets from The Citadel, then Harrison's brigade, as Hampton's division was absorbed into Lieutenant General Hardee's army on its march north from Savannah, burning bridges behind it and fighting delaying actions all the way to Charleston.

We made no move to block the Yankee juggernaut; that would have proven suicidal. Instead, we nipped at him. Skirmish after skirmish, firefight after firefight—at Buford's Ridge, White Post, the Wolf Plantation, Red Bank Creek, and, finally, on the outskirts of Columbia itself—we retreated by night and sought points of ambush by day, trying to slow the advancing blue wave. But it was irresistible.

On February 17, 1865, Sherman's advance divisions began shelling South Carolina's capital city from across the Broad River.

On the very same day, the last Confederate forces left the ruined Holy City of Charleston and also followed Hardee, who slogged doggedly north, intending to join forces with General Joe Johnston and his army in North Carolina.

Defending Columbia was never an issue. What forces we had there were ordered out to join Hardee or had left long before of their own accord. The militia guarding the Yankee prisoner of war camp were the last to get the word. When we rode by the camp gates, crowds of uncertain Federal prisoners were milling about outside. They scattered as we approached, but we cantered past them. Sherman's batteries were arcing shells into the city and we would not stop. The last Confederate troops out of Columbia set ablaze the piles of cotton bales stacked aboard wagons and at every street corner, placed there no doubt for use as street barricades. Instead, they made superb firebrands.

A steadily rising wind began to blow early in the evening, spreading the glowing embers of cotton. Fires flared up in wood piles, on fences and atop the roofs of houses. The first Yankees into the city were bummers looking for food, liquor and plunder. They set more fires to intimidate, to destroy and just for the fun of it. They were joined by bands of young blacks celebrating the coming of their freedom.

That was how Columbia burned. Assigned to rear guard, we watched from a bald knoll north of the city as the sky overhead stayed bright long after the sun went down, first glowing a pale yellow, then brightening into a deep pulsing red that colored the faces of the infantry as they marched, each soldier as he passed unable—like the Biblical Lot's wife—to resist the temptation of looking back over his shoulder to view the destruction of the world.

That night, I made a decision.

While Manse and the boys sat atop that hill, grazing our horses and waiting for the last of Hardee's infantry columns to march on north, I went to Patch. I fed her a handful of small green apples I had scooped out of a yard in Columbia and stroked her satin-sleek neck, blacker than the night. I felt over my saddle for the butt of the .31-caliber Colt pocket revolver Manse had given me. One by one, I removed the copper caps from the rear of each cylinder, meaning that the hammer if triggered would fall on rounds with no detonators.

I had determined not to become the agent of injury or death to another living thing, as long as the war went on. If my life should be forfeit, so be it.

Death was beginning to sound more and more like an honorable and cherished end, one devoutly to be wished.

CHAPTER 11

Capture at Solemn Grove

Over the next three weeks the regiment operated like a disembodied plasma oozing its way north from Columbia to the North Carolina state line, detaching cells of companies to guard railroads, river fords, bridges and crossroads, then reassembling days later only to divide once again when outlying danger alarms sounded. Most of the alarms were false, but we went anyway, until our horses began dropping from exhaustion.

I still carried my Sharps breechloader on my back but had no cartridges for it, for which I was glad. And I still had my father's Prussian saber, which Manse had saved for me after Gettysburg. With it, I could still look the part of a fighting cavalryman even though I no longer was one in fact. I would stick with my friends, but I would no longer fight. My heart was gone out of it.

Patch stood the physical test better than most. Nearly impervious to thirst, she could go for days on a few mouthfuls of grass and a couple of green persimmons. She was young and in her prime, and I determined not to ruin her but to salvage her life if I could. The more I saw of random death and destruction, the more I valued life in any form.

We went into action at places that appear today on no maps: at Strouds Mills and Mount Elon, at Hinnsborough and Phillips Cross Roads, fighting the advance elements of entire army corps. These were Yankees like we had never seen before: rangy, tough, profane Westerners, men who said they had never been whipped in a fight and they acted like it.

Upon leaving behind the grand old Palmetto State, Hampton consolidated his mounted forces and artillery with General Joe Wheeler's division of cavalry. They were Westerners, too, from Mississippi, Texas and Arkansas.

On March 10, 1865, in a broad clearing of a North Carolina pine forest aptly called Solemn Grove, our combined columns bore down before dawn on Union General Judson Kilpatrick's cavalry division, surprised sleeping in its smoking bivouac in and around Solemn Grove. Wheeler's men got bogged down in a swamp, so we went in by ourselves. History books call the fight Monroe's Crossroads.

Southerners prize this minor Confederate victory over many others, perhaps because it was one of the last great feats of Southern arms in the war. I think it is the scent of scandal they savor still, picturing the notoriously horny General Kilpatrick as he lay abed with the infamous Mrs. Boozer, and who, caught inflagrante by whooping Confederate troopers, was forced to flee the field without his trousers as thousands of rebels came pounding down his company streets, shooting and sabering hapless Yankees.

But not all those Yankees were helpless. Enough of them found their weapons and horses quickly, mounted and instinctively formed defense lines. All over that field officers took charge and mounted organized counterattacks; these were ragged at first, coming by squads and platoons, hallooing and shooting in the predawn darkness so that one barely knew friend from foe.

But as night yielded to a cold gray dawn, the volume of fire being poured from their firing lines was heavier and more determined; mounted counterattacks began coming by companies and squadrons. When we heard the first crash of a volley of musketry, we knew Federal infantry had reached Solemn Grove.

Company F crashed through the enemy camp in column of fours, wheeled and charged back up another avenue of dimly lit tents, past lines of skittish picketed horses, in and around two astonished farriers sweating at their iron forge and through a soggy bottomland across which dozens of half-clad Union troopers were splashing as fast as they could hoof it. Our troopers cut from the column to pursue them and the blackness was suddenly illuminated with the muzzle flashes of a hundred rifles from a firing line hidden in the darkness of the trees.

I reined up in a panic, cut away and found myself back among the tents. I steered Patch down a narrow lane, oblivious to the cries of Robert following behind me. The lane became a dead end, so I reined again and turned. Robert came up beside me. Bullets were ripping the air around us.

"Damn but we're in a pickle, Ansel. We've got to find the company." Robert suddenly raised his pistol and aimed over Patch's neck.

"Ansel!" he shouted.

"Surrender, you rebel sons of bitches," shouted a chorus of voices.

I never saw the Yankee who shot Robert but I felt the hot blast of his weapon's discharge against my left cheek. Robert's animal reared and he slumped against me, so I grabbed his belt and pulled him to me in an attempt to get the dead weight of his body over the pommel of my saddle.

Hands were grasping at me, pulling me backward. Instinctively, I reached for my pistol and as I did, a man put one arm over Patch's neck and used that leverage to bring his other arm level with Robert's sagging head and exposed right temple. I never saw the revolver. My hammer clicked on a dead cylinder but not the Yankee's. His pistol spit yellow fire. Robert's head lolled with the blast and a shower of warm blood and sticky tissue spattered my face and mouth. I fell backward off Patch with Robert on top of me and the enraged Yankees surrounded us, pummeling me and poor Robert's corpse with rifle butts and fists.

The blows were like those received in a dream; I barely felt them. I only remember trying to protect my dead friend, and weeping like a child, begging his forgiveness.

Those Yankees must have thought they had killed us both because they left us alone after venting their rage. I did not care. I envied Robert. I would have preferred a quick bullet in the brain to the mental agony that gripped me. I relived the awful moment over and over again, trying to think what I could have done differently. It had happened too fast, faster than thought.

When I finally forced my eyes to open I was sitting against the back of Robert's dead horse. My poor friend still lay on top of me, his mangled head on my breast like a little boy sleeping in his father's arms. I held Robert's cold stiffening form all the more tightly and squeezed bitter tears from my swollen eyes.

It must have been mid-morning, a dirty, gray, overcast morning but I saw them coming, two soldiers, one an officer. He stooped over me and bent so low I could feel his breath on my cheek.

"Take your hands off him, you blue-bellied son of a bitch."

I swan that Yankee leaped back as if stung by an adder. He fumbled for his revolver, then screamed, "Get the colonel!" When he had composed himself, he drew the pistol and kept it pointed at me, albeit very unsteadily. He wore a brass corps badge on the breast of his frock coat; I recognized the acorn device because I had seen it in Columbia: Sherman's Fourteenth Army Corps.

In a moment, I heard the unmistakable clinking music of canteen, cup and bayonet as a column of infantry double-quicked by, a handsome officer at their head, mounted on a magnificent roan stallion. The infantry, in column of fours, kept on jogging, every man as he passed gazing curiously at the dramatic scenario.

The officer reined up and effortlessly dismounted. He snapped an order at the first officer, who sheepishly holstered his revolver.

"Who are you? Are you an officer? Are you wounded?"

My eyes narrowed. I had seen this man before. No, not this man, but one very like him. That black hair, demanding eyes, the strong chin now sporting an imperial in the fashion of Generals McClellan and Johnston.

Yes, this man, my old friend, Parker Pope. Only older now, fitter looking now; the army suited him.

"I am Lieutenant-Colonel Pope, 98th Ohio. You are my prisoner. Do you understand?"

I extended my bruised and swollen left hand, still wet with Robert's blood.

"Hello, Parker. I regret meeting you again under these circumstances. It seems your men have murdered my friend." Under my breath I added, "Remember your pledge."

Pope's eyes slowly widened in recognition. He looked at my hand, then quickly straightened, removed his cap and ran his hands through his thick hair as I had seen him do many times. It meant that he was put out, and worried.

"Lieutenant!" he shouted over his shoulder. "Take a stretcher detail and get this man to a surgeon. Report back to me."

"Parker," I whispered hoarsely, gesturing to where my loyal Patch was grazing a few yards away, oblivious to the smoking battlefield. "My horse. Please."

Parker's eyes flashed. Oh, he was angry at this inconvenience. But he quietly ordered the lieutenant to lead away the black.

Before the stretcher detail came I took Robert's beloved Bible from his pocket, along with a few letters. I composed him as best I could; in spite of his ruined head his face was peaceful. I combed his hair over the gaping exit wound and placed his hands on his breast. I knew how the Yankees would treat him, so I wanted a last image to carry to his folks.

The burial squad happened by first, led by a grizzled, graying sergeant chewing on a stub of clay pipe. He said not a word but his eyes quickly appraised the situation. I looked the sergeant in the eye.

"Please, treat him gently, boys."

At their compassionate sergeant's direction, the Yankees wrapped Robert in a gray blanket and carried him to a flatbed wagon that braked nearby. They placed him among the other bodies with as much dignity as could be mustered. I said nothing but was grateful for the kindness. They were only men, like us, grown respectful of death, hardened on the outside but still capable of being affected by the brutality of war.

The wagon jerked forward.

My own bearers were less gentle. They joked roughly about throwing me on the dead wagon and being done with me. I made no response, but moaned pitiably at every stumble and misstep until each soldier had quieted and one even hissed, "Easy there!"

They took me to a clearing reserved for the captured Confederate wounded, a group of about forty men, most sitting up, glaring from behind half-lidded eyes and faces black with dried blood. The most serious were lying on blankets, a comrade holding their hand. I saw no one I recognized, nor any doctors, not even an orderly.

One of my stretcher bearers left me a full canteen; he looked back at me queerly as he walked away. Concerned, I removed the plug and sniffed at the cork: It was apple brandy, still redolent of the orchard. I raised the canteen in salute and the soldier nodded. I sipped the sweet brandy and shared it with my fellow prisoners, who could not believe I had gotten it from the enemy.

And so, feeling much better, my head buzzing slightly, I greeted the return of Colonel Pope. Like his comrades he treated me with great deference, and spoke as if addressing the nearly dead.

"How are you feeling, Ansel?"

"Pretty damn good, Parker. You?"

"I've brought my regimental surgeon, Major Eskridge, to look you over. Show him where you were injured."

"I cannot."

"What?"

"I hurt all over, goddamnit."

Dr. Eskridge stripped my bloodied blouse. He carefully washed my face and torso with alcohol that stung every cut and sore it touched. He studied the bruises on my arms, back and shoulders, my swollen hand, felt up and down my legs, looked in my eyes.

"Well, Parker, this man has been beaten up pretty well; broken index finger on his left hand," the physician announced. "But he has no serious wounds. Aside from missing a few meals and being slightly drunk, he is in ambulatory condition."

"If you please, sir," I said, emboldened by the liquor. "There are badly injured men here who require care. Will you see to them?"

The surgeon's eyes narrowed. "If it's all right with you, Parker, I will return to our own wounded."

I could see the anger rising in Parker's eyes, the pique that always came over him when he thought he had been bested or tricked.

"Damn your eyes, Ansel, I thought you were dying," he spit out. "What in hell am I supposed to do with you? You have put me in one hell of a spot."

I looked at him, barely able to see through eyes swollen and dry, and replied firmly, "Let me go."

Parker straightened and looked about furtively as if to see if anybody was listening. In that Solemn Grove of death and misery, I doubt if anybody had heard or cared.

Parker stalked off. He had not touched my Yankee canteen. I still cradled it in one arm when I awoke, startled, in semi-darkness hours later.

I was jouncing about in the back of an army wagon, lying atop hundred-weight burlap bags of oats. There were wagons behind and ahead, moving laboriously in a long train. It was early evening and yet in spite of the shadows there was no pretension of secretiveness. The air resounded with the yells of teamsters and the snort of straining mules, creaked with the sound of rusty wagon springs and leather harness.

I remembered sipping a bowl of salty beef broth at the hospital but had had no solid food since the night before the fight. My shrunken stomach was cold as well as empty, so I sipped at my canteen, being careful not to drink too much. As delicious and fragrant as the liquor was, I imagined how much better it would taste in a snug cabin before a warm fireplace, at a table laden with roasted meats, potatoes, gravy, fresh bread and butter, yams baked in molasses, and sugared fruit pies.

Colonel Parker Pope rudely interrupted my reverie, reining up beside my wagon as it lurched suddenly to a stop.

"Come on, you're going with me. Put these on."

I climbed down, sore and aching from the wagon ride and took off my short jacket, stiff with Robert's blood, and regarded it as one might an old friend. Impulsively, I began to pluck off its nine buttons, one by one, stuffing them into the pockets of the fresh sky blue trousers Parker had shoved at me.

"Damn it, Ansel, we haven't all night."

There was a clean flannel shirt, too, for which I gladly sacrificed my cotton shirt, so dirty that it had become a part of my torso; removing it was like peeling away living skin. Then, a Union sack coat buttoned loosely over all. I kept my Confederate slouch hat.

Parker turned in his saddle and tied a familiar horse to the wagon. My jet black Patch, sleek and fit as an otter.

"Mount and let's go."

I fairly flew onto good old Patch's back, ignoring how much the effort hurt. We followed the column for a few hundred yards, then Parker turned off onto a narrow trail through the forest. We did not go far. At a dark crossroads Parker reined up and tossed me a full canteen and haversack.

"There's hard crackers and coffee beans in there, enough for a couple days."

"Parker, come with me. We can ride out of this war."

"Head west and keep going. Travel only by night. You are not likely to run into any of our troops; this corps is Sherman's left flank. But the cavalry are everywhere."

"Parker!"

The colonel only smiled and grasped my hand.

"I truly wish we could turn back the clock, Ansel. But you are what you are and I am what I am. My debt to the past is paid. I will remember you to my sister." He paused. "You expect me to desert my command and run off with you? It ain't that easy, Ansel. I believe in what I'm doing."

He turned to the main road without looking back, and galloped off.

For a moment I was at a loss what to do, where to go. Parker's last words to me burned in my heart; he could not do anything without falling back on his moral superiority. I wanted to wrestle him down and bloody his nose, as he used to do to me when we were combative students. The rascal had just done it again.

I got Patch motivated in the opposite direction, guessing which way was west. My mind seethed with ideas on how to visit retribution upon Parker Pope, but I decided ultimately to forgive Parker for his slight. Being an officer he obviously had other things on his mind. After all, he had risked his career, maybe his life, helping an enemy.

It also occurred to me that Parker rarely did anything that did not directly benefit him. I know later he received the brevet rank of brigadier general and commanded his brigade at the end of the war. I was left to wonder what sort of fantastic story he must have concocted to explain away losing a prisoner. Or, maybe memory has exaggerated my importance; me, an impertinent little cavalry corporal too skinny for the killing.

At daybreak I led Patch far off the road and into a hollow shaded by loblolly pines where she could graze on berries and newly sprouted tufts of sweet grass. Thirsting for fresh Yankee coffee, I tried in vain to start a fire; but I had no matches nor even a piece of flint, and what kindling and wood I could find was soaked through by recent rains.

It is better so, I told myself: No smoke to attract unwanted attention. But with every mouthful of dry hard cracker I choked down my deprived senses could almost taste the heady, aromatic scent of the whole coffee beans in their linen poke bag.

As I ate, I thought. My war was over. I had done my best to be a good soldier, more than many, but one man can only do so much. What good was I anyway, a man with no weapons, not even a knife? There was no point to further sacrifice; the end had come. Those of us still alive and in one piece would have to rebuild the South for the next generation. Yes, the war was over for me. I had decided to heed Parker's advice and find my way home while I still had a good horse and rations. If this was desertion, so be it. I had had my fill of war.

I plucked the eagle buttons from my Yankee sack coat and threw them away, so that I could not at least be shot as a spy. I would replace them with my tarnished palmetto tree buttons when I had a chance.

That night I slept like a dead man, and when I awoke it was with a start, shivering, in total darkness hours before dawn. I lay still as death but heard no sound except those of the pine forest at night. Patch snuffled beside me, then grunted, making road apples where he stood and turning his head as if asking, "Well, how about breakfast?" Was that what had awakened me?

Groggy, I lovingly rubbed down Patch with my hands as best I could, stroking her strong withers and flanks, and inspected her hooves, which were newly shod. A gift from Parker. I led her out of the hollow and down the mist-covered road until the moon climbed into the night sky and shed enough light to see the rough wagon trail we followed. When the mist cleared I mounted Patch and we rode all night through forest and open fields, not seeing a dwelling or a light or another living thing.

When the sky grayed toward dawn I halted and dismounted at the far edge of a pine grove; Patch and I both needed a stretch and a blow. But more, I did not like the look of the terrain ahead. The trace led across a broad, fallow farm field and into a tree line between two forested knolls that might once have been Indian mounds. A perfect spot for an ambush. You must remember, choosing terrain such as this had been a chief part of my soldierly profession for the last three years.

I watched ahead for the better part of half an hour and saw no unusual movements or telltale flashes of steel. I mounted Patch and crossed the field at a trot, uneasy but alert. I no sooner came abreast of the knolls that I heard a familiar rush and clatter behind me.

"Halt!"

Immediately, I dropped my reins and threw up my hands.

"Your prisoner!"

The rider who emerged from the shadows in the tree line more closely resembled a scarecrow than a living man, but there was no mistaking the sapphire brilliance of his eyes or the dusty red of his beard. It was Manse Jolly, leaner of flesh than he had ever been on the farm. Yet his face was impassive as it looked down the barrel of his carbine.

Riders came up from behind, buffeting Patch, making her snort with annoyance. They grabbed at me, lifted my sack coat.

"He ain't armed."

"Manse, it's me, Ansel Fries."

Sergeant Jolly trotted up and looked me square in the eye. He dropped the barrel of his weapon and gazed at me long and hard.

"I am glad to see you, Ansel. We near took you for a Yankee."

"Not on this road, Manse. I haven't seen a Yankee in two days."

We shook hands and the other riders surrounded us. I started to speak but was drowned out by the flare-up of a heated debate that had been going on long before I showed.

"Shitfire, Manse, what'd I tell you?" one long-bearded trooper complained. "We're so far out of this war we might as well be in Californy."

"I heard you, now shut up. Ansel, we're separated from the regiment. There's about fifty of us, mixed companies and regiments. We're short on ammunition, short on rations and short on common sense." He glared at the rangy complainer.

"Are you with us?"

I swallowed hard, suddenly thirsty. "Sure."

"We're riding north. We're bound to strike Johnston's army around Smithfield or thereabouts."

"We ain't a going," the bearded rider snarled. A dozen or so mounted soldiers gathered around him, lean, desperate-looking men. I yearned to go with them. "This here war's over, now."

"Go, and be damned to you," Manse replied with an uncharacteristic weariness.

That was how I came to be reunited with my friend. Henry and Hepsibah were not with him, nor were other familiar faces about whom I inquired; Solemn Grove had badly broken up the company and regiment, wherever they were. I related to Manse the sad news of Robert's death.

"Can't be helped," Manse said tersely. He did not ask or even seem interested in how I had gotten away. I volunteered no information, my heart sinking in my chest until I could no longer feel it beat.

Already far west of Fayetteville, we headed northeast in broad daylight. That night more riders joined us from the retreat from Fayetteville. They reported watching Sherman's troops march in at dusk, regiment after regiment, brigade after brigade, so many Yankees carrying pine firebrands that their columns were lit by fire for miles south of Fayetteville. Then, as in Columbia, the city itself began to glow as Sherman's bummers put the print machine shops near the former federal arsenal to the torch.

We pitched camp north of Averasborough in a grove of trees where a cold mineral spring bubbled out of the ground. I surprised Manse with my hoard of fresh Yankee coffee beans, which were carefully but quickly crushed with stones and rifle butts; the delicious steam of boiling coffee soon pervaded the camp. A new fellow brought out a huge ham that he and his friends had liberated from a party of Sherman's bummers, who had no doubt stolen it from some poor family's smokehouse.

Companies of Yankee foragers blanketed the countryside ahead of the regular troops, absolutely shameless types who avoided any fighting and stole anything they could carry. What happened to the Yankees who provided us with our ham steaks I cannot say, but such men were viewed as the lowest kind of scum. I have no doubt they were hanged or shot, and left to rot.

We ate ravenously and cracked a few smiles but it was not the same. These men were strangers; the old mess was no more. Still, it was so pleasant in that grove, with good water and grazing for the horses, that we stayed two days to rest. It was like a magical place hidden from the war. We saw no troops, heard no sounds of battle. It was all the same to me if we never left. I knew that could not be, and spent several hours by the campfire sewing four of my precious Palmetto State buttons onto my Yankee sack coat.

We reached Smithfield and General Johnston's headquarters on March 15. Confederate troops were in motion on every road, it seemed. Manse reported to no one, fearful that our fifty or so riders would be seized and attached piecemeal to a provisional brigade, and Manse was determined to rejoin the regiment.

From troopers lying with a train of wounded we found out that Major General M.C. Butler's division was somewhere southeast of Smithfield on the Goldsborough road, acting as a rear guard opposing the right wing of Sherman's inexorable advance.

The next day, our numbers reduced by half because of men who had found and rejoined their old commands, we turned down the road toward Goldsborough.

Within hours, we began hearing the unmistakable rumble of battle coming not from ahead of us but from the west—the muted, drumming thunder of artillery and the dim crash of musketry, rolling like breakers on a faraway beach.

At noon we met the head of Butler's column, pared down to fewer than one thousand men, returning at Johnston's orders to Smithfield. Manse eagerly reported to General Butler himself, who ordered our company to fall in.

Riding to the rear of the column, we learned by "soldier's telegraph"—our friends in the thinned out ranks who shouted greetings and news—that old Hardee and Joe Wheeler had surprised two of Sherman's corps that morning and were engaged in a desperate fight around Averasborough. We reined up and waited for the 1st South Carolina Cavalry to come up.

What I saw shocked me; it was no longer the grand old regiment it had been. There were graying, older men I did not recognize, and fresh-faced farm boys, some riding mules, some barefoot. The first familiar face I saw was Baz Hilliard, who stared, by his gaze unsure who I was; then Hepsibah, riding a worn-out mule and leading another, muskets slung over each of his shoulders.

Then came Ab Tucker with his scarred face, his cousin John Lamb, 'Brose Clinkscales, Ragan the young Irishman, and good old Henry Knauff, starved-looking but with his complexion considerably improved; he was as copper-skinned as Manse. Captain Sharpe had shorn his beard and lost so much weight his sword belt was cinched to its final notch.

We shook hands all around but there was no time to jawbone. We rejoined the column. The roads were soft and muddy from recent rain. There was no dust; the air was crisp and scented with pine as we retraced our steps to Smithfield. We bivouacked outside of town for the next two days as General Johnston gathered the remnants of three armies, his Army of Tennessee, Bragg's North Carolinians and Hardee's, which was marching slowly west from Goldsborough to join us.

Here, Johnston meant to fight.

CHAPTER 12

A Long, Bone-Deep Weariness

On March 18, 1865, after stuffing our pockets with cartridges from the ammunition wagons, we were sent back out on the road toward Averasborough. We halted our march at Benton's Crossroads, not far from the town of Bentonville.

Hampton's cavalry was positioned as a heavy screen of skirmishers a mile in front of the long line of trenches our infantry was quickly throwing up to slow the first elements of the oncoming Union Fourteenth Corps.

Hepsibah unshouldered one of his two-band muskets and gave it to me. It occurred to me at that moment how true a comrade he had been, and a soldier, too, as true as any in Confederate service. I am sure that he never doubted it, and it made me ashamed to think I ever did. Yet it gladdened my heart to know that someday history will also know this, because Hepsibah was entered into the official rolls of Company F as cook and teamster. Search the dusty archives and you will see. I put him in the muster rolls and daily returns myself when I was Captain Sharpe's clerk. It was to be the battle of Bentonville, the last major engagement of our Civil War and one of the hardest fought; men I knew who were there compared its intensity to Gettysburg and Cold Harbor.

I still marvel how men could fight so hard for a cause gone belly up, but Johnston's surprise assault routed the proud Fourteenth Corps, veterans of a dozen fights from Shiloh to Fort McAllister, and nearly crushed Sherman's seemingly irresistible left wing. The price the South paid over those three days, from Sunday, March 19 to March 21, 1865, was awful, and it was exacted from the great and humble alike. General Hardee lost his own son, Willie, just sixteen years old. He was one of the last to fall.

In the end, all the blood, toil and effort came to nothing. Before the first shot was ever fired, I was twenty miles away back in Smithfield, on detached duty. At the time, I did not know whether to curse my luck, or to fall to my knees in gratitude for having been delivered from the firing line.

Colonel Black had asked his company commanders to recommend veterans who could take command of provisional companies of state guard and home guard recruits, to be posted at critical points on the roads between Goldsborough and Raleigh in case the army failed. Captain Sharpe sent for Corporal Fries.

"This is your chance to be an officer, Ansel," Sharpe said. "The job carries a first lieutenant's commission. You deserve it."

"But captain—"

Sharpe looked me in the eye and stepped closer to indicate he spoke deliberately, like a man who wants his words remembered. "Someone has to be left to carry on. We can't give up all our best. We have to save some back, or the South is as truly lost as is this war."

Colonel Black cobbled together a provisional company of sixty or so men and boys, the least experienced and most poorly mounted and armed, designated it Company L of the 1st South Carolina Cavalry and put me in command. We were to join any loose units we could find, forage off the country and attempt to hold open the fords and bridges between Goldsborough and Raleigh as an escape route for Johnston's forces.

My commission and written orders were hastily written on separate sheets of cheap paper torn from a schoolboy's tablet; Colonel Black's adjutant had lost his order book at Solemn Grove. Captain Sharpe added a gift to my official papers, an embroidered bluecloth epaulet bearing faded silver first lieutenant's bars.

"It's one of mine, from the old army," he said.

The orders were short and vague: My company was to report immediately to a Colonel Manigault in Smithfield, to join "secondary forces" being assembled there to patrol and protect the roads to Raleigh.

Black had the wisdom to give me a good first sergeant, a veteran South Carolinian from the late Captain Robin Jones' Company H named Hunter Frady; Jones helped Colonel Black recruit the 1st South Carolina Cavalry and, like Buddy Dunn and Frank Hampton, had been killed at Brandy Station. Frady grew his beard thick and long, and looked like any man's graying grandfather. Southern boys instinctively called him "sir." Frady relayed orders in an everyday voice; only rarely did he resort to drill field volume, which, I was to learn, was impressive.

"I will need your help, Frady," I said as we shook hands. "I'm new at command. What do you think of the boys?"

Frady shook his head and spat.

"Scraping the barrel."

"Well, they need fresh mounts, that's clear."

"That's not the worst of it, lieutenant. They's not thirty muskets among 'em; most have shotguns or old flintlock horse pistols. A few have revolvers, none has a saber." Frady looked me up and down. "You've no pistols or sword, sir?"

"Yankees got 'em at Solemn Grove," I half-lied.

I went through what protocols I could recall. We needed a complete muster roll, but Frady already had taken care of that. I relayed our orders and he nodded thoughtfully.

"Well, get 'em mounted and bring 'em on, sergeant."

I rode out to the trench lines being dug by the infantry across the road to Averasborough and trotted out to the cavalry outposts, enduring a few hoots and good-natured taunts from friends who recognized me; news travels fast in the army.

I found Manse and the rest of the reunited Benson House Mess with other men I did not know warming themselves by a cheery fire and sharing a ceramic jug of apple cider. For a little while, it was almost like the old days. Manse thumped me on the shoulders and came close to grasping me in a bear's hug. Henry examined my lieutenant's shoulder strap with exaggerated wonder. We all laughed. Hep took off my sack coat and, with a few passes of his expert fingers, sewed my new rank onto the coat's left shoulder. Then my friends invited me to partake in a chicken they were roasting.

"I can't stay, boys. The troop is waiting for me. I just wanted to say…say that…if we don't meet again…"

I could not get the words out. My throat had closed.

We shook hands, one by one, Manse the last. He gripped both my hands, his blue eyes as seemingly impassive as stars in the night, but who can know what is in a man's heart?

I tried joking, "Guess I tossed a bucket on this bonfire." No one laughed.

In silence I mounted Patch and cantered back to the main line, glad that my friends would not see my eyes filling with tears.

Company L set out at dusk along the main road for Smithfield. It was an eighteen-mile ride, and since my orders seemed to communicate a sense of urgency we kept going all night. Sergeant Frady brought up the rear to discourage straggling. Still, there were a few of my men, especially those on mules, who could not keep the pace. I told Frady if any fell out to make them promise to meet us in Smith-field.

What I left unsaid is what I felt in my heart: If they elected to sneak across country instead and go home, I did not give a damn. Sharpe's words haunted me. I would do my duty, but I would not burden myself with other men's consciences.

I reported personally to Colonel Manigualt at dawn after biv-ouacking the company in a pecan orchard on the outskirts of Smith-field. I told Frady to hunt up the commissary for rations for the men and forage for their animals, then went to look for Manigault.

The colonel had just risen and was not disposed to see junior officers at that time of the morning, or so his adjutant, a Major Meadowcroft, seemed to say with his wearisome attitude.

"Frankly, we have no place for you, lieutenant. We have received no orders from General Johnston as to the disposition of troops between here and Raleigh." The major's clean-shaved visage softened somewhat. "I will add you to the list of provisional troops, so keep yourself in readiness. You do know that, as we speak, Johnston and Hardee are engaging the Yankee left?"

"I know, major. I have just arrived from the field."

The major spread his hands, palms up. As if to underscore his words, the sound of guns rumbled up from the south, rattling the windows of his headquarters office.

I blurted out, "I need rations, and I need firearms for my men, at least forty muskets and plenty of ammunition."

The major nodded curtly. "That, I can help you with."

He quickly scrawled two orders and gave them to me. I snapped up the papers and turned on my heel, disgusted with myself and angry. I should be with my friends, sharing their dangers, instead of becoming a rear echelon coffee cooler.

I turned out the company and marched them to the ordnance park, the last wagons of which were harnessing up to take the road to Bentonville. My small command traded in its shotguns and flintlocks for three-band Springfield and Enfield rifle-muskets, mostly battlefield pick-ups in varying condition. The ordnance sergeant also issued leather cap boxes stuffed with copper percussion caps and four cases of .58-caliber cartridges, appropriate for either weapon. I traded in my unfired two-band musket for a .36-caliber Navy model revolver, which I carefully loaded and tucked into my belt.

Sunday, March 19, was a beautiful day, springlike, dry, with a delightfully warm breeze that smelled of green, living things. When I got back to camp, First Sergeant Frady and several troopers were putting the finishing touches on a combination lean-to and tent that was my quarters.

I peered inside; the floor was planked and strewn with fresh straw.

"It ain't much to look at, lieutenant."

"It'll do fine, sergeant. Thank you. Thanks, boys."

The men were frying salt pork at their fires, crumbling hard crackers into the grease to make a crude stew. I knew the aroma well. Satisfied that for the time being I had taken care of them, I spread blankets on the rough, pine-smelling floor and dropped into an untroubled sleep, oblivious to the thunder in the south.

We stayed in camp all that day, and the next day, and the next. Frady and I passed the hours drilling our green troop, on foot and on horseback, until we were confident they knew at least the rudiments of skirmish fighting and field movement.

One of my boys, a tailor named Farrell, fashioned a crudely-stitched company guidon from two dark blue cotton shirts; it featured the white crescent moon device South Carolina soldiers have served under since the Revolution, and beneath it a solid white letter L in block style.

I appointed Farrell a corporal and troop color bearer on the spot, and instructed him that he was to ride at my side on the march.

"That's fine work. Find a staff for it, corporal."

Farrell grinned and saluted, his straw-colored hair sticking out from beneath his cap. His eager youthful face, so hungry to see the elephant, is one of those which still haunt me.

By Monday afternoon the first wounded from Bentonville began to straggle in, some in wagons, many on foot. By Tuesday, the trickle had become a stream; soldiers were coming in still armed and unwounded, in small groups. By noon on Wednesday, we knew Johnston was in full retreat and that Hampton and Wheeler were screening the army's withdrawal.

It tortured me knowing my old comrades were out there, fighting and perhaps dying while I sat on my commission, rested and got fat. Our rations were monotonous but steady, better I warrant than those enjoyed by those in the field.

Johnston's army slogged back to Smithfield defeated but in good spirits and with their heads held high; they had dealt Sherman's army a hammer blow and sent it reeling so hard that the Yankees went into camp at Goldsborough to lick their wounds, there to linger for the better part of three weeks.

Believe it or not, within a few days the race track outside of town was soon hosting horse races once again. I was tempted to try old Patch at the course, but in spite of the amount of Confederate specie that was changing hands at trackside I could not bring myself to do it; it seemed frivolous, even blasphemous somehow, to gamble while soldiers were suffering and dying at the field hospitals.

One of the largest hospitals sprang up on the grounds of the Johnston County Courthouse, which served as Johnston's headquarters. Each morning I walked through the tents and among the hundreds of wounded lying haphazardly on the bare ground until one day a familiar, musical voice hailed me from beneath the bare limbs of an oak tree.

"Ho, Ansel! Look, 'Brose, who 'tis." The voice could not be mistaken: Patrick O. Ragan, harpist and sweet-spoken poet. A man lying next to him struggled up on his elbows, smiling weakly: Ambrose Clinkscales.

I was glad to see them and gave them each a biscuit with some ham I was carrying.

Poor 'Brose had been hit in the thigh, but he said when the surgeon went to probe for the bullet it was so close to the surface he was able to make a small incision and pop out the slug with his thumb and forefingers. His thigh had swollen to twice its size, and if the wound became septic 'Brose might still lose his leg.

As for Ragan, I could sadly see he would never again play the harp; his right hand was swathed clublike with bandages. A piece of exploding shell had clipped off three of his fingers, "neat as you please," he said cheerily, as if the subject had been the weather.

When I inquired as to the rest of the boys, they looked glumly back over their shoulders. "Still out there, with Butler's rear guard," said Ragan.

"Gentlemen, the war is over for you. Don't do anything foolish like getting better too soon."

'Brose winked, wincing with pain as he lay back down. I promised to visit every day and bring them more blankets, or a quilt if I could find one.

Incredibly, on April 1, General Johnston ordered a review of the army, to be held at the race course. North Carolina Governor Zebulon Vance and other dignitaries came down from Raleigh as the general's guests for the occasion, and with them a fair number of well-dressed and handsome ladies. They buzzed like bees around the balding Johnston, who never smiled but stood impeccable in his dress uniform.

"Don't they know there's a war on?" grumbled Sergeant Frady, who stood by me at the track fence to watch the show. He sucked his pipe angrily, no doubt thinking, as I did, of friends dead and gone. Was this what their sacrifice had been for?

Company L did not participate in the review, as we had no official command to attach ourselves to. Not that I was ashamed of our boys, not one whit. And when I saw what passed as Joe Johnston's army I was thankful. It was appalling, frankly: Rank upon rank of bearded, bedraggled men, brown and gray uniforms tattered and patched, many of the infantry barefoot, many even without firearms.

"Saddest spectacle I ever did see," commented Frady. He, too, had been at Brandy Station and remembered the grand review of Stuart's divisions that gentle June morning when our hearts were still young and many now dead still had life.

I remember the languid days we spent in Smithfield before the end came as if they were a dream, a dream pathetically trying to remember itself, to replay memories and fantasies that never were in a vain effort to halt the inevitable. But the dream ended abruptly, and after the bubble popped events began to unravel very quickly.

Within days of the review, rumors began to circulate that Federal troops had entered the Confederate capital of Richmond on April 3. Morale, I admit, had been unrealistically high since the review; now spirits plummeted. Desertions increased to the point where entire Home Guard companies were disappearing overnight and dispersing cross-country, each man heading for home.

Frady and I put the company in readiness for the move we were sure was to come, making certain every man had rations and extra ammunition. Food was plentiful. The townspeople pressed upon us flour, bacon, chickens, even jugs of fresh milk. "Rather you boys get it than the damn Yankees," they said. They knew, as did we, the army could not defend Smithfield. As soon as Sherman moved, Johnston would retreat to Raleigh. The army's only hope was to link up with Lee, then still defending Petersburg or so we believed.

And so we waited for orders, and waited. On the afternoon of Sunday, April 9, 1865, most of the 1st South Carolina Cavalry marched into Smithfield. Colonel Black set up his headquarters in a private home not a city block from our encampment. When I reported, I was proud to inform him that I had a wagonload of rations for his men and forage for horses ready and waiting in Company L's camp. Sergeant Frady saw to its distribution.

During a hasty meeting of company commanders—I counted seven besides me; three companies, including Company F, were still with Butler's rear guard—Black reported that Sherman's army would strike camp in Goldsborough the next morning to begin its march on Raleigh.

"You have seen hard service," Black said gravely. "Your men need a respite. I can give them none. Johnston will move his army on the morrow. Our task is to block the road between Goldsborough and Raleigh, delay the Yankees, give up as little ground as possible."

I stepped forward. "Colonel, I have sixty men, well rested and armed, ready to move."

Black regarded me with weary but expectant eyes. "Thank you, Lieutenant. Your company will move out tonight. The Moccasin Creek swamp, just east of here. Make yourself familiar with it."

"I have no maps, sir."

"Take mine. Colonel Twiggs." The lieutenant-colonel handed over a well-worn and tightly-folded square. "I know the damned thing by heart. Good luck, my boy."

Our night ride was mercifully short, less than seven miles in all according to the map. But, made in darkness and in ignorance of the lay of the country, it took us until well after dawn to reach the strong point being prepared on Moccasin Creek.

We crossed the Neuse River east of Smithfield without incident, then rode east until we struck the bed of the North Carolina Railroad. We had ridden too far east, so we retraced our steps until we found the right road south and cantered into the encampment just as the sun was rising. Already the troops there were up and working, strengthening trenches and cutting trees for breastworks and head logs.

I reported to Major Lipscomb of the 6th North Carolina Cavalry, commander of the Moccasin Creek ford. He looked warily at my small company.

"Any more coming?"

"I don't know, sir."

Using my map, Lipscomb quickly briefed me. Johnston was using companies of North Carolina state reserves and the Home Guard, shored up by veterans of Butler's and Wheeler's divisions, to block every road from Goldsborough for as long as possible while Johnston's army escaped to Raleigh.

"Can we hold this line?"

Lipscomb regarded me coolly. "With your company, I have fewer than four hundred muskets. No artillery, no reserves. My last dispatch tells me the first division of Mower's Twentieth Army Corps is eight miles down that road, five thousand strong. What do you think, lieutenant?"

Major Lipscomb personally directed us to our section of the line, just west of the road from Goldsborough, a wagon-rutted trail which bisected the breastworks his troops were building.

The road crossed Moccasin Creek at what had been a shallow, swampy ford and climbed a small bluff on the way to Raleigh. Our trenches extended for half a mile along the bluff, facing southeast. Engineers had broken up a mill dam upstream, flooding the creek below to two or three times its usual depth and creating a muddy, flowing moat nearly fifty yards across.

We picketed our horses just below the north side of the bluff, as close as I could get them. I instructed Sergeant Frady to tell the men to build fires and to cook and eat all their cookable rations and save their crackers; there was no way to predict when, or if, more would be available.

He was also to organize details to fill canteens. Tell every man to be ready to leave his hole at a moment's notice. Have them load and prime. And wait.

"There's another thing, sergeant. If something happens to me—"

"Lieutenant, don't worry about the boys. They will do just fine."

"That is not what I mean," I said. "I want you to promise me: Thirty rounds, no more, then get them out, orders or none. Do you hear? Head toward Raleigh, but before you get there give the company a choice: surrender with Johnston, or go home. Cut loose every man who wants to go. Will you?"

Frady picked at his pockets, searching for his pipe, but could not find it.

"I know the boys'll do fine."

"That's not enough, Hunter. Not enough. I want every one to come out of it. I want every one to go home."

Frady nodded. "Yes. Home. I promise, lieutenant."

Riders clattered in and out of the camp all afternoon, carrying messages for Major Lipscomb. One brought news that raced through the camp like wildfire, that Lee had surrendered his army in Virginia the day before, on Palm Sunday. That the war was over. Lipscomb immediately called a meeting of his commanders.

"The dispatch noted only rumors. There has been no confirmation from Johnston's headquarters," the major announced. "I expect every man here to do his duty."

In spite of the news—which smothered like a blanket the very spirit of every man who heard it, regardless of whether or not he believed it—I felt light of heart that afternoon. I had done everything I knew to do and I was ready for whatever was to come.

It was well past three in the afternoon before we heard the popping of musketry as the first elements of the Federal army engaged our outlying pickets. They did as they were told, harassing the lead units, bloodying their noses, then retreating half a mile to another prepared ambush. But in less than an hour they were galloping back to the bluff, their horses breasting the flooded creek.

The Yankees, when they came, approached piecemeal, in foraging parties, like theater-goers late in arriving for the first act. These were the infamous bummers who preceded Sherman's army like an infestation of locusts. They parked their wagons and carts, laden with loot, well out of musket range and studied our works. They waited.

Before long, the fields in front of us began to fill with columns of Yankee troops, veterans who double-quicked to their positions in the forming battle line with practiced ease, their bayonets glinting rank upon rank in the late afternoon sunlight. Squads of raucous skirmishers fanned out for a quarter mile in front of the surging blue lines, which appeared to be a full brigade of infantry at least two thousand strong.

Behind the infantry a six-gun battery of artillery deployed at a dead run, each team wheeling in its turn and presenting the business end of the three-inch ordnance rifle it hauled, then grinding to a halt so the gun crew could unharness the field piece from its limber and move it into position.

I had no field glasses and needed none. I was watching the opening act of an epic tragedy unfold before my eyes. With those guns behind them, the Yankee skirmishers alone could easily push us off this hill. More likely, I thought, the artillery will keep us in our holes while the skirmishers pour on frontal fire. Then the infantry will find a ford upstream or down, get a regiment or two across and flank us.

"Damn!" said First Sergeant Frady, cursing our bad luck.

Unconsciously, I had been thinking aloud, weighing our thin chances for survival for anybody to hear.

"Well. Do you agree, Hunter?"

"'Pears to be certain, sir," Frady glumly replied.

With their fellows in force behind them, the bummers in our front got cocky and opened a ragged and desultory fire on our works, most of which went well over our heads. Their contempt made me angry.

"Shall we give it to them?" I shouted to Frady, who needed no prodding. He jumped onto the parapet.

"Company, take your aim. Fire! Fire at will!"

Our little volley sounded mighty, when followed up by the rest of Lipscomb's battalion in successive blasts. I swear, those bummers tumbled heads over heels in their sudden desire to leave the field. Every one melted back into the woodline, slinking between the ranks of the oncoming skirmishers, who jeered at them unkindly.

"Cease fire!" I shouted down both sides of the trench line. "Cease fire, boys. Save your rounds. Every man, load and prime."

I climbed out of the trench to join Frady on the brow of the bluff. We could see Major Lipscomb on his horse a rod away, using an eye-glass to study the Yankee columns.

"You take the boys from that dogwood tree on," I told Frady. "I will direct the first section here. When you hear me yelling 'pull out,' you and your boys run for the horses."

At that moment the Federal guns opened up from more than one thousand yards, first one, then two, then two more quick detonations—pum pum pum pum—and the shells arced overhead with a sharp soughing sound, dropping far behind the brow of the bluff.

Two more rounds per gun, I knew, and they would have the range. Of all the services in that war the Federal artillery was the most to be feared. Because it was perfect and relentless.

The initial small arms fire was surprisingly weak and ineffective but that did not last. Before long the volleys were coming hot, heavy and well-organized: the infantry had come up. Our return fire was as heavy as we could make it.

Many years later, late in middle age, I visited San Antonio and consulted the one hundred twenty-eight volumes of the "Official Records of the War of the Rebellion," to see what they said about the fight at Moccasin Creek. The reference I found contained a single report from the colonel of the 123rd New York Infantry, who accurately noted the designation of the Confederate units he had faced, reported three men killed in action and added, "The rebs kept up a galling fire before retiring."

The good colonel neglected to comment on the ferocity of the Yankee firestorm; from our viewpoint, it was Old Testament in noise and scale. Shells were bursting over our heads, hurtling chunks of hot iron in every direction. My men were afraid to even shoot from under their head logs for fear of being struck by the storm of lead that was being poured into our positions.

I could see a Yankee column passing behind its firing line around their left flank; they had found a ford downstream. I made the decision it was time to vacate the premises.

"Frady! Frady!" I screamed, but it was like trying to be heard in the mouth of a hurricane. I waited for a lull in the firing, then jumped out of my hole and like a frog crouched along the line, telling the men to get out, run for it, go for their horses.

Through the smoke I could see troopers on my right emerging from their trenches and making for the rear, whizzing shrapnel and zipping Minie balls kicking up dust around them.

First Sergeant Frady squatted in the open cradling his Enfield, waving frantically to the rear with his left arm. I went from hole to hole to be sure everyone was out, then ducked and ran for it, making it unhurt to the brow of the bluff and down into the ravine where Patch was screaming and rearing, tied to a young, white-blossoming dogwood.

That is the last thing I remember: Patch's sleek black flanks, her great head twisted in alarm, mouth agape, just as the ground erupted beneath me, lifting my feet and twisting my body, while something like a fist punched me hard on my right side, just below the ribs, pushing the breath out of me, and, I thought then, the very life.

I awoke again and again, short of breath, in pain, unable to breathe without pain, until blackness again took me.

I awoke for good lying in darkness on a soft quilt on the cold floor of a house. My side ached. I was tightly bandaged there and every breath made me wince, but I was clear-headed and hungry. The room was redolent with the coppery smell of blood; men stirred and sighed, coughed, moaned.

A candle bobbed in the dark and a form that smelled of fresh soap came to me, enveloped my face with a warm, moist hand. "What news? Miss?"

"The war is over." Her breath was as sweet as mint, and I drank it in. "Rest now."

Instead my body shook uncontrollably in spasm and I wept, not from joy nor even from pain, but from the great emptiness that filled me. I wept for Newton's leg and my dead brother Tom, and Manse's five brothers; for Buddy Dunn, Ezra and brave Robert and their poor folks; even for Siegfried and Lettie, my horses lost. I wept for the starvation and disease, the agony and death that had been suffered by millions, all for nothing.

It was at last over, and my emptiness became a long, bone-deep weariness.

Another Word

A Brief Note to the Patient Reader:

I feel constrained to explain that, at this point in the narrative, my mental faculties utterly drained and my overworked right hand wrapped in a sling, all communication with the late and Honorable A.W. Fries ceased for nearly nine months.

When, after much needed rest and long hours of astral probing on my part, our consciousnesses again touched—suddenly, and with the shock of crossed live electrical wires—we resumed the work we had set out to do, like any good author and his loyal transcriber.

In spite of Mr. Fries' advanced age at passing and the decade (in earth years) he had already spent on the Other Side, he is clearly possessed of a strong and relentless spiritual presence which demands to be heard. Thus, I willingly consented to be his secretary.

Mr. Fries' narrative continues in the next book, titled "The True Story of Manse Jolly, Part II," which takes the reader on his long journey at war's end home to South Carolina. He also, almost by way of apology, attempts to explain the lawlessness and violence committed by federal occupiers and ex-Confederates alike in the months following the reestablishment of the Union, and provides a participant's account of a landmark court case of the era, still referred to today by South Carolinians as the "Browns Ferry outrage."

Further, Part II chronicles the westward migration of many disenfranchised Southerners who sought new lives and prosperity on the wild and dangerous Texas frontier.

Although the publisher has cleverly conspired to print my mentor's tale in two separate volumes, in order to squeeze twice the profits from an unsuspecting public, I strongly assure you that my reward in this transaction barely covered my considerable investment in time and labor. I gave willingly of both because I believe there is merit to this tale.

That, at least, is the fervent belief of this humble transcriber, who, whatever skeptics may say, continues to be a wholly uninvolved and objective third party. The enlightened reader will envision my role as akin to that of a telephone cable, connecting this world with the next.

I remain the Patient Reader's obedient servant,

Julian K. Dent, Esq.
Ft. Worth, Texas
29 March 1940

A Roster of
Company F, 1st South Carolina Cavalry

Name & Hometown	Rank	Service
Sharpe, Elam Pendleton	Captain, com- manding Co. F	Surrendered at Bennett's Farm, N.C., April 1865
Dunn, Buddy Pendleton	Lieutenant	Killed at Brandy Station, Va.
Fries, Ansel W. Townville	"	Commissioned commander Co. L, March 1865; wounded at Moccasin Swamp, N.C., April 10, 1865
Grew, Willie Pendleton	"	Killed at Brandy Station, Va.
Hilliard, Bassett * Anderson Dist.	"	Surrendered at Bennett's Farm
Noggle, Bill Anderson Dist.	"	Wounded near Columbia, S.C., Feb. 1865
Whitner J.B. Anderson C H	"	Transferred to Company E
Jolly, Manson S. Anderson Dist.	First Sergeant	Served through War; no discharge Rec'd.

Name & Hometown	Rank	Service
Post, Cater Anderson Dist.	Orderly Sergeant	Killed at Gettysburg
Frady, Hunter York Dist.	Sergeant	Transferred from Co. H, promoted 1st Sgt. Co. L, March 1865
Barrineau, Tom Anderson Dist.	Corporal	Killed at Gettysburg
Clayton, A.T. Pickens Dist.	Corporal	Died typhoid fever, James Island, S.C., August 1864
Fries, Ansel W. Townville	Corporal	Wounded Kellys Ford, Va., 1863
Knauff, Henry Anderson C.H.	Corporal	Surrendered at Bennett's Farm
Blassingame, A.J. Pickens Dist.	Private	Listed as deserter, July 1864
Burrell, Bright Pickens Dist.	Private	Surrendered at Bennett's Farm
Burrell, Butler Pickens Dist.	Private	Killed at Gettysburg
Clinkscales, Ambrose Anderson C.H.	Private	Wounded at Bentonville, N.C., 1865
** Evers, Hepsibah Anderson C.H.	Negro cook & teamster	Surrendered at Bennett's Farm
Lamb, John Disputanta, Va.	Private	Wounded at Brandy Station
Largent, Walter Edgefield Dist.	Private	Listed as deserter, 1865
Ragan, Patrick O. Charleston	Private	Wounded at Bentonville, N.C., 1865
Sitton, Ezra Pendleton	Private	Wounded & Captured at Gettysburg
Sitton, Robert Pendleton	Private	Killed at Solemn Grove, N.C. 1865

Name & Hometown	Rank	Service
Syms, Raleigh Anderson C.H.	Private	Discharged May 1862; enlisted 14th S.C. Killed at Spotsylvania C.H., 1864.
Tucker, Absalom Disputanta, Va.	Private	Wounded at Gettysburg
Welborne, R.J. Anderson Dist.	Private	Wounded near Goldsborough, N.C., 1865
Whitley, J.D. Laurensville	Private	Died at Camp Hampton, S.C., June 1862
Spurgeon, Dr. Walker T. Columbia	Captain, Medical Corps	Captured at Upperville, Va., June 1863

* South Carolina was divided into districts, not counties, until 1868.

** Enlisted under Cpl. H. Knauff's mother's maiden name.

Bibliography

Barrett, John G. The Civil War in North Carolina. Chapel Hill: University of North Carolina Press, 1963.

Battles and Leaders of the Civil War. Vols. I-IV. Reprinted from Century Magazine. New York: Castle Books, Thomas Yoseloff, Inc., 1956.

Biondo, Steve. "The Legend of Manse Jolly," Part I of a series. The Anderson Independent. S.C. Edition, 12 April 1981. Sec. 1, p. 1A, col. 1-4; p. 8A, col. 1-5.

Biondo, Steve. "Manse Jolly: The Man." Part II of a series. The Anderson Independent. S.C. Edition, 19 April 1981. Sec. 1, p. 1A, col. 3-6; p. 6A, col. 1-2.

Black, J.L. Crumbling Defenses: Memoirs & Reminiscences of Colonel John Logan Black. Unpublished postwar manuscript printed privately in Columbia, S.C., 1961.

Blackford, Lt. Col. W.W. The War Years with J.E.B. Stuart. New York: Scribner's and Sons, 1945.

Brooks, U.R. Butler and His Cavalry in the War of Secession, 1861 1865. Reprinted. Germantown, Tenn.: Guild Bindery Press, 1994. South Carolina Regimentals Series.

Editors of Time-Life Books. Arms and Equipment of the Union and of the Confederacy. Two volumes. Alexandria, Virginia: Time-Life Books, 1996.

Herd, E. Don Jr. The South Carolina Upcountry, 1540-1980: Historical and Biographical Sketches. Vol. II. Greenwood, S.C.: The Attic Press, 1982.

Jolly, Manson Sherrill. Unpublished 1861 army furlough, photos and postwar letters, 1866-69. Archives of Olin D. Johnston Library, Anderson College, Anderson, S.C.

Jones, Walter Burgwyn, Editor. Confederate War Poems. Nashville, Tenn.: Bill Coats Publishing, 1959.

Lord, Francis A. The Civil War Collector's Encyclopedia. Vol. 4. West Columbia, S.C.: Lord Americana and Research, 1984.

Moorhead, Lewis D. Image collection of the Anderson, S.C., photographer.

Mulligan, A.B. Dear Mother & Sisters: Letters of Capt. A.B. Mulligan. Spartanburg, S.C.: Reprint Co., 1992.

Newspapers: Anderson Intelligencer and Anderson Gazette, 1865-66, Anderson County Library; files of the Anderson Daily Mail and Anderson Independent, 1981-82, ibid; Alamogordo, N.M., News, 1936.

Reed, Emmala Thompson. Unpublished wartime and postwar journals of the daughter of Judge J.P. Reed, 1865-67. Anderson County Museum.

Reid, Crayton L. Unpublished biographical sketch and family papers of C.L. Reid, Company C, Palmetto Sharpshooters. Originally dictated 1914, transcribed 1951.

Thrift, Joanne. "Manse Jolly: Warm-Hearted Hero. Letters Donated to Anderson Collection Reveal Local Hero's Family Affection." The Anderson Independent. 29 January 1976. Sec. 2, p. 1B, col. 1-8.

Vandiver, Louise Ayer. Traditions and History of Anderson County. Atlanta: Ruralist Press, 1928.

War of the Rebellion: A Compilation of the Official Records of the Union and Confederate Armies. Washington, D.C.: U.S. War Department, 1880-1901. 128 volumes. Vols. 6, 14, 21, 25, 27, 29, 33, 35, 42 and 47.

About the Author

Author
Gettysburg 1976

Steve Biondo was born near Champaign, Illinois, in 1950.

He studied journalism and creative writing at Ohio University, and holds an M.A. in English from Virginia Tech.

Since 1974, he has written for seven daily and weekly newspapers in eastern Virginia and Upstate South Carolina.

Long a student of the Civil War, Biondo followed the Old Flag on fields of mock battle from Pennsylvania to Florida. He continues to live and work in Upstate South Carolina.

0-595-23800-9